Julia's head swam as she stared at her mother, the room around her growing blurry.

She's done it. I didn't think she could, but she's found a way.

It was the very thing she had feared. Mama had somehow managed to force a match, or was at least trying her very best to, and Julia grasped the back of her chair as her legs suddenly felt too weak to bear her up.

"No, Mama. Mr. Beresford has done nothing wrong. In fact, he was helping me—you can't punish him for that."

With desperate eyes she saw Samuel glance at her, his own blank with shock. He was still standing just inside the doorway, only a few paces from her mother, but he seemed miles away, probably so gripped by dread that he wished himself in another place altogether.

Mrs. Livingston drew herself up to her full height. "You were seen."

Author Note

The inspiration for *Their Inconvenient Yuletide Wedding* came from the comfortingly cheesy films that are always shown during the run-up to Christmas, in particular the (usually early noughties) ones where nobody realizes the heroine's beauty until after she's taken her glasses off. It always seemed ridiculous that the hero could fail to notice the love of his life before this tiny alteration and it made me want to write a similarly clueless man of my own—which is where Samuel Beresford makes his entrance.

Samuel has known Julia Livingston all his life and spent much of his childhood teasing her for her unusual yet striking looks. Julia in turn always harbored a secret liking for her tormentor, but after an unexpected reunion as adults, it's Samuel who now finds himself at the mercy of an unwanted attraction. Since he last saw her, Julia has undergone the 1800s equivalent of a teen-movie makeover and he realizes he's in danger of getting far too close—not that Julia now has any intention of letting him try.

I had a lot of fun writing this book, and I very much hope you'll enjoy getting to know Julia and Samuel as much as I did.

JOANNA JOHNSON

—

Their Inconvenient Yuletide Wedding

HARLEQUIN
HISTORICAL

ISBN-13: 978-1-335-59584-3

Recycling programs for this product may not exist in your area.

Their Inconvenient Yuletide Wedding

For questions and comments about the quality of this book, please contact us at CustomerService@Harlequin.com.

Harlequin Enterprises ULC
22 Adelaide St. West, 41st Floor
Toronto, Ontario M5H 4E3, Canada
www.Harlequin.com

Printed in U.S.A.

Joanna Johnson lives in a little village with her husband and too many books. After completing an English degree at university, she went on to work in publishing, although she'd always wish she was working on her own books rather than other people's This dream came true in 2018 when she signed her first contract with Harlequin, and she hasn't looked back, spending her time getting lost in mainly Regency history and wishing it was acceptable to write a manuscript using a quill.

Books by Joanna Johnson

Harlequin Historical

The Marriage Rescue
Scandalously Wed to the Captain
His Runaway Lady
A Mistletoe Vow to Lord Lovell
The Return of Her Long-Lost Husband
The Officer's Convenient Proposal
"A Kiss at the Winter Ball"
in *Regency Christmas Parties*
Her Grace's Daring Proposal
Their Inconvenient Yuletide Wedding

Visit the Author Profile page
at Harlequin.com.

For everyone who wishes
Twelfth Night balls were still in fashion

Chapter One

Pretending she hadn't heard the library door creak open, Julia Livingston slid down in her chair, holding her book higher in front of her face. If she didn't make eye contact, perhaps her brother wouldn't notice her sitting in front of the fire, trying to make herself invisible as his heavy tread came to a halt beside her.

'Julia.'

She didn't look up. She knew exactly what he would say and she didn't want to hear it, instead huddling deeper into her armchair as if it could hide her from the conversation she'd been trying to avoid.

'Julia. Ignoring me won't make me go away.'

A finger hooked over the top of her book and tilted it down, at last forcing her to look up at the figure looming above her.

'Oh, Harry. Apologies. I didn't see you there.'

Her brother snorted and fell into the chair on the other side of the fireplace, resting his boots on the fender. For a moment he watched the flames, their cheerful glow battling against the winter chill that prowled outside Highbank's tall windows, but then he turned to her and she felt her shoulders slump at what she knew was about to come.

Harry cleared his throat, opened his mouth…and grimaced.

'Don't look at me like that.'

'Like what?'

'You know *like what*. You're giving me the same sad eyes my greyhounds do when I won't let them off the lead.'

It wasn't a particularly flattering comparison, although she couldn't deny its accuracy. Her eyes were indeed fixed on him with the earnest entreaty usually only dogs could manage, wordlessly imploring him not to continue with the inevitable, but he faced them down with a weary shake of his head.

'Come on. If it was up to me, of course you could stay here for as long as you liked, but you know *she* won't give either of us a moment's peace until you're back beneath her roof…or better yet, have one of your own.'

Julia dropped her abandoned book onto the table beside her, her straight eyebrows drawing into a frown. Once objects of ridicule, those same full brows had recently come to be considered an asset to a face now deemed worth looking at; something that would have been very difficult for her to believe when she was younger.

There had been universal surprise when Alice King's daughter wasn't born an obvious beauty. Once the toast of Guildbury society, even now, nearing fifty, Mama could turn heads when she entered a room. Julia's father had been the lucky man to win her hand—as the richest and most handsome suitor, naturally—and their son had inherited a combination of their good looks that made him as popular among the young ladies as his mother had been with the gentlemen in her day. With such well-favoured parents it had seemed a surety their next child would be just as blessed, which was why, when Julia came along four years after her brother, she had instead seemed as out of place as a sparrow in an aviary of exotic birds. Somehow, Mama's wide-spaced eyes had found themselves set below Papa's powerful brows, with Alice's superb bone structure fighting against the decided Livingston chin and the long limbs that suited Harry so well made Julia as ungainly as a foal. The mixture of such strong features had entirely overwhelmed her for much of her life, and since her recent return from Europe Julia felt she had merely exchanged one set of problems for another, all of them caused by the outer shell she wouldn't have chosen for herself.

'It's the most ridiculous double standard.' She leaned forward to stoke the fire, jabbing the poker into it with more vigour than was strictly required. 'You're older than me and yet because you are a man you're seen as more eligible with every passing year, whereas just because I haven't leapt at my first sniff of a proposal…'

'You're teetering on the brink of spinsterhood at the grand old age of twenty-one? An oddity who refuses to wed even when showered with offers?'

At the sharp turn of her head Harry produced a sheet of paper from his pocket. 'Our mother's words. Not mine.'

'Oh.' The sight of the letter settled a weight over her chest. 'She's still angry, then?'

'Possibly not. The tone is more wounded martyr than anything else.'

'Heaven help me. That's *worse* than angry.'

It was Julia's turn to gaze into the flames. Yet again she'd proven a disappointment and the heaviness in her chest grew more oppressive as she recalled what had driven her to seek sanctuary at her brother's house.

Mrs Livingston's mouth had sagged with horror when Julia came bursting out of Burton Lodge's parlour, the two almost colliding as Mama stood with her ear pressed against the door, and Julia's rejected suitor had barely left before the screaming began. Whatever had possessed her to spurn the advances of one of the richest men in the neighbourhood was beyond understanding, and the fact it was the *third* time she'd turned down an offer was not to be borne. Mr Sydenham was wealthy, of an appropriate age and not *un*attractive in certain lights, and there was absolutely no reason for his dismissal other than Julia's stubborn refusal to do as she ought.

Never mind that he'd been among those who tormented me for years, joining in when the others laughed at my clumsiness or how I blushed like a radish every time someone glanced in my direction. Why wouldn't I jump at the chance to wed a man who helped make my life a misery?

As a girl there had been no chance of her remaining unaware of her various shortcomings. When forced by her parents to leave the safety of Burton Lodge's library, where she'd preferred to spend her days reading instead of venturing outside, her flaws were pointed out mercilessly by the prettier young ladies and the neighbourhood lads in a constant catalogue of her failings until she could barely stand to look in the mirror. Harry had done his best to protect her but his own good looks meant he never fully understood how much *gentle teasing* could hurt, and once he'd left for university, she'd had to weather that mockery alone. For years she'd been convinced of her own hideousness, and just because she was now celebrated for the same unusual countenance that had once garnered such scorn didn't mean she had forgotten the feeling of being trapped in her own skin.

So many stupid jokes at my expense—and most of them started by the same person. How I rejoiced the day he left town, off to be a thorn in someone else's side...

Her conscience gave a faint tweak.

Fine. Perhaps that isn't entirely true.

The day *that person* had left Guildbury to embark on the Grand Tour had indeed been a blessing, but it would be a lie to pretend she hadn't also been secretly grieved. *He* had been barely eighteen and she two years younger, given to blushing whenever he entered the same room and more likely to grow wings and fly than utter a word in his presence. Every girl in the neighbourhood had fancied herself in love with him, with his tousled chestnut hair and confidence surpassed only by his good looks, and every lad had looked to him as their model. So when he'd first made a jest at her expense it hadn't taken long for others to follow suit. He had by no means been the worst of her persecutors nor the cruellest, but he'd certainly set the example for everyone else, and she was sure that without his involvement her childhood could have been marginally less miserable.

Belatedly, she realised she was sucking in her bottom lip. It was an unconscious habit she'd had for as long as she could remember, something she'd always done when anxious or unsure, and she stopped hastily as soon as she became aware she was doing it again. The action lingered as a relic of the sad, uncertain girl she had once been, and she was determined never to feel like that again, not now she had come to know her worth.

She'd come to understand something in the years since *that person* had left town. It didn't matter how good-looking a man was. It was his nature that really counted, a kind heart the most important thing; and no comely face nor bulging pocketbook would now make her overlook a rotten core.

An awkward cough brought her back into the present. Harry was folding and unfolding the piece of paper on which Mama had made her anguish known. 'It *was* your third proposal since your return to England. Three offers in two months? I don't agree with what Mother said or how she said it, but I wonder...' He tailed off when Julia looked ready to seize hold of the poker again.

'Yes, I've had three—from three equally unappealing men. I might not have minded so much if they'd approached me pleasantly, perhaps leading with an apology for their unkindness when we were younger, but they don't. They just ooze.'

Harry looked faintly revolted. 'They *ooze*?'

'You know. Charm, compliments...frothy words none of them were uttering before I went away with Aunt Marie. Where were all my admirers then? Certainly not praising my sense of humour or grasp of

French, which I possessed long before I was regarded in any way pretty.'

Kind, stylish Aunt Marie had always showered her sister's offspring with love, and it surprised nobody when she chose her unhappy niece to accompany her and her husband on an extended tour of warmer climes. Such a lengthy separation was scant hardship for Mr and Mrs Livingston; after all, it would give them a break from the ceaseless question of what to do with a shy, stooping daughter nobody wanted to marry, who every day caused them to shake their heads and wonder what went wrong.

But then Italy had happened. Wonderful, balmy, cultured Italy—and Julia hadn't been the same since.

Beneath the Mediterranean sun she found herself surrounded by more appreciation than she'd known in her entire life. To her amazement the men there *praised* the wild darkness of her untamed curls, and her almost black eyes were likened to gleaming obsidian, or ebony, or a hundred other things that made her flush a rosy pink. The strong planes of her face were suddenly admired—not possessing the delicateness so favoured at home, perhaps, but striking in a different way, distinctive and so arresting that soon Julia found herself in the novel position of being very much in demand.

One gentleman begged to paint her. Another left flowers outside her door every day for a month, until Uncle Cecil finally intervened. At first, Julia thought they were mocking her, their attentions based in the same ridicule she'd grown so used to, and to realise they were sincere was the single largest shock of her life.

Sensing the moment had come, Aunt Marie had

swung into action. A fashionable French modiste was
employed to subtly shape Julia's heavy brows, enhancing their bold shape in a flattering frame for her large,
expressive eyes, and a local woman skilled in the art of
managing curls was brought in to teach Julia's lady's
maid how to properly dress her hair. Mama had always
thought she was a lost cause but a little gentle encouragement was all it took to bring out her unique beauty
and her confidence had gradually begun to rise, each
day climbing a little higher from the mud into which
it had been trodden by others' cruel jokes.

Arriving back in Guildbury a year and a half later,
she had known herself to be almost unrecognisa-
ble. Glowing with self-assurance, she was graceful,
collected, radiating an inner vibrancy that eighteen
months of happiness had lit to burn inside her like a
flame. She didn't shy away when spoken to any longer;
instead, she met every eye and joined every conversation, and she'd barely been back at Burton Lodge a
fortnight before the first gentleman left his card. The
ugly duckling had become a swan at last, and Mama's
surprise was matched only by her delight at finally
having a daughter she felt she could be proud of, little
realising the person inside was very much the same as
before. The old Julia still lurked *just* beneath the polished veneer and nobody knew how hard she worked
to maintain the illusion, her newfound poise looking
effortless, although in truth anything but. It was only
by careful concentration she now managed to prevent
herself from dropping teacups or fumbling with her
gloves as had happened so frequently before Milan
transformed her life.

A silence had settled over the library. Aware Harry was patiently waiting for her to finish, Julia shook her head.

'I won't have any of the men who want me now, no matter how much Mama might desire a match. When I take a husband, it will be a man who values me—*me*, for who I am inside rather than out—and I won't settle for anything less.'

She stood, pretending to stretch her legs as she strolled to one of the windows overlooking Highbank's fine gardens, the grass sparkling with frost beneath a sky so bright it hurt her eyes. This house was her haven and she wished she didn't have to leave it, the prospect of returning to her parents making her lips twist. Mama would throw herself into the role of the injured party, sighing and making much of bravely bearing her immense disappointment, and Papa would sequester himself in his strictly off-limits study. There would be no lively conversation, only quiet rooms and disapproving glances, and Julia's spirits dropped further to imagine the cold reception that awaited her return.

Behind her she heard her brother get to his feet. He'd never been one to enjoy discussing feelings, and she could tell he was uneasy as he came to stand beside her.

'I sincerely hope you find such a man. In the meantime, however...'

'I know. It's time for me to go home.'

Harry pushed a hand through his hair, looking apprehensive. 'Take heart. It's not long until Christmas. There are all kinds of parties and agreeable distractions in the next few weeks to take some of her attention from you.'

'Nothing will distract her,' Julia replied despondently, picking gloomily at a flake of loose paint on the windowsill. 'She won't rest until I'm wed. With every party her eyes will be on stalks for single gentlemen to parade me in front of, and I'll be forced to dance with one after the other until my legs give out.'

'I'll be there to pick you up.'

'You? You wouldn't notice even if I dropped into a dead faint. You'll be surrounded by young ladies the moment you set foot in the ballroom—and don't try to deny that's the way you like it.'

Her brother at least had the good grace to pretend modesty. His face was acknowledged locally as almost more of an attraction than his fortune, but his blushes were saved when the sound of the front door knocker made both Livingstons turn away from the window.

'Are you expecting someone?'

'Not at this hour. I'm shooting with Langtree but not until later this morning. He must have come early.'

Despite her low mood Julia couldn't help a small smile. 'In that case I think I might go to see about packing my things. Colonel Langtree is a very pleasant man but I'm in no hurry to be trapped in another conversation with you two about pheasants. Last time I made the mistake of being caught up the topic was hunting, and I only understood about one word in three.'

Harry's huffed laugh followed her as she made for the door and stepped onto the landing. Her rooms were at the other end of the corridor and she moved briskly towards them, listening for footsteps on the stairs. It would be the height of bad manners if the Colonel caught her beating a hasty retreat—but the thud of ascending boots told her she hadn't hurried *quite* fast enough.

There goes my chance of escaping more talk of guns.

She stopped, throwing one wistful look towards her distant bedroom door before adopting a welcoming smile. The Colonel really *was* a very pleasant man for all his relentless talk of things she had no interest in, and she readied herself for his usual bluff greeting as his head rose into view.

But it wasn't Colonel Langtree's affable, weathered face that appeared above the carved oak banister. It was a different one entirely—one that made Julia freeze where she stood.

The man paused on the penultimate step as he noticed her, his eyes meeting hers to send an unpleasant shock through her suddenly taut insides. Their deep blue scrutiny swept over her, giving the impression of taking in every detail with one glance, but then he bowed and any hope of speech died in Julia's tight throat.

'Good morning, ma'am. I apologise—I wasn't aware Mr Livingston already had company.'

He straightened up again, easily able to look down at her even while standing a stair below. By the polite pause he seemed to be inviting her to reply, but Julia found for the moment that was quite out of the question.

She looked up at him into a face she'd studied hundreds of times and always with admiration. She hadn't seen it for five years, of course, and would have gladly gone twice that time again without catching sight of that aquiline nose and lips always teetering on the brink of a smile; but he'd broken that winning streak, ambushing her now in what she'd thought was her safest place, and she felt a hot wave of displeasure to realise he had only improved with age.

He was tanned now, his skin taken on the same

olive depth her own had developed in Italy, and sun-bleached streaks glinted among his chestnut hair. It was as disordered as it had always been, artfully arranged to look casually undone, and for the most fleeting of hideous moments she recalled how her younger self had longed to run her fingers through those tousled waves, one glance enough to send her mind spinning backwards to days she now tried to forget.

When she didn't speak he continued, a faint furrow appearing between his brows. Perhaps her expression gave him a hint of what was unfolding behind her frozen mask but he pushed on, so civil now that it made Julia want to grind her teeth.

'The butler trusted me to escort myself upstairs. My name—'

'Is Samuel Beresford.' She cut him off abruptly, her tongue at last ungluing itself from the roof of her mouth. 'I already know your name, sir. Just as you know mine.'

'Do I? I'm sorry. I'm afraid I can't quite place...'

He climbed the final stair, narrowing the space between them, and Julia almost flinched away. Only her determination to appear unmoved held her in place, and as she met his questioning gaze she felt a fierce pride that she hadn't stumbled backwards, another victory over the innate awkwardness it had never been so important that she conceal.

It was the *Honourable* Samuel Beresford if she was being pedantic. The son of Viscount Maidwell, heir to a vast estate and confident in the knowledge he was respected and revered wherever he went—and quite possibly her least favourite person in all the world, the very man she would have been quite happy never to lay eyes on ever again.

It had been *his* jokes that set the tone for how the others had mocked her so mercilessly from the tender age of twelve, when the other girls began to blossom but Julia did not. *He* had been the first to notice how she stuck to the sides of every room, too shy to venture out into the open, and how she so often seemed to trip over her own feet when Mama forced her to dance. His *playful teasing* had paved the way for far more vicious treatment and even if he hadn't been the worst he had still been the most to blame, and it was only thanks to Aunt Marie that the damage he started with his thoughtlessness had at last been reversed.

He was examining her closely and she made sure to keep her chin raised. She *would not* blush under his scrutiny—not anymore, no matter how much the passing years had honed his boyish good looks into a grown man's handsomeness. There was power in his jawline now and a new firmness to the set of his shoulders, the impressive height that had made so many young ladies swoon matched by a breadth of chest that he hadn't possessed as a youth. In all, he was a man to catch the eye and was undoubtably aware of it, and Julia felt her hackles rise to admit her own attention might, too, have been piqued if she hadn't known who he was.

But I do know.

It was maddening that he could have had such an effect on her life while she had evidently left little trace on his, and her shoulders tensed further when he dared offer her a smile—one far more charming than she liked.

'Forgive me, ma'am. I've been away for some years.

If we were acquainted before that—' Suddenly, the faint puzzlement gave way to dawning realisation. 'Wait. It can't be Julia? Julia *Livingston*?'

Her stomach contracted as frank disbelief flashed over his face. It was far from a flattering reaction and her aversion sharpened as she watched him collect himself, trying to cover his amazement with a veneer of courtesy.

'It's a pleasure to see you again. I'd never have known you. You look…different.'

'Yes.' Her voice was like ice; deliberately so, and she took a grim satisfaction in seeing his uncertainty. Probably he expected her to wilt as she would have five years ago, delighted and mortified by his undivided attention, but she would have to disappoint him now.

'It's been widely noted how much I've changed in recent years. I used to be regarded by certain people as something of an oddity—but then, who would know that better than you?'

Looking down into her cold eyes, Samuel realised it was too late to avoid causing offence. He shouldn't have allowed his surprise to be quite so obvious, probably, although surely anyone who had last known Julia Livingston as a girl of sixteen could be excused for feeling some shock at seeing her so changed. *Then* she had indeed been slightly strange, painfully quiet and always with her nose buried in some book, but now…

Good Lord. When did this happen?

Catching his first glimpse of her as he came to the top of the stairs, he had felt a flicker of involuntary admiration at the sight that greeted him. Tall, beautifully dressed and crowned with a lavish abundance of coiling dark hair, she'd been a striking picture, waiting to welcome him to Highbank with a smile that had slipped the moment she saw his face. It wasn't quite the reception he might have expected, the delight of young women usually growing stronger at his approach rather than rapidly diminishing; but then again, he thought as he watched a muscle move below her clenched jaw, wondering when exactly her neck had become such a supple curve, *that* was what had caused him his current trouble in the first place.

The minute raising of a now well-shaped eyebrow, probably to prompt him into some reply, rescued him from thoughts of what he had left behind in Venice. He'd returned to England to put that mess behind him, and an encounter with a childhood acquaintance was as valid a distraction from his torment as anything else… as long as he made sure not to dwell on the bewildering new refinement of her bearing or glossy splendour of her once uncontrollable hair. Those were the kinds of things he never intended to notice in a woman ever again, his heart still in Italy even if the rest of him had found its way home, and the idea of Miss Livingston in any way rousing his attention was as unwanted as it was baffling.

He took in the frigid elegance of her posture, more graceful now than he would ever have believed but radiating dislike that was almost tangible.

I always thought she liked me…although by the looks of things, perhaps not anymore.

Samuel tried another smile—one that to his mild puzzlement was again not returned. What had he done to earn such a frosty reception? The Julia he remembered, the younger sister of one of his boyhood friends, had been endearing in her ineptness; a sweet, timid thing he'd been unable to resist subjecting to a little good-natured teasing for continually treading on the hems of her dresses and banging her elbows in doorways. She had never complained, however, and he could hardly imagine what he could have done in a five-year absence to warrant such treatment on his return, her bashful smiles now replaced by a glare that could have curdled milk.

She allowed the slightly uncomfortable silence to linger for a beat before she continued. 'You're here to see my brother, of course. If you'd come with me, I'll take you to him.'

Without another word she swept past him, holding the now pristinely un-stepped-on hem of her gown away from his boots as if he was contagious. She moved like a dancer, her head high and shoulders perfectly squared, and he found himself left with no choice but to follow or be left behind. The subtle sway of her waist as she walked—or glided, rather, no longer slouching along as she would have once—drew his eye with renewed amazement, although he made sure to disregard it as she stopped to call through a half-open door.

'Harry. Your visitor.'

With obvious unwillingness she waved him inside, coolly averting her eyes from his nod of thanks. For a moment it seemed she was tempted to leave but reluctant good manners evidently prevailed and she followed him—at a safe distance—into the room.

Harry was standing beside the roaring fire, his back to the door, and he turned as he heard them enter.

'Langtree. You're earlier than—' He broke off. 'Beresford? Samuel Beresford? What are *you* doing here?'

At once, he came forward to grasp Samuel's hand, pulling him in to slap his shoulder. 'This is an unexpected pleasure! When did you arrive back in town?'

'Only last night, under cover of darkness. I sneaked into Rookley Manor like a thief and almost scared my mother to death.'

'I imagine she barely recognised you. What has it been—four years since we saw you last?'

Samuel shook his head. 'Above five. I was eighteen when I went away and you just shy of twenty. I can't say you've changed much with time, though—you still look the same.'

It was the truth and he considered briefly how strange it was that one sibling could be so unaltered when the other had almost become another person, uncomfortably aware of Julia's presence at his back. A glance over his shoulder showed she watched him, her eyes slightly narrowed, and the short hairs on his nape stirred inexplicably.

Just as well I didn't come here to see her. What the devil's gotten into the girl?

Pushing the question to the side he accepted the chair Harry offered, glad to draw nearer the fire. The winter chill was made even colder by Julia's unfriendly gaze, and he deliberately didn't return it as she arranged herself in an armchair beside her brother's, warily settling herself among the cushions.

Fortunately, Harry appeared not to notice anything was amiss. 'So. You're home again. And you didn't send word you were coming.'

'No. I left Italy too quickly even to write to my par-

ents, and then I thought to catch them unawares by
showing up unannounced.'

'Is that so? What made you quit the place in such a
rush?' Harry's curiosity turned quickly to a grin. 'No.
Don't tell me. My guess is you paid a little too much
attention to the wrong signor's daughter. Did you have
to flee before you were made to marry her? Perhaps at
the end of a shotgun?'

He laughed and Samuel attempted to force one, too,
although he felt his stomach plummet. Quite accidentally, Harry had strayed too close to the truth, and Samuel had to work hard not to let his smile slip, hoping
the stiffness of his lips wouldn't betray him.

If he hadn't found out Lucrezia's secret he would
indeed have married her, although out of choice rather
than force; and, like a fool, he'd be thinking himself
lucky to be the man who could call her his wife.

With great effort he tried not to let his mind turn towards her but it was too late. Harry's throwaway joke
wrenched open the floodgates, and the memories Samuel was trying to hold back poured through, picture
after picture from what he had imagined would be the
happiest time of his life now soured into raw regret.

Her vivacity was like a dancing flame, warming him
with her mere presence, and now he was left alone in
the cold. From the first moment he had seen her, alighting from a gondola and shielding her eyes from the
Italian sun, it was as though for him all other women
had vanished. Everything about Lucrezia Bianchi had
taken perfection as its blueprint: the raven waves of her
hair and her laughing eyes, the same deep brown as
the strongest coffee, and the way she smiled with her
long lashes half lowered as though to stop anyone but

him from reading her thoughts. She was vibrant and passionate and he'd been so sure their love would be the kind poets spoke of, a connection that would grow year by year until the only thing to part them could possibly be death.

But he had been wrong.

From somewhere he found a careless shrug, praying neither Livingston noticed the rigid set of his shoulders. It wasn't a tale he wanted to tell; not now, while Julia watched him with the strange hostility he didn't understand, and not later when he might have spoken to Harry alone. His pain was private, rooted inside him like a malignant growth, and he had no wish to share either his suffering or his shame with the world.

'I suddenly decided I'd had enough of it. Nothing more dramatic than that.'

The lie didn't come easily but he made himself deliver it with all the nonchalance he could muster. 'After so many years... I simply felt the urge to return home.'

Out of the corner of his eye he saw Julia frown. She was inspecting her fingernails now, although her furrowed brow suggested some question had occurred to her. It seemed unlikely she would choose to voice it but he turned to her regardless, determined to change the subject before anyone could delve any deeper into things he wanted left alone.

'Do you live here now? With Harry rather than your parents?'

She looked up from her study of her cuticles. He'd already noticed her ring finger was bare; she hadn't married and gained a house of her own, then, during his time abroad. Once that wouldn't have shocked him, the Miss Livingston he'd known perhaps not an obvious choice for a bride, although now as she sat near the fire, the light playing over her face to emphasise the height of her cheekbones, he had to admit a glimmer of surprise.

Who would have known she'd turn out like this? That somewhere beneath the gorse bush hair and hunched shoulders a handsome woman was waiting to break free?

If he'd been inclined to fall prey to another striking countenance he might have been in danger from Julia as she was now, her features no longer overshadowed by heavy eyebrows and the line of her profile like tawny stone. There was more colour to her skin than he remembered, as though she had been overseas herself, and for the first time he felt a twinge of unease.

The more he looked at her…the more he studied her sable hair and eyes surrounded by lashes so thick… Did she remind him, in the smallest possible way, of…?

Her voice was as brittle as fractured ice. 'No. I have been staying for a while but will be returning to Burton Lodge shortly, most likely today.'

She smoothed down the lap of her skirts, pointedly looking away from him. 'I don't have the luxury of being able to stay away from home for as long as I wish. That's something I find only men are able to enjoy.'

It was almost an accusation, sharp enough for even Harry to realise something was wrong, but Samuel hardly registered it. His stomach had dropped another notch as he tried to dismiss the unwanted thought dawning on him, the movement of Julia's full lips sketching a parallel to another pair he wished now he had never kissed. The idea she could remind him of the woman he'd left behind was so unexpected it threatened to knock the breath out of him, suddenly caught between the desire to watch the familiar yet different face and the instinct to get up and walk away.

In this light, when she tilts her head towards the fire...

There was a definite resemblance, he acknowledged unwillingly, tamping down a leap of unease.

Signora Bianchi had been lively, bright and warm and so magnetic he hadn't been able to resist her pull—whereas Miss Livingston was like a statue carved from ice. Julia was so cold that she possessed none of Lucrezia's allure, her charms restricted to the glacial beauty that she'd somehow managed to acquire in his absence. Once he had gotten over the surprise of seeing her so altered, any discomfort she caused him would fade, he assured himself, and until then he would simply keep his distance.

That, at least, should be easy enough.

He risked one more swift glance, wishing he hadn't when he noticed the delicate shape of her collarbones above the invitingly low neckline of her dress.

It seems Julia takes little pleasure in my company now and would welcome my avoiding her—although as to why I still couldn't say.

Samuel determined to set the question aside. It was a reunion with Harry he had come for, not his peculiar sister, and what an admittedly attractive young woman thought of him didn't matter. After the debacle in Venice he was resolved never to be led by a beautiful face ever again, and when he inevitably came to wed it would not be to anyone in any way like the woman he had loved before.

Harry coughed, breaking the tension that Julia's tone had spun like a chilly web. Obviously, he didn't understand her manner any better than Samuel did, but with his usual cheerfulness he carried on regardless. 'I'm expecting Colonel Langtree later this morning. We're going over to Brookland to shoot. You'll come with us, I hope? I have all the things here you'll need—spare gun and so forth.'

'I'd be glad to.' Samuel managed a slightly more normal smile. What he needed was to be among friends again and he felt a flicker of relief when Julia rose to her feet.

'I imagine the Colonel will be here soon. As the three of you now have an engagement, I shall wish you good morning and withdraw to pack my things.'

She dropped him a curtsey as stiff as it was perfect and turned away, her gown rustling as she went. Again, she moved with enviable grace and the overwhelming temptation to watch her swept over him, so powerful only Harry's voice stopped him from surrendering to the urge.

'Wait, Julia. How soon are you going? You won't have left for Burton Lodge before I return?'

'I may have.'

Julia paused to look over her shoulder, her curls gleaming like a pile of black pearls. She smiled at her brother, but when she met Samuel's eye it vanished like sugar in a puddle.

'Suddenly, being back under Mother's roof rather than this one doesn't seem so bad.'

Chapter Two

Lady Fitzgerald's ballroom was hot and airless and Julia knew she must be flushed as she smiled up at her partner, suppressing a wince when—once again—he stepped heavily on her foot.

'I beg your pardon, Miss Livingston. I'm afraid I'm not quite as nimble as I once was.'

'Not at all.' Julia twirled, privately grateful for a partner who wouldn't notice if she stumbled herself. It was more difficult to maintain her studied poise when moving at speed, and Sir William's mistakes made it easier to conceal any of her own. 'If anything, it's a challenge for me to keep up with you.'

Sir William beamed, his good-natured face shining with exertion, and Julia found her own smile growing as he manhandled her across the floor. As Papa's friend since before she was born, the old knight was a secure pair of hands to be in, fond of her in a grandfatherly way with thankfully no undertones of anything more, and despite the ever-present danger of his trampling feet, for the first time that evening she felt herself begin to relax.

For the duration of this dance she was safe—from both her mother's scheming and the men who watched her every move—and the moment it was over she'd be at their mercy once again.

Her card was already full. At Mama's insistence she'd accepted every offer, under constant threat from a slender hand on her arm that was far stronger than it looked. If she took too long to graciously agree the hand would tighten, almost pinching the sensitive skin inside her elbow, only loosening when the gentleman had written his name into her little book and her fate was sealed. There was scant enjoyment to be had in a dance under duress, none of her partners aside from Sir William men she would have chosen for herself, but at least for one small mercy Julia was very grateful indeed.

Samuel wasn't there.

She'd made sure to check the moment she'd arrived and was relieved to find him absent from among the jostling crowds. Probably Lady Fitzgerald thought it an unforgivable snub for Viscount Maidwell's son not to attend her famous St Nicholas's Day ball, but for Julia it made the evening slightly more bearable. She hadn't been back to Highbank since their accidental meeting for fear of risking another, preferring to pretend as far as possible that he was still in Italy where he arguably belonged, although the stir his return had made among Guildbury's high society made such pretence difficult. If Samuel had graced the ballroom with his presence Mama would have been at his side at once, trying to engineer some hideous agreement where Julia would have had to endure him for a whole dance, and she felt her spirits lift slightly to think of her lucky escape.

'You're kind to favour me, my dear. I'm sure there are many other young men you'd rather be dancing with.'

'You're quite wrong. If it wouldn't cause eyebrows to raise, I'd dance with you and only you all night.'

Sir William chuckled, Julia's own laugh ringing out as she turned in a thankfully graceful circle, her new gown of green silk glistening beneath the chandeliers. Out of the corner of her eye she caught a glimpse of Mr Sydenham among the onlookers surrounding the floor and quickly returned her attention to her enthusiastic partner, a creeping unease stealing over her at the expression she'd seen on the younger man's face.

Did he—and the rest of her unsuccessful pursuers—have to watch her *quite* so intently, clearly hoping she might change her mind? At times it felt like she was a joint of meat in a butcher's window, their gazes hungry and looking to her to fulfil their appetites. She didn't like it and never would, and as the dance ended she made sure to slip away before anyone could make a move to stop her.

A tall window was set into an alcove to one side of the room and Julia threaded her way towards it, moving through the throng as quickly as she could. Much of the glass was obscured by a heavy velvet curtain and with a swift scan about her she ducked behind it, immediately relieved to at last find herself away from prying, predatory eyes.

She leaned against the window frame, relishing the opportunity to finally *breathe*. The ballroom was so hot, and the constant scrutiny so wearing, and when someone else poked their head around the curtain to intrude into her sanctuary, for a second she thought she might cry.

'Are you hiding?'

She felt herself unclench as she recognised the newcomer. Her cousin Eliza was always welcome company and Julia gave a guilty shrug as she waved her into the alcove.

'Perhaps.'

'I thought you didn't do that anymore. Aren't you supposed to be the pride of Guildbury since your return from Italy?' Eliza raised an eyebrow but with none of the judgement Mama could express with that same movement. 'Here. Take this. You look as though you're about to fall over.'

Her cousin held out a glass of punch and Julia seized it gratefully.

'My saviour. How did you know I'd be thirsty?'

'I saw Sir William Forsyth throwing you around the floor. After that, anyone would need some refreshment.'

Eliza slid into the corner next to her, twitching the curtain farther open to cast a considering eye over the masses that covered every square inch of the ballroom.

'You acquitted yourself well, I thought, despite your bruised toes. Your smile didn't falter for a moment, just as when you danced with Mr Ollerton.'

'You've been watching?'

'Of course. There's little else I can do, is there?'

Eliza rested a hand on her midriff, where the outline of a neat bump was just beginning to show beneath her skirts. 'Watching you try to avoid being trampled by a procession of men is almost as entertaining as dancing myself.'

'I can imagine. Harry was supposed to stand by in case I needed rescuing, but as always…'

With one accord both women glanced towards the end of the room, where the top of Harry's head was only just visible above an encirclement of ladies. Any conversation was too far away to be heard above the din of raised voices, but the flirting of fans and winsome smiles were enough to suggest he was being fascinating indeed.

'Good old Harry. At least he's consistent.'

His audience erupted into distant laughter and Julia couldn't help but smile herself. 'That's certainly one word to describe him. Wherever my brother goes, you know the most eligible debutantes in the county are sure to be nearby.'

Her cousin's mouth twitched. 'Speaking of which…' Eliza scanned the room again. 'Where's my Aunt Livingston? I thought she'd stay just as close to you in turn. How did you manage to shake her off?'

'I slipped away after the last dance but she'll be here somewhere, prowling about for husbands,' Julia muttered darkly, shooting a wary glance over her shoulder as if her mother might have crept up behind. 'It's no accident I chose this shadowy corner to hide in until the next.'

'You're still no closer to making a decision, then, I take it?'

'As to which of my ever-present suitors I might wed? Since they insist on following me around now like a pack of lost puppies, just because I've learned to shape my eyebrows and stand up straight?' Julia wrinkled her nose. 'Oddly enough, no.'

She watched Eliza incline her head thoughtfully, the

feathers in her auburn hair swaying. 'Yes. It can be so difficult to decide.'

Her cousin had married only the year before, while Julia was still abroad, and by her faintly wistful look it seemed she found the experience of being pursued by multiple admirers an agreeable memory—until suddenly her lips moved into a shrewd smile. 'Perhaps that's not surprising, in your case. I suspect there's one man you're waiting for to declare himself.'

'Who do you mean?'

'Samuel Beresford, obviously. You were so in love with him when we were younger it's no surprise if you've set your cap at him now that he's back. You'll have to be quick, mind. From what I hear he's much in demand by ambitious mamas all over Hampshire, and you don't want to miss your chance.'

Julia's fingers tightened around her empty punch glass.

Was that just Eliza's misguided opinion—or, excruciatingly, were others thinking the same thing?

The muscles of Julia's face felt so rigid that her mouth barely moved. 'I was not in love with him and I'm certainly not waiting for him to make me an offer. It was a stupid girlish liking and one I've long outgrown. I'd rather marry a kind man three times my age than allow *him* anywhere near me, and if you hear anyone saying otherwise I hope you'll correct them.'

To her rising dismay Eliza's smile didn't diminish one bit.

'Don't look at me like that. It's the truth.'

Her cousin studied her closely, the blue keenness of her eyes like twin searchlights. 'Is it, though? Why should you be so set against him? He's as handsome as ever. If I wasn't married to Robert...'

'His appearance isn't the problem.'

Julia tried—with limited success—to keep her voice level. She wanted to cut this conversation short, nipping it in the bud before some throwaway word gave Eliza more cause to believe she harboured some secret yearning for Samuel *blasted* Beresford.

'It's his character I object to now. Don't you remember the constant jokes he made at my expense, which encouraged others to do worse? It would be strange indeed if I was keen to make a match after how he treated me.'

'Oh, that.' Eliza waved a dismissive hand, the gesture betraying the fact that her own share of the Livingston good looks meant she'd never suffered an insult in her life. 'We were children then. You can't hold a man accountable for what he did as a boy.'

Eliza's airy indifference hit the same nerve Mama's disregard had played on since Julia was twelve. There was no malice in it, only a complete lack of understanding, but still it stung.

'He may have been a boy when it started but the effect of his words lasted far longer, even after he left town,' Julia replied quietly. 'Have you forgotten how relentlessly I was bullied, until I was ashamed of my own face and my person in general? He was the instigator of much of my unhappiness whether he meant to be or not, and it makes me ill disposed to regard him fondly. If my aunt hadn't taken pity on me and spirited me away for a while I might still be hiding in my bedroom, despairing of my awkwardness and with a shawl thrown over the mirror, even now.'

Some of Eliza's playfulness ebbed away. 'Oh.'

She touched Julia's arm, immediately contrite. 'Well. I'm sure you know best. He doesn't seem to feel the same, however. I've noticed him regarding *you* on a number of occasions since he arrived...though whether fondly or otherwise I couldn't quite tell.'

Julia started. 'Samuel's here? I didn't think...'

She bit off the end of her sentence, cursing herself when Eliza's eyes glittered with renewed interest.

'You must be mistaken. I hadn't realised Samuel was here, but even if he is... He must have been watching some other lady. Certainly he has never looked at me but to find more things to laugh about.'

The corners of Eliza's mouth turned down doubtfully. 'Is that right? He didn't seem to be laughing when you were dancing with Sir William.'

An unpleasant ripple snaked down the back of Julia's gown. Eliza was peering past the curtain at something—or someone—among the crowds, and as she turned Julia braced herself for what she might find.

It was small wonder she'd missed him. Samuel was half-hidden in another alcove set into the opposite wall, a group of his cronies and adoring young ladies all but concealing him from view. He'd been back in Guildbury less than a week and yet it was as if he'd never left, once again surrounded by hangers-on no doubt eager to agree with his every word and Julia was about to turn quickly away again when her heart gave a sharp lurch.

He'd seen her.

There could be no mistaking it. The moment their eyes met she saw him snatch his away, switching his attention to whatever the lady at his left was telling him, although Julia wasn't fooled. For one beat their stares had locked, his deep blue fixed on her almost black, and to her intense dismay she felt heat rush into her already flushed cheeks.

She gritted her teeth on frustration, her heart thumping hard. It was *his* fault she'd turned to look at him; *his* fault that a split-second connection had crackled between them from opposite sides of the room, but now...

Now he's going to think I still admire him. That one glance from him is enough to set my cheeks on fire, just as it was before I knew better.

Eliza's bright scrutiny flitted over Julia's glowing countenance. 'Is something the matter?'

'No.' Quickly, she flicked open her fan, using it to cool herself as well as to hide her face. 'It's just hot in here, that's all.'

'It certainly is. I wonder that Lady Fitzgerald invited quite so many people. I realise it's the first festive ball of the season, but even so...'

Her cousin chattered on but Julia was hardly listening.

Had Samuel really been watching her earlier, as Eliza claimed? And if so, why, when caught in the act now, would he bother to pretend otherwise?

Standing with her back turned resolutely towards him she felt exposed, the nape of her neck tingling as though a fingertip had traced across it. Samuel's admittedly striking blue eyes might be trained on her once again for all she knew, taking in the narrow span of her waist and the gilt flowers twined into her hair, and despite herself she couldn't help wondering if he'd like what he saw.

Not that I'd care if he did. Nothing about him is of interest to me now.

Unease gripped her and refused to let go, squeezing so tightly that for a moment she almost forgot where she was.

Through the haze of her confusion she saw Eliza's attention fix on something over her shoulder.

'Julia…'

The tone of warning came too late. Before she could collect herself she felt a presence behind her, a rustle of expensive skirts that did nothing to ease the racing of her mind.

'There you are, dearest. Don't loiter about behind curtains. It looks furtive.'

Her mother's voice managed to cut through the noise of the ballroom, and Julia briefly screwed her eyes shut. Apart from Samuel himself Mama was the last person she wanted to see, and she took a moment to arrange her face before turning around.

'Sorry, Mama. I didn't—'

She stuttered to a halt, her mouth instantly dry as she took in the two people standing in front of her.

Oh, no. Please, heaven spare me.

Mama's hand was on Samuel's arm, gripping it with the unwavering determination Julia knew all too well. He had no hope of escape and her speechless mortification grew to new heights to realise her mother must have dragged him over. He looked down at her, as accursedly handsome as a Greek statue, and Julia looked silently back; and it would have been difficult for an observer to decide which seemed the most uncomfortable to be brought so unwillingly face-to-face.

'You remember my Julia, don't you, sir? My son Harry's younger sister?' Mrs Livingston waved towards her, continuing smoothly before Samuel could answer. 'Let me reacquaint you. I think you'll find her much altered from the girl you knew.'

Dimly, Julia saw Eliza drop a discreet curtsey and begin to move away, pausing only to take the punch glass from Julia's hand. Her now-empty fingers tried to seize hold of her cousin's sleeve, to keep her there as a barrier between herself and whatever fresh hell Mama was plotting, but Eliza evaded her desperate grasp and disappeared into the crowd.

With nobody now to save her Julia felt her alarm grow as Samuel bowed. 'Good evening, Miss Livingston.'

For some reason he seemed to prefer to address the space over the top of her head rather than her face before he turned back to her mother. 'In fact, ma'am, we've already met since my return. I had the pleasure when I visited Harry at Highbank last week.'

'Did you? She didn't tell me.' Mrs Livingston gave Julia a hard look that the next second segued into her most gleaming smile. 'But don't you think she's changed? She's spoken of now as the handsomest young lady in Guildbury, you know. Isn't she grown into a beauty?'

The moment the words left her mother's mouth Julia braced herself against them, preparing for the inevitable wave of humiliation about to break over her. It was always the same: Mama forcing some unfortunate victim into singing her daughter's praises while the daughter herself wished the ground would swallow her up. It would never occur to Mrs Livingston that in proclaiming Julia only a recent beauty she emphasised how much she believed had been lacking *before*, a hurtful statement made all the worse for coming from a mother's lips. For almost the entirety of her childhood Julia had longed for acceptance that never came, and to know Mama only deemed her worthy now she was considered pretty never lost its sting, a secret pang she would much rather not have to endure while Samuel stood so close by. Probably he was groping for some polite reply, some way to acknowledge as tactfully as possible that she had indeed once been a lost cause, and she fixed her eyes fiercely on the ground, determined he wouldn't see the shame in them when the blow finally came—

'Beauty is subjective, I find. What is more universal is character, and I think I recall Miss Livingston never lacking in that regard.'

Too surprised to stop herself Julia looked up sharply, regretting it as soon as she met Samuel's deep blue gaze. She'd expected him to agree with Mama but somehow he had succeeded in turning the question aside, not *quite* paying a compliment but certainly not rubbing salt into an already open wound, either. She found she wasn't sure what to make of it until her mother broke in with a falsely delighted laugh.

'What a gentleman you are! Clearly, your time abroad was spent honing your skill in flattery.'

Without allowing Samuel any time to make another unsatisfactory answer she turned back to Julia, a sudden edge of menace behind her smile. 'Dearest, I'm sure you'll want to favour the Honourable Mr Beresford with a dance. He's been away five years, you know, and I dare say he's been longing for one the entire time.'

Immediately Julia took a smart step backwards.

'My card is full, Mama. I have no space for another partner. Even if I *wished* to dance with him—' she broke off to pay Samuel a pointed glance that she hoped left him no room for interpretation '—I could not.'

Expecting her mother's annoyance, she was surprised to be met instead by another tinkling laugh.

'Not so. You have Mr Clinton for the next and he has gone home with a sprained ankle. I'm sure Mr Beresford would be only too glad to take his place.'

Julia blinked, careful not to let herself look in Samuel's direction. By slightly turning her shoulder she could hide him from her line of sight and she did so, fixing on her mother with fervent pleading in her eyes.

'I'm getting tired. Perhaps I might sit this one out…'

It was as if she hadn't spoken. With one deft move Mrs Livingston had snatched up the little book that hung from Julia's wrist and pencilled Samuel's name over the top of the unfortunate Mr Clinton's, returning it to her daughter with a satisfied smile.

'There. That's all arranged.'

At her shoulder Julia thought she heard Samuel mutter something but the room was too loud to know for certain. His close presence made the hairs on the backs of her arms stand on end, the low murmur of his voice far more masculine than it had been five years before, and she felt an involuntary thrill to know he was near enough to touch—and, whether she liked it or not, would soon be closer still. She would have to concentrate on keeping up her facade of composure like her life depended on it.

Mrs Livingston's smile was firm. Under cover of brushing a loose curl from Julia's forehead she pulled her closer, dropping her voice to whisper into her daughter's ear.

'This is your chance to make up for the three times

you've disappointed me. You could find yourself as a future viscount's wife if you do as I say—and earn my severe displeasure if you don't.'

Unease twisted through Samuel as he took up his place in the set. Julia's eyes were carefully averted as she stood opposite him but that didn't mean he couldn't see her face, brilliantly lit by the light of a hundred candles, and his discomfort grew with every second he looked her way.

The curls that had once run so wild were tamed now, piled at the back of her head and strewn with glinting petals as though she'd been sprinkled with gold. In a gown of rich green she glowed like an emerald, the colour flattering the newly sun-kissed cast of her skin, and Samuel clenched his jaw tighter.

While he'd believed Julia to be merely cool and reserved he had been able to dismiss her startling good looks, their single meeting at Highbank all the proof he needed that ice now ran in her veins, and any fleeting attraction to Harry's provoking sister would be sure to wither once her resemblance to Signora Bianchi became less of a novelty. The two women weren't so alike after all, he'd determined, Miss Livingston like his former love in face only…although after this evening he wasn't so sure.

Arriving unforgivably late he'd been trying to slip inconspicuously through the crowds when a flash of green silk had caught his eye: a dark-haired young woman in a jewel-toned dress dancing, alive and animated as she laughed up at her partner, and his heart had given a painful jerk as he recognised her radiant face. In that moment Julia was every man's focus, impossible to ignore as her vitality and presence filled the space around her, and to Samuel's alarm he'd realised he couldn't look away. It was the same ungovernable pull he'd felt the first time he'd seen Lucrezia, so mesmerising no one could have resisted, and the glimpse of Julia's smile came at him like a ray of sunshine punching through the thickest cloud.

Where had she found that confidence? That gaiety so completely at odds with the glacial hostility she'd shown him on Harry's landing, when it had seemed she'd lost the ability to laugh? As she twirled with one partner after the next she hadn't been the shy girl of five years prior *or* the hostile Miss Livingston he'd encountered in her brother's house. She was a third version of the same person; another Julia he hadn't known lived within that disapproving skin, and it was that smiling incarnation that had put him so sharply on his guard.

She wasn't so lively now, however. Shimmering beneath the chandelier Julia worried at her lower lip without seeming to realise what she was doing, holding it between her teeth in an unconscious movement he suddenly recalled from years before. When they were younger he'd seen her do the same thing countless times and it appeared even as a refined lady she couldn't stop herself, that one small gesture the tiniest crack in her otherwise impenetrably perfect shell.

He glanced to the side, wishing the couples above them in the set would hurry up and move. The sooner the dance began the sooner it would be over and then he could escape, turning his back on Julia and the novel notion that a ghost of the girl he'd once known might still be buried somewhere her new glossy exterior couldn't quite reach.

Was it possible some of that person might remain—the endearingly shy, uncertain one who had the habit of biting her lower lip? It wasn't something he wanted to consider; her former sweet personality combined with her present looks was a far too tempting prospect and inwardly he cursed her interfering mother for making him wonder, Mrs Livingston's attempt at fishing for compliments not having quite the effect she'd intended. It was honeyed words she'd been after, hungry for admiration for her daughter that she could somehow take credit for herself, but it had been the expression on Julia's face rather than her features that had prompted his unintentionally honest reply.

It only lasted for a half a moment but I saw it clear as day: unhappiness at being reminded of her previous shortcomings.

Her embarrassment had caught at him, laying down the first hint she might not be *entirely* carved out of ice, and the decades-old nibbling of her lip now only built on that foundation.

If she does still carry some traces of who she was before her transformation, then in that regard at least she's less like Lucrezia than I thought. There could still be some softness hidden away beneath Julia's sophisticated surface—whereas Lucrezia never had any to begin with.

The thought was not a comfortable one and he tried to disregard it, determinedly forcing himself to not frown. At last, there seemed to be some movement farther along and as the couple beside him finally began to step out, Samuel saw Julia take a deep breath like one about to face their doom.

He paced forward, extending a hand that she took as hesitantly as if it had been made of dynamite. She refused to look up at him as they circled one another, first turning one way and then the other, her slender fingers holding his with the lightest possible grip. It felt as though the smallest excuse would have made her drop them altogether and Samuel tensed, keenly aware of his every movement in a way he strongly disliked.

I blame her mother for this. I meant to keep my distance but that woman's meddling left me with no choice.

He didn't speak aloud but perhaps his expression spoke for him.

'I didn't mean for Mama to force you into dancing with me.'

Glancing down, he caught the tail end of a sideways glare, the first time Julia had deigned to turn her dark eyes in his direction. 'I had no intention of partnering with you tonight and wouldn't have if my mother hadn't contrived it. Just so that you're aware.'

Despite the warning bells' discordant chiming, Samuel couldn't help a wry smile. *There* was the Julia he was more at ease with: the ice queen, hiding all traces of both the vivacity and hidden vulnerability he'd glimpsed that had, just for a moment, given him cause for concern.

'Are you sure? You seemed so enthusiastic at the prospect.'

She looked up at him sharply. 'Difficult for you to believe, I know. I imagine your attentions are usually far more welcome.'

They parted to walk around another couple, Samuel only able to reply when they came back together to join hands once more.

'My attentions were a result of your mother's intervention, just as you said. If she hadn't insisted on my going to talk to you I would have left you alone, as I'm sure you would have preferred.'

'You'd be correct to think so.'

Julia rose onto her toes, bobbing up and dropping down again and Samuel did his best to ignore how gracefully she moved. When she'd been dancing she'd seemed to glide on air and even when having her feet flattened by Sir William she hadn't stumbled, any hint of the clumsiness he might have associated with her in the past entirely absent.

Side by side now they advanced forward, her light fingers warm in his palm, and despite himself he again felt that glimmer of ill-judged curiosity.

Why was she *so* determined to dislike him? For everybody else he'd seen her with that evening she had a smile, a polite word and sometimes even a laugh, but for him there wasn't even a pretence at tolerance. He knew he shouldn't care and certainly shouldn't ask, but somehow the words made it past his lips before he could snatch them back.

'Since my return your manner towards me has been markedly cool. Might I ask why?'

Her head turned with the quickness of a cracking whip. 'You can't think of any reason?'

'I'm afraid not.'

Julia's lips pressed into a tight line. The dance called for them to part again and she sailed away from him, apparently using the few scant seconds of distance to collect herself.

'If you don't know, I don't feel inclined to tell you.'

They circled each other once again, wary as a pair of hunting wolves, and Samuel had to brush aside a faint prickle of impatience.

If she was displeased with him, why keep the cause a secret? If he'd wronged her somehow she would do much better to tell him so that he might make some amends, rather than hold on to her grievance for the rest of their acquaintance...but that, he realised, could be risky.

He didn't *want* her to like him. If she turned the same charm on him that had so ensnared half the men of Guildbury he might make another mistake, the same disastrous error that had led him to place trust in Lucrezia that she ultimately hadn't deserved. Julia had already turned down three proposals, if what Harry had told him was true, and doubtless had the ability to break countless more hearts just like any other beautiful woman; but his own would *not* be one of them.

Glancing to the edge of the dance floor he saw they were not unobserved. Mrs Livingston was following their every move from her place among the spectators, her sharp eyes missing nothing while beside her a young man couldn't tear his gaze from Julia's rigid face. Samuel didn't know his name but he recognised others in the crowd—Sydenham, Ollerton, Captain Jacobs among them—watching with clear envy as he took Julia's hand for the final time.

The musicians were nearing the end of their piece. Reluctantly, he drew Julia closer, the last stance bringing them almost chest to chest, and he couldn't help a reflexive swallow as she stopped mere inches from his face.

She was tall but still she had to tilt her chin to look up at him and her eyes held him motionless, as dark and secretive as the midnight sky. As a young girl they had seemed set a little too far apart but now the effect was deer-like rather than strange, almost otherworldly in a manner he couldn't explain. She kept him prisoner for one long beat, not saying a word and not looking away, until the audience broke into polite applause and she stepped back—slightly unsteadily, for the first time showing the smallest trace of something less than perfect poise—as if an invisible thread between them had been abruptly severed.

Ollerton was beside them at once.

'That was enchanting, Miss Livingston. I hope you'll still have the energy to partner me in the next.'

Julia turned towards him and Samuel could barely hide his amazement at the instantaneous transformation that swept over her. In the blink of an eye she became a different person: from sullen to sparkling as if a switch had been pressed, her smile so bright and engaging it could have lit up the room as she took Ollerton's outstretched arm.

'Be assured of it, sir. I'm sure the Honourable Mr Beresford would be dismayed if he thought he had in any way disrupted our evening.'

She didn't look at him, her full attention instead fixed on Ollerton's rapt face, although Samuel could have sworn the colour in her cheeks now burned hotter than ever. What he'd seen in her eyes was compelling, an unwanted but undeniable heat beginning to kindle beneath his skin, and he made no move to delay her departure when Ollerton began to lead her away.

He made sure not to watch her go but all the same a stark warning descended like a cold mist, chilling him as it wrapped around his heart.

I never imagined Julia Livingston could be so dangerous.

A woman like that could never be a safe match and he almost pitied the string of hopefuls that followed her jealously with their eyes. There would always be someone tempted by her, hovering on the periphery waiting for the day he might get a chance to strike... and then any chance of happiness would shatter, just as it had for him on the day Lucrezia had revealed the truth that had sent him reeling. In one moment he had watched his plans for the future crumble, and he'd known nothing could be salvaged from the wreckage. All he could do was walk away and so he had, leaving his heart and his trust behind on the streets of Venice, and determined not to make the same mistake twice.

The band members were readying themselves to play again, a few tentative scrapes of a violin catching his ear. His partner for the next dance would be waiting somewhere for him to claim her—a pleasant young lady whose name he had already forgotten and posing none of the same hazards as Julia, although he couldn't quite quell his unease as he moved through the crowd.

Never again would he target the woman to whom every eye turned when she danced. It would be far safer if from now on he made sure to give her a wide berth.

Fortunately, that's the only thing she seems to want from me.

In spite of his determination not to, Samuel couldn't

resist one single glance over his shoulder at Julia's re-treating back—at the same moment she looked round likewise, her head turning away again as their gazes met but not quickly enough for him to miss how fresh colour rushed into her cheeks.

If, of course, her word can be trusted...which I know now, from experience, one should never assume.

Chapter Three

The air was bitterly cold and Julia's breath hung around her in little white clouds as she trudged down the lane that led back to Guildbury, careful not to let the contents of her basket spill onto the frozen mud. It had taken most of the morning to fill it with holly destined to become Yuletide decorations for Burton Lodge, a task she always enjoyed, and the prospect of a pleasant afternoon spent making kissing balls beside the fire was almost enough to take her mind off the other things vying for her attention.

Almost, but not quite.

A vague disquiet accompanied her with every step as she blew on the numb fingertips of her free hand. Mama had been in a suspiciously good mood since Lady Fitzgerald's St Nicholas's Day ball and she had the uneasy feeling she knew why. It was that dance with Samuel—that stupid, unavoidable misstep she wished had never happened—that had made her mother so pleased, setting cogs whirring on any number of terrifying schemes and it made Julia flinch just to imagine what they might be.

'A future viscount's wife', Mama had said, the threat of what would befall her daughter if she didn't comply hanging like the blade of a guillotine. The determination in that hushed voice was the stuff of nightmares for a young woman resolved to make her own choice.

She can't make me pursue him. She's tried before to force me into a match, but even she can't broker one where neither party is agreeable.

Can she?

The most comforting answer was *no*, but she knew her mother too well to relax her guard. One glimmer of weakness, one minuscule inkling that Julia might entertain the idea of looking favourably on Samuel and Mama would be upon her at once, pushing and pushing until a ring was on her finger and the terrible deal was done.

Because it *would* be terrible. Julia scowled at nothing as she walked, the empty fields that bordered the lane innocent of any wrongdoing but bearing the brunt of her discontent all the same. Samuel Beresford had no idea how he'd wronged her—even having the nerve to *ask* her, as if it wasn't the most obvious thing in the world!—and was still the very last man she'd consider marrying even if he made an offer. Just because he'd said something unexpectedly agreeable in the face of Mama's tactlessness didn't mean she'd change her mind, and neither did the fact that the touch of his hand on hers had done strange, fluttery things to her stomach...and *that*, she was adamant, was the end of *that*.

With her head lowered Julia strode onwards, picking her way over the rutted ground. A short distance away the lane split into two: one fork offered a longer but less hazardous route to Guildbury while the other posed a speedier path through a small ford, and for a moment she hesitated.

The river would be high and the crossing precarious, but a gust of frigid air down the back of her neck helped her make up her mind.

'The sooner I can get home, the better,' she muttered into the wind, pulling her cloak more tightly together at the neck as she turned left. 'I'll catch my death staying outside much longer, and then how will my mother fill her time?'

She struggled over the frosty mud, grumbling beneath her breath as she went. If anyone had overheard they might have been surprised at her vehemence but it seemed there was nobody around for miles, only the bright blue sky and scudding clouds keeping her company as irritation nagged at her like a persistent itch.

If she were to be honest, the root of her annoyance wasn't really the wind or the cold, or even Mama's plotting. It was her own disloyal reaction to Samuel that truly irked her as she stumbled along—although she would rather have eaten the spiky contents of her basket than admit it out loud.

Nobody would ever know how borderline impossible it had been to maintain her glacial calm while in his hold. The first moment he'd taken her hand her heart had turned over, an involuntary flip she'd tried to ignore, but her pulse had insisted on leaping higher with each choreographed step they'd taken together across the floor. As a girl the idea of dancing with him had been a secret dream, and to find that, as a grown woman, his warm palm against her glove could still send ripples right through her was not a welcome revelation, a constant threat to the serene elegance she took such pains to convey.

Her only consolation was that he didn't know the commotion he'd caused and she clung to that knowledge as she gathered her skirts, clambering over a stile with as much dignity as she could. She'd made her feelings for him—or lack of them—perfectly clear. If he'd believed for one minute that she still harboured any liking for him, surely there was no danger of him doing so *now*, when she'd looked up at his aggravatingly handsome face and told him how much their being forced together revolted her; and if some contrary little part of her had enjoyed the sensation of his fingers grasping hers then she would just have to snuff it out.

The sound of rushing water grew louder as she walked. Just past a screen of skeletal trees the river stretched out before her, swelled by weeks of rain that had only recently given way to clear mornings sparkling with frost, and slowing her approach Julia ran a doubtful eye over the ford.

The water was so high it had reduced the crossing to steppingstones barely visible above the surface. With her hands full it would be difficult to maintain her balance and she realised she was holding her breath as she cautiously stepped onto the first tiny island, thankful she'd thought to wear her stoutest pair of boots as she felt the slick surface beneath their soles.

Slowly, she moved away from the bank, making her careful way towards the middle of the river. Water ran over her feet, demonstrating at the worst possible time that her boots weren't quite as sturdy as she'd thought, but she braced herself against the chilling wetness of her stockings and stretched out to the next stone. Holding her skirts clear of the water she wobbled, for a horrible moment fearing she might slip, but then her foot came down and relief washed over her to find herself safely perched on another outcrop of rock.

If she kept this pace she'd be across before she knew it and she pressed forward again, growing in confidence as she reached the halfway point. There were only a few more islands to hop and she'd found her rhythm, keeping her eyes fixed downwards to know exactly where to tread—

A sudden bark directly behind her made her jump.

If it was just the slipperiness of the stone she had to contend with she might have been able to regain her balance. What pushed her too far was the dog leaping up to greet her, a soggy blur that knocked her off her feet and was the last thing she saw before she felt the water rise to wrap her in its freezing embrace.

She landed with a loud splash, merciless cold immediately seeping into her bones, and she sucked in a ragged breath, her muscles seizing at once. The water wasn't deep but it was fast flowing and she strained to keep her head above the surface as she tried to push herself up, jagged stones digging into her palms. Her basket had floated free to be borne swiftly away downstream and Julia felt a stab of panic that she might join it, terrified to realise she couldn't stand. The unbearable iciness of the water was so intense it felt like burning, and her throat tightened as she fought against the current, her wet skirts tangling around her legs and trying to hold her down.

'Don't struggle. I've got you.'

A strong hand found her arm and hauled her upright. Her bonnet had come loose and it slipped down to cover her eyes, making her stumble as her unseen saviour half carried her to the river's sloping bank and together they waded ashore.

The hand guided her down onto a fallen tree and Julia hunched forward, wrapping her arms around herself as she tried to catch her breath. Her cloak and dress were soaked and she shivered violently, too frozen to choke out any words from between blue-tinged lips. Meaning to thank her rescuer once she'd managed to regain the feeling in her tongue, the thought fled when he crouched in front of her and lifted her waterlogged bonnet from over her eyes.

'Sit there for a moment. Are you hurt?'

She stared at her saviour with rising horror, her already thumping heart skipping faster. Her brain was still sluggish from the freezing water and her lips too numb to move, and it took what felt like an age to force out a reply.

'N-no.'

Her teeth chattered on the single word but she couldn't make them keep still. Samuel was before her, his face scant inches from hers, and she had to use all her self-control to not groan out loud.

Why him? Why did I have to fall over in front of him?

His brow was creased with concern and she couldn't completely deny the sight of it was a momentary distraction. His blue eyes swept over her and she felt a small shiver of a different kind, recalling the last time they'd been close enough for her to have been able to touch the subtle cleft in his chin. As they'd come to the end of their unintended dance he'd drawn her towards him, so near she'd had to tilt her head back to hold his gaze, and her face had burned as his eyes had locked with hers and she hadn't been able to prevent herself from stumbling when she could finally back away.

'You're certain? You're sure you're not hurt?'

Julia nodded mutely, the movement made jerkier by a particularly strong shiver as she huddled in a miserable, wringing wet heap. The bitter air attacked every sodden inch of her and yet the disloyal working of her own mind was almost as bothersome as the ferocious cold.

She pushed back her hair, unpleasantly aware it hung around her in damp ribbons. Samuel was still watching her, still crouching far too close by for comfort, and she was glad when a movement over his shoulder caught her eye.

A brown-and-white shape was splashing merrily in the water and a welcome surge of righteous anger rose to chase away the thoughts she had no wish to entertain.

'Is that your d-dog?'

Samuel glanced behind him. 'My father's pointer. Nelson. He's only a pup and has yet to learn his manners.'

He rubbed the back of his neck, his concern momentarily tinged with a faint trace of amusement. 'I'd no idea he was such a menace. If I'd known he'd try to drown someone I wouldn't have let him run free.'

The gleam of ill-timed humour made Julia's already rigid frame stiffen. Was he laughing at her again, just as he had when they were younger? Again making jokes where they were least wanted?

As a girl she'd allowed him to tease her because she'd been held captive by her foolish infatuation, but now she knew better. A handsome face didn't mean its owner could get away with treating others however he liked, and the look she turned on him was almost as cold as the water inside her boots.

'You should have been more c-careful,' she shivered furiously. 'What if it had been someone elderly that your d-dog had knocked into the river? Or in poor health? They c-could easily have died from the cold water and you'd have found yourself before the local m-magistrate for murder.'

His faint amusement flickered like a candle in a draught. 'Doubtful, considering the local magistrate is a close family friend, but I take your point. I'm sorry. I should have had Nelson under control.'

He stood abruptly, Julia leaning backwards as he rose. His eye ran over her again, serious now, and she was suddenly grateful that the chill stopped her colour from rising.

'You're drenched. You'll need dry clothes at once or you could catch a dangerous fever.'

She scowled up at him. Now he was standing she could see he was half-soaked himself: his breeches clung to his legs even more than their tapered cut first allowed, emphasising the strong shape of his thighs, and Julia immediately switched her attention to the far safer hem of her muddied skirt.

'What a k-keen observation. It hadn't occurred to me that sitting around like this might not be a good idea.'

Gingerly, she slid off the trunk, grimacing to feel the full saturation of her boots as she stood up. 'I'm near home. I daresay I'll be w-warm again before you are.'

Samuel frowned. 'Unlikely. Burton Lodge is at least

another mile and a half away while my parents' house is less than five minutes.'

He hesitated. His frown deepened and his jaw appeared to tense, enhancing the line of it so sharply Julia almost forgot her irritation.

'I think… Yes. You'll have to come with me.'

She stared at him. 'What?'

'I said you'll have to come home with me.'

'Don't be ridiculous.' She backed away, gripping her soggy cloak to her chest. 'Why would I go anywhere with *you*?'

To her intense annoyance Samuel seemed on the verge of rolling his eyes. 'Perhaps to avoid frostbite? You need to be inside as quickly as possible. It makes far more sense for you to dry off at the closest house rather than risk walking farther than you have to.'

He folded his arms, one of the few men in Guildbury tall enough to be able to look down at her. 'You might have decided you don't like me any longer for reasons of your own, but is your aversion to me truly worth dying for?'

'Of course not.'

'Then come with me. I'm staying at my parents' house until my own is made ready following my return—with them present there can be nothing improper.'

Julia wavered. The largest part of her wanted to refuse, her pride unwilling to bend, but the chill in her marrow was persuasive. Her blood was beginning to feel like icy water and she tried again to supress the chatter of her teeth as she huddled deeper into her uselessly wet cloak.

'Fine. I'll accept your invitation. But only b-because it's your fault I'm in this predicament in the first place.'

Samuel turned away, probably to allow his hidden annoyance to cross his face without her seeing it. 'Good. Nothing would make me happier.'

A retort leapt to the tip of Julia's tongue but she swallowed it the next moment. He was taking off his coat, shrugging it from the broad shoulders she'd been so careful not to notice.

'Put this on.'

She blinked at the proffered coat, horribly aware that a blush was threatening to overcome the frost in her cheeks. 'I couldn't. It's yours.'

'Yes. But I think at present you need it more than I do.'

Samuel thrust it towards her and she had no choice but to catch it. The coat was heavy, obviously made with the English winter in mind, and as Julia swung it around her she revelled in its immediate warmth.

It wasn't just the wool that warmed her, however. The heat from Samuel's body still lingered inside along with the unique scent of his skin: soap and cedar and so appealing that she pulled her ruined bonnet back on just to hide her face.

'Thank you.'

He nodded vaguely, looking around for the dog. It came to his whistle and without another word Samuel began to stride away, the pointer bounding at his heels and Julia following behind, her head bowed and too many thoughts to count jostling inside it.

Samuel purposefully increased his pace as they approached the stone stairs leading to Rookley Manor's front door. Each step was unpleasant, his boots water-logged and his breeches horribly damp, but it wasn't just physical discomfort that made him so keen to reach the safety of the manor's grand entrance hall.

Once they were inside, Julia would become his mother's responsibility, and that moment couldn't come soon enough.

The sound of her squelching footsteps behind him had been a constant reminder not to look back as he'd led her over the field towards his parents' house. Huddled into his coat Julia seemed smaller, again showing a tantalising glimpse of the secret vulnerability he'd caught at Lady Fitzgerald's ball, and he'd determined not to glance at her again. There was something instinctively alluring about a woman borrowing a man's oversize clothes; intimate and faintly arousing, and he was thankful she couldn't see how tightly he now clenched his teeth.

Bantry, his parents' long-established butler, was far too experienced to express any surprise at Samuel's bedraggled appearance, and he merely bowed respectfully as he and Julia dripped onto the polished parquet floor.

'Good morning, sir, ma'am. I wonder might I be of some assistance?'

Under other circumstances the dry query might have made Samuel laugh, but not now. Out of the corner of his eye he saw Julia slide off her spoiled bonnet, still wrapped tightly in his coat, and he turned sharply away again, removing his own hat as he spoke.

'Would you have my mother fetched, please? As you can see, Miss Livingston is in need of her help.'

Bantry took the hat but to Samuel's alarm the butler shook his head. 'I'm afraid Her Ladyship is not at home, sir. She and His Lordship have gone to visit Lady Marten. I understand they don't mean to return until tomorrow morning.'

Samuel froze in the act of pulling one clinging trouser leg away from his thigh.

Of course he knew his parents wouldn't be at Rookley—he remembered that now, so vividly he could have cursed out loud. His mother had told him the night before that she and his father were going to meet her goddaughter's new baby, but in the chaos of the morning he had entirely forgotten. The only person left to host Julia was him, and dread closed its fist around his chest as he realised exactly what that meant.

The same thing must have occurred to Julia herself as he heard her take a step forward, her boots squeaking on the wet floor.

'Your mother isn't here?'

'No. An oversight on my part.'

With great reluctance he turned towards her, wishing he didn't have to when she gazed back at him with wide eyes. If her vibrancy at the ball had been attractive then this new soggy appeal was almost as strong. Her lips had taken on a bluish tinge but the shape of them as they formed into a horrified circle was still prettier than it had any right to be.

'You needn't worry. That doesn't mean I'm going to send you back into the cold.'

The situation teetered on the brink of impropriety. For a single man and a single woman to be alone together in a house would set tongues wagging, but what choice did he have? If he refused to help her it would be his fault if she fell ill—or worse—and with what felt like a rock forming in his stomach he made up his mind.

'Bantry. Would you take my coat and Miss Livingston's cloak and have them dried, please? And ask a couple of the maids to come. Our guest will need to be made warm and dry as quickly as possible.'

'Yes, sir. At once.'

The butler gestured towards the servants' corridor and immediately a pair of maids came forward. They descended on Julia and began to peel away the layers that swaddled her, first his coat and then the cloak that hung around her in damp folds. With every deft movement Julia murmured her thanks, attempting to smile with those numbed lips, but it wasn't her mouth that now drew his reluctant eye.

Her wet dress hugged the contours of her body in a manner almost indecent, making imagination unnecessary if he was to wonder what lay beneath the sprigged muslin, and Samuel felt his mouth run dry. He ought to look away—wanted to, even—but something made it damnably difficult, the secret line of her hips and the sweep of her waist seizing his attention and not willing to let go. With her back to him he could easily make out the slender length of her legs and the soft roundness above them, and he only had time to briefly give thanks he couldn't see the front of her before he tore himself away.

'Ellen and Martha will take care of you. If you'll excuse me, I'll go to change.'

He walked away without giving her time to answer, making for the grand staircase at the back of the hall. Behind him he heard the maids fussing and Julia's shaky voice in reply, but he didn't stop until he was safely in his own rooms and could shut the door more firmly than necessary, in a hopeless attempt to block all thought of her out.

Forty-five minutes later, hastily bathed and in clean shirt and breeches, Samuel frowned at himself in the mirror above his bedroom mantelpiece.

The picture of Julia's enticingly transparent gown tried to offer itself again and he batted it back, his frown turning to more of a scowl. He had to do his duty as a host and those kinds of images weren't helpful, an alarming interest somewhere ungentlemanly making him press his fingers against his eyes.

I'll go down, check she hasn't keeled over, and then she can leave. Surely, the maids will have dried her off by now?

Harry would never forgive him if he allowed Julia to succumb to frostbite beneath his roof, Samuel thought darkly as he made himself cross towards the door. For some reason Livingston was fond of his wretched sister, and as Samuel was fond of Harry in turn, he knew he ought to make sure she was comfortable—even if the idea made him very *un*comfortable indeed. The sooner she left Rookley, the better, every minute she spent there a minute too long, and he gritted his teeth as he descended the staircase again and made for his mother's best parlour.

It was the warmest room in the whole house and it came as no surprise to find Julia sitting close to the fire, her chair drawn so near to the flames it seemed she was trying to get into the grate with them. What he *hadn't* been expecting was her appearance—or how swiftly he would realise there didn't appear to be a gown beneath the blanket drawn around her shoulders.

She looked round when he opened the door, pure panic flashing over her face as she saw who had entered the room. For half a second they stared at each other in wordless horror, but then Julia pulled the blanket more tightly around her and Samuel feigned a sudden fascination with the chandelier hanging above his head.

'I'm sorry.' He addressed the crystal droplets, fixedly inspecting each one as he sensed Julia trying to sink lower in her chair. 'I thought you'd be dressed. It wasn't my intention to intrude.'

To his dismay his voice sounded strangled and he winced internally, glad when Julia's seemed every bit as strained.

'Your maids took my gown to have it washed and dried. I'm afraid it's me who will have to intrude on your hospitality a while longer until it's ready. They said your mother's parlour had the best fire, so they brought me in here to stay warm while I waited for them to come back.'

Samuel nodded, still squinting up at the chandelier, although his heart sank. For how *much* longer would she need to stay at Rookley, her presence so unsettling in ways he didn't want to admit? What he wanted was for her to have been fully dressed and waiting to go, and he could have drawn a line under this whole unfortunate episode with a large glass of port.

'There's no rush,' he lied. 'I just came to see how you fared and to ask if you have everything you need.'

There was a soft sound as Julia shifted in her chair, apparently managing to knock a cushion onto the floor, which he heard her hastily retrieve. 'Yes. In the absence of my own things they were kind enough to find me one of your mother's shifts to wear until mine was dry. I hope she wouldn't think that an imposition.'

'I can guarantee she would not,' Samuel assured the ceiling. 'If anything, she'd much rather you borrow one than be...'

He let the end of his sentence die, belatedly aware in which unacceptable direction it had been going.

She'd much rather Julia borrow one than be naked under that blanket? Is that what you were going to say?

The image of her clinging gown burst upon him again and it was all he could do to prevent his mind from going further still, hauling himself back from the brink with all the strength he could muster as temptation tried to carry him away...

To his relief Julia was the one to break the awkward silence.

There was a rustle of blankets, another creak of her chair and then her voice so low it was almost lost to the crackle of burning wood.

'Thank you,' she mumbled. 'For this and for pulling me out of the river. I'm not sure what would have happened if you hadn't come to help.'

Surprised, Samuel wasn't quite quick enough to prevent himself from glancing down. It was the first time she hadn't sounded angry, or haughty, or any of the other disagreeable sentiments she managed to convey with just her tone, and he was about to answer when the sight of her made it suddenly difficult to find the right words.

Each curl of her raven hair gleamed in the firelight like a ring of the most expensive jet, her eyes sparkling with the reflected dancing of the flames. The blanket covered her right down to her feet but her sun-kissed throat was exposed, turned a rich sepia in the shadows, and that single flash of bare skin above her collarbones sent a tremor through him he didn't want to understand.

She was beautiful, and when she wasn't scowling at him or turning up her nose she was more beautiful still—and that novel civility was even more danger-ous than her face. It hinted at the sweet-natured per-son he suspected might still exist beneath the pretence she insisted on, someone far less brittle and far more human, and if she dropped her disdain in favour of it there would be nothing to stop him from wanting to get closer still. *That* would be a mistake that couldn't be allowed to be repeated, leading to possibilities he had no desire to entertain, and he knew he sounded brusque as he replied.

'As you said, it was my fault you were in there in the first place.' Samuel wrenched his gaze away from her, turning it resolutely back towards the chandelier. 'The very least I could do was make sure you didn't freeze to death afterwards.'

When two pairs of footsteps sounded in the corridor beyond, Samuel offered up a prayer of thanks that the maids must be returning with Julia's gown.

Unfortunately, he was wrong.

The parlour door burst open and both he and Julia started, neither prepared for the suddenness with which it swung inwards. A figure stood on the threshold, bathed in the pale winter sunlight streaming in from the hall, and if Samuel had felt uncomfortable before, *now* his stomach sank down to his boots.

'Madam. This is an unexpected pleasure—'

Mrs Livingston sailed into the room as though she owned it, ignoring the cowering maid at her back and taking in the scene with one slash of her narrowed eyes. They flicked from Samuel to Julia and back again and he could have sworn there was a glimmer of triumph when she delivered her verdict.

'Spare me the pleasantries, Mr Beresford. I see what you've contrived.'

There was a quick movement as Julia stood up, her once tawny countenance now blanched. She took a step towards her mother but was checked with one regally raised hand, his own legs feeling strangely leaden when Mrs Livingston fixed him with a direct stare.

'I was informed that this was where I would find my daughter. I didn't quite believe it, and yet here we are.' She gestured to the room at large. 'It seemed impossible that a man of your standing should do such a thing but perhaps I was too trusting. You've compromised an innocent young woman, sir. If talk of *this* were to leak out, Julia would be ruined.'

Mrs Livingston's expression was severe but Samuel was certain he caught a hint of a smile behind her thinned lips. She looked more like someone who was pretending offence rather than truly feeling it, but all such thoughts were eclipsed by a dawning realisation beginning to take hold of his insides. A coldness was spreading through them, like frost forming on a window, and even before she'd finished he knew what she was going to say.

'I think you know what must be done,' she continued, still with that poorly concealed satisfaction. 'There can be no alternative. You will have to marry my poor daughter now you have dishonoured her—and you will have to do it fast.'

Chapter Four

Julia's head swam as she stared at her mother, the room around her growing blurry.

She's done it. I didn't think she could, but she's found a way.

It was the very thing she had feared. Mama had somehow managed to force a match, or was at least trying her very best to, and Julia grasped the back of her chair as her legs suddenly felt too weak to bear her up.

'No, Mama. Mr Beresford has done nothing wrong. In fact, he was helping me. You can't punish him for that.'

With desperate eyes she saw Samuel glance at her, his own blank with shock. He was still standing just inside the doorway, only a few paces from her mother, but he seemed miles away, probably so gripped by dread that he wished himself in another place altogether.

Mrs Livingston drew herself up to her full height. 'You were seen.'

'By whom?'

'Mrs Heston,' she answered at once. 'It was she who

told me where you were. She saw you coming out of Gaters Lane, soaking wet and wearing Mr Beresford's coat around you. Now I come here and find you like this—practically naked in his house, with only a blanket to preserve your modesty, and you say he did nothing wrong?'

The victorious undercurrent in her voice made Julia's stomach knot. Her mother's outrage was a charade: in truth, Mama was delighted that her daughter had compromised herself with the richest and most eligible man in town, and Julia realised she was shaking now as much as she had when she was pulled from the freezing river.

'You know this is Viscount Maidwell's house and not Samuel's own,' she persevered, struggling to frame the words. 'He didn't realise his parents wouldn't be here. His only intention—'

Mrs Livingston cut off any argument with a flick of her wrist. 'Who knows what his true intentions were in bringing you here? The facts are that your dignity has been injured and that of our family. He must wed you now whether he likes it or not.'

Almost unable to breathe for horror, Julia snatched another look at Samuel. He was watching her mother as if he couldn't believe what he was hearing, his shoulders rigid and his face an expressionless mask. Mama was slandering him shamefully and yet he couldn't seem to speak, forcing Julia into the unthinkable position of trying to defend him herself.

Until that morning her opinion of him had been in little danger of changing. Even after dragging her out of the water he'd tried to make a joke of it, the same unwanted humour that had bitten so deep when they were children rising again to the fore, but then he had taken her by surprise. Surrendering his coat to her was the act of a gentleman and taking her into his home, despite his obvious reluctance, showed more kindness than she might have expected. She still didn't like him, but she couldn't in all good conscience allow her mother to cast aspersions that he didn't deserve.

Julia released her grip on her chair, stumbling towards her mother on unsteady feet. The blanket was still draped around her and it dragged along the floor like the train of a wedding dress—something that unless she acted fast she might soon be forced to wear.

Samuel moved backwards as she staggered past but she didn't turn her head. Even while stunned he was too handsome by half and there was nothing to be gained by noticing it, instead training her eyes full on her mother as she seized her arm.

'Please, Mama. Please don't say these things. Mr Beresford was my saviour today, not the reverse. If you do this—'

'*I'm* not doing anything.' Mrs Livingston again snipped off the end of her daughter's sentence. 'It has nothing to do with me. It wasn't *me* who insisted you go to a man's house without a chaperone to end up in a state of undress. Once Mrs Heston has spread word of what she saw, tongues will begin to wag, and if she's guessed what followed…'

Julia's mouth moved but nothing came out.

What was there to say? Loath as she was to admit it, her mother was right. Mrs Heston was a notorious gossip and she used rumours like currency, buying her way into the centre of society by always having the latest news. There was no hope she would keep what she'd seen to herself and it was naive to think she hadn't already begun to speculate what had happened once Julia reached Rookley Manor, although Samuel had evidently yet to accept that as fact.

He paced away, going to stand beside the fire as if a distance of a few yards could make all the difference. 'Madam. As much as I respect your daughter, I never had any thought of taking her as my wife. Perhaps this lady—Mrs Heston—might be persuaded not to speak? There must be another solution, one more acceptable to Miss Livingston as well as myself.'

Mama immediately and vehemently shook her head, her hand tightening over Julia's. 'There is not. You know so. Surely you wouldn't try to flee what your honour demands? Even if Mrs Heston hadn't seen you, you have still brought about my daughter's shame by bringing her here and forcing her into such an undignified situation.'

Julia tried to pull away, humiliation and misery coursing through her, but her mother held firm.

'How am I to believe you didn't intend to use her ill? I doubt other mothers would be quick to trust you with their daughters if I were to tell them how you treated mine.'

Her mother raised her eyebrows ominously, steely determination radiating from her, and Julia felt any last desperate hope of a reprieve shrivel and die. Between Mrs Heston's loose lips and Mama's willpower, it seemed the battle was lost and she thought her trembling legs might give way when her mother abruptly released her hand.

'I must go to find your gown. I may not have arrived quickly enough to save you from your initial shame but

I can at least shorten its duration now. You can't stand around wearing naught but a blanket and shift, even if the damage has already been done.'

Mama swept away, beckoning imperiously to the maid still hovering at the door. Poor Ellen looked helplessly to Samuel for instruction but Julia saw he didn't notice, desperate unhappiness growing in his eyes.

'You argued that our spending time together unsupervised has ruined your daughter, madam. How is it that you'll willingly leave her alone with me now?'

Her mother almost allowed her triumph to show for a moment. 'I'd have thought that was obvious. What's the point in shutting the stable door once the horse has bolted? There's little danger in leaving you alone for a few minutes now that there's an understanding between you…is there?'

Julia stared at her bleakly, knowing exactly what she intended. If the two of them were left alone again it would add more fuel to the fire, giving further opportunity for Mama to claim some line had been crossed. They could only incriminate themselves further and Julia thought her tight chest might burst as Mrs Livingston followed Ellen from the room, barely able to keep a smile from her scheming lips as she went out and closed the door crisply behind her.

A terrible silence fell over the parlour.

Julia wavered, not knowing whether to chase after her mother or to stay where she was. Her limbs felt like water and hurrying anywhere was out of the question, although when Samuel dropped heavily into a chair beside the fire she found the strength—just—to stagger a wary step towards him.

He was holding his head in his hands, his face hidden from view. For an untold span of time the heavy silence continued, taut and agonisingly tense as both Julia and Samuel remained trapped in their private horrors, each trying to make sense of how their worlds had just fallen so spectacularly apart. It was unbelievable, impossible, and as Julia stared down at Samuel's bowed head she wondered how on earth they were supposed to proceed.

At last, after what could have been a few minutes or a few hours, Samuel lifted his head. He still didn't glance up at her as she hovered near his chair, instead turning so only his flame-lit profile was visible.

'Did you plan this?'

His voice was hoarse. His silhouette was sharp against the flames and even her turmoil couldn't make Julia blind to it, the combination of her numb dismay and the chiselled lines of his face making it hard to make sense of the question.

'Plan what?'

'This.'

He twisted in his chair, at last meeting her eye. 'A situation to force me into an engagement. Was this your ploy from the start? I suppose someone must have told you I walk by the river with Nelson every day. It would have been easy for you to arrange to be there at the same time I was.'

Julia gazed down at him, her heart beginning to thump harder beneath the thin linen of her borrowed shift. 'I beg your pardon? Are you accusing me of dragging us into this position *on purpose*?'

She saw Samuel's neck flex as he clenched his jaw, perhaps biting back further accusations, but she gave him no chance to voice them. Angry amazement built inside her in a rising tide, the shocking injustice of his allegation cutting far too deep. When she'd entered the parlour she'd been so cold she'd thought she might never feel warm again but now heat spread beneath her skin, the idea that he thought she *wanted* to be in this awful predicament too much to bear.

'Have you run mad? I believe I made it clear I had no interest in spending time with you. Why, then, do you flatter yourself that I'd willingly sentence myself to a lifetime at your side?'

To his credit Samuel didn't flinch. Only the telltale movement of the muscle in his neck betrayed he was not as calm as he appeared.

'I don't know. I don't have the first clue how your mind works. How am I to understand what goes on inside your head? You profess to dislike me but won't say why, and now this… All I know for certain is that what you say and what you mean are clearly not the same thing.'

He stood abruptly to stride away from her. Pacing the floor he was like a caged animal and Julia watched him without moving, frozen in place by her leaping anger and frustration that he could be so recklessly *unfair*.

She'd been wrong to think he could be a gentleman. When he'd given up his coat and brought her to shelter at Rookley Manor, she'd wondered if there might be another side to him to contrast with the boy she'd known, but now she saw that wasn't so. Clearly, his merit only stretched so far: he was as arrogant as ever if he imagined she'd deliberately set out to ensnare him, and then didn't even have the grace to believe her when she told him the truth.

Still pacing he threw her a dark glance. 'I don't see that we have much choice,' he went on grimly, each word like a pinprick to her skin. 'What your mother said is true. Your reputation would suffer if people heard of this morning's situation. The rumours would only exaggerate the tale until people believed I brought you here to ravish you, which would reflect just as badly on my eligibility as it would yours.'

He crossed to the fireplace and rested his fists on the mantel, turning his burning eyes to her in the mirror above. Their reflected heat was scalding but it was Julia's turn not to flinch, returning their intense unhappiness and distrust with just as much force.

'Do you truly think I want this? To marry a man who has so little regard for me that he doesn't trust my word?'

His back was to her but the mirror image of his face showed his thoughts as she raised her chin, challenging him with all the power and dignity she could muster.

How could he think *he* was the wronged party? That their enforced connection was in some way more agreeable to her than it was to him? He was everything she'd sworn she never wanted in a husband but fate had conspired against her, perversely matching her with the person she would have chosen last of every man on earth. Thanks to him she'd had to bear years of mockery and low confidence, and now she would be stuck with him for ever, the cruel irony of it stinging her eyes.

Why he was so set against marrying *her* couldn't be clearer. He still thought of her as an ungainly oddity, she had no doubt, never for a moment considering her anything more. Even after so many years had passed he still didn't see her as a desirable woman, and shame added an even sharper edge to Julia's tongue.

'I could have had my choice of men but instead I waited. I wanted a man who would love me, value me for myself instead of what was on the outside…and instead I get *you*.'

She blinked rapidly to fight back the tears threatening to bead her lashes, fiercely determined he wouldn't see her cry. Samuel's gaze never strayed from hers, and she thought she saw him stiffen further when she pulled her blanket up higher to hide her aching throat.

After a tense pause he summed up their predicament with succinct bleakness.

'Then we're agreed. Neither of us wants this marriage, and yet we must go through with it regardless.'

His curled fists pressed the mantel as if trying to crack it beneath his hands, solid stone barely a match for his dismay. Julia merely stood like a statue, and she delivered her own conclusion with all the emotion of a shard of ice.

'So it would seem, Mr Beresford. As you said, we don't have much choice.'

Samuel watched from the window of his study as the Livingstons' carriage bore Julia and her accursed mother away, feeling as though all his hopes for the future were being taken along with them.

Even after the carriage had disappeared he didn't move away from the glass. He stared out at the frosty grounds below, Rookley's hedges and fountains sparkling in the cold sunlight, and dimly he wondered how he had allowed things to spiral so catastrophically out of control. When he'd gotten up that morning he'd had no idea what lay in store, and now he wished more than anything he could turn back the clock.

Engaged to Julia Livingston. How the hell did I let this happen?

He closed his eyes, although it made no difference to the images that flitted past them.

Julia in her clinging gown, every curve and contour laid bare…how pleasant it had been when she'd briefly spoken to him with something other than dislike…and then the fury that had blazed from her as she'd denied all wrongdoing, so powerfully attractive in her passion that despite his own anger he hadn't been able to look away…

He slowly butted his head against the glass as if to knock some sense into himself. It was true he'd had no option but to consent to an understanding. If he'd refused it would bring disgrace down on his family, and allowing his parents to suffer for his stupidity was out of the question. Whether Julia herself should shoulder some of the blame he still wasn't sure, her intense denial certainly very convincing…

The parallels with Lucrezia were so vivid he felt himself shudder. Another ebony-haired beauty who captured the attention of every man around her, possessing the same vibrancy and pulling him closer with no effort at all: was that to be his fate?

'Perhaps I'm cursed,' he muttered to the silent room around him. 'Perhaps it's my destiny to go through life tied to a woman who'll never give me a moment's peace of mind.'

The memory of the final time he'd seen Lucrezia tried to circle back but he turned his face away, determined it wouldn't intrude again. In that sunny half hour she'd finally spoken the truth, ripping the scales from his eyes with cruelty he hadn't known she possessed, and there had been no going back. His trust was damaged almost beyond saving and there was no chance Julia could be the one to repair it, the very opposite of the safe wife he had one day intended to find.

He turned away from the window, withdrawing into the shadows of the study. What he wanted was a drink: a large one, and then another and then however many more it took to stop the alarm bells from shrilling in his ears. How long would it take Julia to betray him in the same way Lucrezia had? If she was telling the truth— which he doubted—and she hadn't contrived to bring their situation about, then there was even less to stop her from seeking amusement elsewhere. Julia would never lack opportunities to turn to another, and if she disliked him as much as she claimed then his wedding ring on her finger would surely count for nothing.

With unthinking strides he made for the bell pull hanging beside the empty fireplace, pulling it more sharply than he'd intended. Sick dread swirled in his stomach and he steadied himself against the wall, taking a deep breath that he held until his lungs burned.

At least Mother and Father will be pleased. The marriage of their heir will surely mean a fine grandson in time to carry on the Beresford name. What a consolation for having a faithless wife—assuming any child will be mine at all.

An unobtrusive knock at the study's door heralded Bantry's arrival. He came to stand just inside the doorway, waiting politely to hear the reason for his summons, and Samuel managed to find a grim smile.

'Would you have the port brought up, please? I think the whole decanter.'

The butler would never presume to argue, although Samuel caught his eyes flick towards the clock. It was indeed far too early for a gentleman to start calling for liquor, but under the circumstances an exception must be made, the morning's events calling for the sweet oblivion only fortified wine could provide.

'Very good, sir.'

The butler bowed and turned to leave, only pausing when Samuel spoke again.

'Oh, and Bantry. You can be the first to congratulate me.'

'Congratulate you, sir?'

'Yes.' Samuel smiled a little wider, the tautness of it making his lips hurt. 'It would seem I'm to be wed.'

Chapter Five

A dinner party to honour an engagement would usually be a joyous affair, Julia supposed as she sat at her dressing table, waiting for Fenshaw to finish wrestling her hair into an elegant knot. The bride-to-be would smile and blush and her fiancé adopt an expression of modest pride, and everyone would toast the happy couple and shower them with the congratulations they deserved. It would be an evening of laughter and merriment and everyone should be delighted, not least the two people who would soon be joined as one.

Julia's lips turned down at the corners, her expression in the mirror one of sour regret.

That was the scenario she'd always hoped for when she finally came to celebrate her match—not this debacle Mama had planned, where neither the bride nor the groom wanted to sit next to each other for the length of one meal let alone a lifetime afterwards. Ever since her mother had announced she'd invited Samuel and his parents to dine at Burton Lodge Julia had barely slept, three nights spent staring up at nothingness until weak dawn light crept beneath her curtains, and as she gazed at her reflected face she saw dread in her eyes as well as shadows beneath them.

She hadn't seen Samuel since the disastrous day that had ruined her life, and the idea of encountering him in her own home sat inside her like a brick. Lady Maidwell had sent a letter of warmest wishes, the Viscountess's excitement seeming to rival even Mama's, but from her reluctant fiancé himself there had been nothing but the most resounding of silences. Clearly, the space of a few days had done little to kindle any enthusiasm in him, and for Julia's part her misery only grew hour by hour, watching the clock with morbid fascination as the time until her next humiliation dwindled.

'There, ma'am. Finished.'

Fenshaw at last took a step back, surveying her creation with one eye expertly closed. 'Up at the back as your mother requested, but a frame of curls left at the front as I know you prefer. I think the combination looks very well.'

Julia gave her a wan smile. 'Thank you. I feel sometimes you should have been a diplomat rather than gone into service.'

Her lady's maid looked gratified and Julia turned her head slightly to examine the finished result. Her hair was indeed a masterpiece in diplomacy: the crown of ringlets swept up off her neck showed her delicate nape and the collarbones beneath, both gifts for which Mama was adamant she be grateful, while the cloud of tiny curls at each ear made her feel as though she had something to hide behind, a carry-over from the shy years she could never fully escape. Their dark gloss contrasted with the cream of her gown and under other circumstances she might have been pleased by the reflection that stared back at her from the glass...

But not tonight.

Hardening herself against the urge to lay her head down on the dressing table's polished surface, Julia tucked a stray wisp back into place. It hardly mattered how she looked. Samuel wouldn't find any beauty in her whatever she wore or however many hours poor Fenshaw had to slave to tame her spiralling curls, and if she thought otherwise she'd soon be disappointed. He still thought of her as he always had: as Harry's strange, awkward younger sister with little to recommend her, and his reaction to having to make her his wife left her in no doubt as to how much the prospect filled him with disgust.

A far-off knock at the front door made her stiffen in her chair.

They're here.

At once, her heart leapt. Samuel and his parents were on her doorstep and she had no choice but to see them, weathering an evening she was sure both she and Samuel would have rather pitched themselves into the River Avon than endure. To make matters worse, Harry wouldn't even be in attendance to act as a good-natured buffer. Her brother was suffering from a heavy cold and under strict orders not to leave Highbank lest he catch a chill, but even with his aching head and streaming nose, Julia would have switched places with him in an instant.

'That will be Mr Beresford, I imagine, ma'am.'

Fenshaw was tidying away the silver-backed brushes but Julia still caught a trace of concern on her down-turned face. There could be no secrets between a lady's maid and her mistress, and Julia felt a pang of appreciation that at least *someone* was willing to acknowledge her engagement might not be the happy event her parents were pretending.

'Yes. I suppose I'll have to go down.'

She stood up. The largest part of her wanted to collapse straight down again but she made herself pull her shoulders back, lifting her chin as Fenshaw gave the ribbons at the back of her gown a final tweak.

'You look wonderful, ma'am. I only hope Mr Beresford realises it.'

The lady's maid stepped backwards and Julia gave her another bleak smile as she rustled past on her way to the door.

'It's very kind of you to say so, but I think we both know that he won't.'

Her heart raced like a hare through a field as she descended the staircase that swept into Burton Lodge's hall. The hall was empty, and with colossal unwillingness Julia followed the hum of voices to her mother's parlour, having to stop to take a deep, calming breath before she pushed open the door.

Mama and Lady Maidwell sat together on a sofa, absorbed in some conversation clearly of great interest to them both, while Papa and the Viscount stood near the fire. Only Samuel was alone, staring out the window at the darkness beyond with his back resolutely toward the rest of the room—and it was to him that Julia couldn't help but look as she entered, her breath catching as he turned and their eyes met for the briefest of agonising instants.

There was an immediate flurry and Julia looked round, her already skipping heart picking up its pace even higher. Papa and Viscount Maidwell offered suave bows but it was their wives who had sprung into life, Mama and Samuel's mother falling on her at once.

'Miss Livingston—Julia! Oh, you lovely creature. Come here and let me kiss you!'

She had no time to collect herself before she was captured in a surprisingly firm embrace. The Viscountess must not have known how Mama had forced Samuel into their engagement, Julia thought with a dart of uneasy relief. Surely if she had she wouldn't be nearly so delighted, hugging her soon-to-be daughter-in-law so tightly now that it was a miracle nobody's stays cracked.

'It's the most wonderful news. I can't tell you how happy Maidwell and I are to be welcoming you into our family!'

Still pressed against a perfumed bodice, Julia glanced over the Viscountess's shoulder. Samuel was watching, his face tight, although even his strained expression didn't make him any less handsome. His jaw was enhanced by being held so firmly and his shoulders broader for their tension, and as she patted Lady Maidwell's silken back, Julia prayed for the strength not to scream.

Why did she still have to find him so cursedly attractive, even after everything he'd done? It made it harder than it should have been to maintain her rigid dislike, drinking in the clean line of his profile and the way his hair fell *just so* over his brow without being able to stop herself. By the look of him he hadn't been sleeping well, either, and Julia almost felt a gleam of sympathy, the circles beneath his eyes matching those under her own. If he'd reacted with even a fraction less revulsion to their predicament they could possibly have found some common ground, perhaps even re-building what his boyish unkindness towards her had destroyed—but his distrust of her word and obvious disgust for her person had pushed her too far to forgive him now. They would both just have to grit their teeth and get on with it, and Julia bit the inside of her cheek in a warning not to glance at him again.

At last, the Viscountess released her, and Julia forced a smile, hoping it didn't look as pained as it felt.

'It's an honour to have you here, Your Ladyship. I thank you for your good wishes and am glad to have your kind approval.'

It was the line Mama had coached her to parrot but it seemed to hit its mark. Lady Maidwell beamed, her smile genuine, although any tentative relief Julia might have felt vanished when the Viscountess waved towards the sofa she and Mama had vacated.

'You and Samuel should sit there now. I want to look at the two of you together.'

Julia froze. The very last thing she wanted to do was sit down on a far too small sofa with a man she de-tested, but four pairs of eyes were trained on her, and inwardly cursing the day she'd been born, she slowly moved for the sofa and sat rigidly at its farthermost edge, trying her very best not to fall off the end.

With manfully supressed reluctance Samuel came forward, the sofa creaking ominously as he sat down beside her. It could only comfortably hold two *small* people, and Julia's heart fluttered like a trapped bird when Samuel's hand accidentally grazed her arm, a sudden shower of sparks glittering through her. Out of the corner of her eye she saw him hesitate, perhaps torn between apologising and pretending it hadn't happened, the awkwardness between them so tangible that her toes curled inside her silk slippers.

She sat motionless, trying not to breathe. The same tantalising scent she'd caught on his coat the day he'd pulled her from the river hung about him again now—clean and slightly woodsy and so enticing that she was tempted to lean closer—and it was almost a relief when Lady Maidwell seated herself directly opposite.

The Viscountess looked from Julia to Samuel and back again, leaning forward to take the full measure of the scene set out before her.

'Don't they look well together, Mrs Livingston? As handsome a couple as any I've ever seen.'

'Oh, yes. A perfect pair.'

If the Viscountess hadn't been sitting in front of her, Julia would have shot her mother a black look. To call herself and Samuel a pair of *anything* was beyond the pale, his tense form at her shoulder never less welcome. She was horribly aware of every tiny movement he made, even down to the undulation of his chest as he breathed, and she didn't dare speak for fear nothing of sense would come out.

If Samuel was struggling, however, he was doing a good job of hiding it. He was staring straight ahead, bearing his mother's scrutiny with admirable patience, and he even managed to control his face when she leaned forward again to pat Julia's hand.

'Dear Julia. To think we've known you for so many years, and now this happy event… We had no idea, did we, Maidwell?'

She stopped to peer expectantly at her husband. The Viscount was still leaning against the fireplace, he and

Papa like a set of bookends at either side of it, but he immediately shook his head.

'No. No idea at all.'

Apparently satisfied with this scant input, the Viscountess continued. 'Samuel and Harry have always been friends, of course, but I confess I hadn't foreseen a match with you. With you both recently returned from Italy, however, I suppose you've more in common now than before my son went away. Perhaps I should have expected this after all.'

Julia was trying to think up some response when Samuel turned towards her.

'You were in Italy?'

His straight brows drew together, for the first time since she'd entered the room something other than discomfort edging into his expression. It was the first time he'd directly addressed her, too, his tone less flat than she might have expected, and she wasn't sure she liked the flicker of *something* that leapt up as a result. 'Whereabouts did you visit?'

Her own forehead creased. Why was he asking? It wasn't as though he would care whatever she replied, but with so many people watching she had little choice but to answer. 'Milan. I went with my aunt and uncle. We stayed for about eighteen months and I came home again in September.'

Samuel watched her for a moment and Julia silently pleaded with her cheeks not to redden. An unreadable look passed over his face as if he was thinking something he didn't intend to share, but then he looked away again with a single dip of his chin. 'It's a beautiful country.'

There was something in his clipped reply that raised

questions. His unexpected interest disappeared as quickly as it had come although for some reason Julia wasn't convinced he was quite as unmoved as he was trying to appear.

'Yes. I would have happily stayed there longer but Uncle Cecil's business called us back to England.'

Samuel nodded again, now looking down at his hands rather than at her. He didn't seem inclined to speak but even if he had been, his mother got there first.

'I'm amazed you didn't know that, Samuel. Did you actually speak to poor Julia before you made her an offer?' The Viscountess laughed, far too loudly to Julia in her current state. 'Or perhaps *speaking* didn't come into it. I suspect your heart made up its mind at first sight.'

The swirling pattern of the Persian carpet became instantly mesmerising as Julia stilled, staring down at the expensive weave as if her life depended on it. Heat roared up from her neck, mortification flooding her entire body and making her palms prickle with sudden sweat.

Lady Maidwell, please stop talking. I beg of you.

Already keenly attuned to every move Samuel made, she thought she felt him stiffen, his discomfort so obvious she could hardly believe his mother would miss it. The Viscountess didn't seem to notice, however. In a striking similarity to Mama it appeared she didn't always require a reply, in her delight running on without pausing for breath.

'You can't be blamed for that. I don't know that any man could see her and not be intrigued. That's

how it was, I suppose? One glance—probably at Lady
Fitzgerald's—and you decided you had to ask?'

Julia knew she must be the colour of a beetroot
as she sat perfectly still, misery coursing through her
from head to toe. Probably her silence and flushed
cheeks looked to the Viscountess like modest shyness
at being praised, not suspecting that in truth she was
fearing she might die of shame at any moment.

Of all the corners to back him into…

There was no chance whatsoever of Samuel dredg-
ing up even the smallest compliment to assuage his
mother's curiosity, and Julia's insides twisted to wonder how he would escape. It must be intolerable for him
to hear her spoken of in such glowing terms when he
couldn't even bring himself to glance at her. Her vi-
sion began to blur as she stared down at the carpet's
fringed edge, willing someone—anyone—to change
the subject. He *didn't* find her beautiful and he *hadn't*
wanted to offer his hand, and to try to force him to
admit either of those things was sure to feel like a slap
in the face when in reality he wanted no more to do
with her than she did him.

She felt him shift position on the sofa. Probably he
was also experiencing the sensation of sitting on hot
coals, and she fiercely studied a particularly frayed
tassel as he mumbled something indistinct. It was the
most noncommittal of responses but it seemed to please
Lady Maidwell, whose turn towards Mama Julia caught
out of the tail of her eye.

'Have you considered yet how lovely the children
will be? I wonder if they'll favour Julia's dark hair
or Samuel's fair. In any case, I'm certain they'll be a
sight to behold.'

Julia's watering eyes flew wide.

Children? What children?

Just when it seemed the situation couldn't get any worse, the Viscountess had managed to outdo herself. Julia was aware that Samuel had tensed even further, now leaning slightly away from her, and she clung to the last vestiges of her self-control as the urge to get up and flee came at her from all sides.

The notion of children hadn't even crossed her mind and she felt her skin flame hotter at the very idea. She wasn't so much of a child herself that she didn't know how they were acquired and the knowledge that she would be expected—no, *required*—to provide the Beresford heir made her head swim.

Samuel could hardly bring himself to look at her, and when he did she knew all he saw was the same unhappy girl she had once been. How were children to follow when the prospect of making them must be so abhorrent to him—even if the thought of the intimacy it entailed made Julia's heart skip a beat?

When she'd imagined having children it had been with a husband who loved her. Any son or daughter would have been born of a union based on real affection and trust, building a family on a solid foundation of mutual care and respect. *That* could never happen for her now. In place of a man who loved her for herself she had Samuel, who neither liked nor trusted her and whom she felt similarly about in return, and not even the ungovernable attraction she felt to him could compensate for what had been lost. Perhaps in her children she might find some solace, but again the problem of begetting them came back to taunt her, Samuel's horror at having to offer her his hand something Julia knew neither she nor he would ever forget.

The carpet's pattern whirled before her and she was at last forced to look up, growing dizzy as it danced in front of her eyes. Lady Maidwell was smiling and Mama likewise, and even the two fathers at their post by the fire seemed to have found some interest in what was going on at the other side of the room. Only she and Samuel sat like blocks of ice, unmoving beneath the weight of their torment, and they might have found some comfort in their shared dread if each hadn't been the cause of the other's dismay.

The Viscountess's smile took on a coy edge that would have come as a warning if Julia's mind hadn't been elsewhere.

'We're all very much looking forward to meeting them. I only hope you won't leave us to wait for too long. For my part, I'd like to have grandchildren while I'm still young enough to enjoy them.'

It was the final straw. There was only so much she could endure, and before she realised what she was doing Julia found herself standing, both mothers' brows rising in well-bred surprise as they peered up at her.

'Would you excuse me for just a moment? It's so warm in here, my head's beginning to ache. I'm just… I'm just going to go…'

Giving nobody the chance to stop her, Julia all but ran for the door, feeling Samuel's eyes on her as she went. If she was made to stay in the parlour a moment longer she might lose her wits, and she staggered out into the corridor, closing the door a little too firmly behind her.

For a moment she sagged against the opposite wall,

tipping her head back to stare up at the ceiling. Her heart was pounding and her face so hot she could have used it as a griddle pan, and she wished desperately there were somewhere to hide…

The library. I'll be safe there, and it's only at the end of the corridor.

The cosy room was dark and soothing after the candlelit glare of the parlour, the only light coming from the small fire flickering in the hearth. It cast long shadows over the rows of leather-bound books, and a thin trickle of relief wound through her as she stood still, breathing in the scent of ink and paper that she'd loved since she was a child. If there was a place in which she felt most at home it had to be here, where silence reigned and the world could be forgotten for hours at a time, the books carrying her away on their pages to places she could only dream of visiting for real. Lady Maidwell's questions couldn't find her in the library and Mama's schemes couldn't intrude, and her pulse slowed a little as she crossed unsteadily to one window and tweaked the curtain aside.

The moon threw silver sparkles over the frosted lawns, the cold of it touching the glass in front of her to drench her in its chill. Goose bumps rose on her bare arms but she didn't move away, instead drawing closer to the window so the night air could cool her cheeks. Probably she'd been inexcusably rude in running away—but what else could she have done? With Samuel sitting so close beside her his every breath had caught her attention, a constant reminder that a broad chest rose and fell with each one, and when his mother had begun her questions it had all been *too much*.

She sighed, briefly closing her eyes to let the moonlight play across the lids. She'd have to go back in a moment. There was no way she could stay in the library all night and she knew it, and she was just pressing a warm hand against her forehead when a voice—a deep, aggravatingly attractive voice—made her jump.

'Hiding behind curtains again? I'm starting to think that's a habit of yours.'

Samuel had to brace himself when Julia looked over her shoulder. In the moonlight her eyes were darker than ever and her hair as glossy as a crow's wing, and not even the weight sitting in the pit of his stomach could make him immune to noticing the slender curve of her neck.

It was her reaction to hearing him speak that really caught him, however. She'd started, an entirely instinctive response completely lacking the poise he'd come to expect, and it gave an intriguing insight into how she behaved when she thought she was unobserved. Before she'd realised he was behind her the line of her shoulders had been more relaxed, even slouching slightly in a manner that took him right back to when they had been in their teens—yet another reminder that the old Julia might not have been completely eclipsed by the new, and not a prospect on which it seemed a good time to dwell.

Her lips tightened. Evidently, she wasn't any more pleased to see him than he was to be there, the high colour in her cheeks still plain despite the gloom. 'You didn't need to come to check on me.'

'On that we agree. It wasn't my idea.'

She frowned. 'So who made you? Your mother or mine?'

'Both. It was a two-pronged attack.'

Julia huffed a humourless laugh, turning back to the window so all he could see was the back of her curl-crowned head. Her bare nape gleamed much paler than the skin of her face, and he fought down the sudden unacceptable urge to trace a fingertip across it, wondering if it could be as soft as it looked. She'd pulled her shoulders back, hitching her usual elegance firmly into place again after giving him an unintended glimpse behind it, and the taper inside him his mother's thoughtless probing had already lit threatened now to burst into flames.

The Viscountess had been beside herself with delight when he'd broken the news and he hadn't the heart to tell her what had forced his hand. She'd heard the tattle, of course, of what Mrs Heston had seen out in the wintry lane, but his mother knew him too well to believe any of the more unsavoury rumours that followed. As far as she was concerned he'd simply been assisting the woman he'd already chosen to marry, and if anyone suggested otherwise then to her that was mere proof of a vulgar mind. She had no idea Julia's mama had impugned his honour and he would never tell her, her excitement too pure to be tainted by something so grubby as the truth.

Now, as he stood close enough behind Julia to be able to count every pearl strung into her hair, he felt aching tension in his own shoulders. With unnerving accuracy his mother had managed to put her finger on the very subjects he had no desire to discuss: his feelings for Julia and the children that would come from their marriage, and he wished more than anything that he could have been spared that test. It had taken all his discipline to keep his face from betraying his inner thoughts, Lucrezia's tear-stained countenance streaking through his mind, and it was damnably difficult to separate what had already happened from what he feared might still yet occur. Julia could very well turn to one of the other men who admired her just as Lucrezia had, possibly laying a child in the Beresford cradle that she'd swear was his own blood, and what could he do to stop her? With his shattered trust and apparent inability to tell real regard from lies he was at her mercy, the net closing around him one he still wasn't sure whether she'd played a part in weaving, but there could be no turning back now.

Julia's quiet voice broke into the chaos of his thoughts.

'That must have been distasteful for you to listen to.'

She was still facing away from him, gazing out the window at the moonlight beyond. She spoke as if they were in the middle of a conversation and he was supposed to know what she was talking about, but Samuel found himself at a loss.

'What must?'

'The talk in there.' Julia nodded to one side, in the direction of the parlour. 'All that talk…of children.'

There was an undercurrent in her tone that Samuel couldn't quite decipher. Embarrassment was part of it, certainly, of the kind any young woman might feel at the things his mother had been suggesting, but there was something else…something he didn't have a name for but that captured his attention at once.

He folded his arms, the constant unease he felt in her company increasing. Did she really want to discuss what had just happened? It had been mortifying for both of them, and given the choice he wouldn't re-visit it.

'Distasteful? No. Uncomfortable? Absolutely.'

A pause settled between them. It went on for what felt like a long time, and Samuel was just wondering if he'd have to be the one to break it when Julia turned.

She looked up at him, so near they were almost touching, and he gave an involuntary swallow 'You needn't lie to me. If we're to marry, we may as well be honest from the start…if indeed you believe me capable of such a thing.'

There was a hint of a challenge in her eyes and Samuel met it with boldness of his own.

'I've yet to decide what I think you're capable of.'

'Ah.' A faintly ironic smile twisted Julia's lips. 'You still distrust my word. I expected nothing less.' She shrugged, although it seemed to Samuel there was precious little nonchalance in the gesture. Whatever she was driving at mattered to her, he could tell; if she'd only spit it—whatever *it* was—out.

'I know the mention of children must have disturbed you. I realise the idea must be objectionable to you in the extreme.'

Samuel folded his arms more tightly across his chest as if it could ward off the temptation to stare at that wry smile. 'What do you mean?'

'Just that such a prospect mustn't fill you with enthusiasm. I know how you regard me.'

In the light of the fire fresh colour had risen across her cheekbones and she glanced away from him, her gaze resting on one of the bookshelves on the other side of the room. A tendon twitched at the corner of her jaw and Samuel realised she was clamping it shut, perhaps regretting having raised a subject she no longer wanted to pursue.

Still, she had been the one to begin it. He hadn't wanted to linger over the sensitive topic that had the potential to bring him so much pain—but Julia had refused to let it drop, and he felt a growing curiosity to know what she was now so reluctant to say.

'Please. Enlighten me. How is it that you think I *regard* you?'

'You'd be cruel enough to make me say it out loud?'

Her eyes darted towards him and away again, only resting on his face for a fraction of a second but even that was enough to make Samuel's gut tighten. It was as if she'd pulled the shutters down on her inner self, any light that had gleamed in those eyes now deliberately hidden from him, and when she spoke it was with the mechanical precision of one separating any emotion from their words.

'Very well. If you insist on hearing what you already know. I'm aware you don't see what the other men of Guildbury admire about me. You can't fathom how I might now be considered an attractive woman. To you I am still Harry's strange, shy sister and that's how it will always be—no more than that but quite probably eventually even less.'

She closed her mouth firmly, signalling she had nothing more to add, and for a moment Samuel found he could only stare.

'Is that what you think? That I don't find you attractive?'

'Of course. I know it to be the truth.'

Again, her voice was carefully flat, whatever she was feeling still concealed behind that cool facade.

'You were always so quick to laugh at my flaws when we were younger, and given your reaction to being forced to take me as your wife I see your low opinion of me hasn't changed. Surely you knew I'd realise that bringing a child into the world with me isn't an idea you'd relish?'

She made a slight movement, as though intending to turn away, but she mastered the urge. With nerve that would have impressed him if he hadn't been so confounded, Julia stayed where she was, still not looking at him but standing her ground, although Samuel wished she *would* distance herself as her meaning hit him squarely between the eyes.

That was what she imagined his objection to their marriage was? That he *didn't* feel a quickening of his pulse every time she was before him?

He took a breath to reply but nothing came, only empty air as he studied her upturned face and wondered how the hell he was supposed to answer. Her head was up and her shoulders straight and even if she wanted the ground to swallow her she gave the impression she'd rather die than admit it. In that moment she couldn't have been more different from the shy girl he'd known and it struck him as bizarre she could ever think otherwise.

'You're wrong.'

The words jerked out before he could stop them but there was no hope of holding them back. Her sooty eyelashes were too long and the memory of her in that wet gown far too enticing, and it would have been a man of stone who could stare down at that face and not see the beauty in it that he was powerless to deny.

'The truth is exactly the opposite,' he managed unevenly, knowing even as he spoke them that each syllable was a mistake. 'I can see your merit just as well as everybody else—if not even more.'

At once, Julia's gaze flashed upwards.

'You're lying.'

Her startled uncertainty was almost as appealing as her forcefulness. It gave another glimpse of the softer side she was so determined to conceal from him, and he realised it called to the same thing inside himself, a vulnerable underbelly Lucrezia had made him so wary to share with anyone else. He was playing with fire confessing his attraction and he couldn't think what had made him do it apart from the strange magic Julia now wielded, the very thing he'd been resolved to avoid. He couldn't trust her, surely, her face and vibrancy too like her predecessor's to inspire much faith, and whether she'd played a part in their farce of an engagement had yet to be discovered…

And yet it was *she* who accused *him* of deceit?

It should have made him angry but he didn't seem able to muster any ire. Instead all he could think was how she could be so wrong, believing him indifferent when the reverse was true, and with each heartbeat the battle not to show his weakness became harder to win.

He saw her throat move, delicate above the tantalisingly low neckline of her gown.

'I'm not sure why, but I'm certain you must be. Why else would you say this now, when you never—' She broke off as she took another breathless glance at his set face. 'What are you doing?'

He'd stepped forward without being aware he'd moved, reducing the space between them to barely a hand's breadth, and he felt his breathing quicken.

'I don't like being called a liar, madam. With your permission, I'll show you that *I*, at least, can be relied upon to tell the truth.'

He heard her gasp, the faintest whisper of a sound that was sweeter than anything she could have said. It came too instinctively to be a refusal and Samuel felt his head swim as he realised it could mean only one thing, perhaps an answer that shocked her as much as it did him.

Yes.

She was tall enough that he didn't have to stoop to slant his lips across hers and as he captured their petal softness, relief he hadn't known he was holding back crashed over him like a wave. For how long he'd wanted to kiss her he couldn't say, only that now her mouth was under his he didn't want to surrender it, blindly reaching for her when she swayed against him and winding an arm around the curve of her waist.

She shivered, the ripple running the length of her narrow body, and he held her tighter to his chest, revelling in the heat that flared from her as if they wore no clothing at all. His free hand slid up to cup that tender nape and his legs weakened to finally touch it, proving beyond all doubt that the skin there was indeed the softest on earth. It felt like warm velvet and he traced across it over and over again, his fingers tangling in an unwary ringlet but Julia making no attempt to pull away as he gently twisted the silken strand, another sigh against his lips making him want to pull the pins from her hair and bury his face in that abundance of rose-scented curls.

He felt a hand skim over his chest and he choked back a groan as she brushed his jaw, setting the skin there smouldering with a single touch. With her lips parted wider and her questing fingertips *just* dipping inside the collar of his shirt, Samuel felt his arousal peak sharply, an ache spreading through him so physical he knew of only one way to quell it.

He'd known that sensation before—and it was enough to bring him to his senses, rationality finally wresting back control from the far baser reflexes that had seized it. Julia's lips were so pliant, so naturally skilful that he wanted nothing more than to keep kissing her until it was she who pulled away first, but the kernel of doubt ever present in the back of his mind spoke too sternly to be ignored.

Reluctantly, he slackened his grip on her waist, still steadying her as he withdrew from their heated embrace. Her eyes had been closed, those long eyelashes brushing her flushed cheeks, but now they opened again, dazed and blinking as he elbowed aside the urge to abandon all good sense and pull her to him once again.

'Is that proof enough that I'm not a liar?'

She gazed at him, the faint sheen of her lips so tempting he felt another sharp pulse of helpless desire. It seemed he had stumbled across the sole way to render her speechless and he almost smiled, only the steady beat of wariness growing inside him making his mouth remain in a straight line.

'You're a beautiful woman, Julia, and no one can say otherwise. It's the very thing that makes you so dangerous.'

Her striking eyebrows pinched together. Apparently, even dazed confusion couldn't keep her quiet for long, and she took an unsteady step backwards that held none of her usual gracefulness, glancing down at Samuel's hands as they slipped away from her waist.

'I don't understand. How could you ever be in any danger from me?'

She shook her head in unfeigned bewilderment. Whatever had just passed between them hadn't been something she'd foreseen, that much was clear, and Samuel wondered—with a stab of *something* beneath his ribs—whether she was regretting it already.

Should he have kept himself under better control? The obvious answer was *yes*; and yet the power of Julia's kiss awakened something in him he'd never thought to experience again…

She was all but leaning against the window now, about as far from him as it was possible to get, and he made sure to back away. There were too many things to think about, too many decisions to be made, and he wouldn't be able to attend to any of them while Julia watched him with those big, dark eyes.

'It doesn't matter. Forget I spoke.'

He tried for a smile but it refused to come. Disquiet was beginning to steal over him, blotting out the surge of desire that had so made him lose his head, and the question as to whether he ought to regret his conduct was becoming easier to answer. His unfightable attraction to Julia and her bafflingly concealed sweetness had made him overlook his former scruples, even if for only a moment—but that was still long enough to make a mistake, and as he turned away he felt the tension return to his spine.

'We should rejoin the others. They'll be thinking we got lost.'

Chapter Six

Gazing out the carriage's window, Julia tried not to let her apprehension run unchecked. Many of Guildbury's most fashionable were taking advantage of the sunshine to display their winter finery, and the tree-filled avenue was packed despite the bitter cold, although she could hardly focus on anything but the wriggling of her insides. She'd been to Fairclough Street many times before—widely acknowledged as among the most exclusive addresses in town and therefore, one of the best places to be seen—but never for the reason she was now, the carriage beginning to slow as it drew closer to a large and handsome house surrounded by an ornate iron fence.

Her anxiety grew more intense as the horses drew to a gentle stop, the carriage rocking on its wheels. The thought of what she was there to do was unbelievable, and yet she'd had little choice but to agree.

The invitation to tour Samuel's house had come from his mother rather than the man himself, but how could he have objected? He'd barely spoken a word after they'd returned from the library, sitting through dinner in the same stunned semisilence that had afflicted Julia, too, and when the Viscountess insisted the future mistress of Larch House should go to view it, the matter had already seemed decided. There were a few more little details that needed seeing to before the young couple could move in, delaying the wedding until St Thomas's Day four days before Christmas, but in the meantime Julia could at least see the place she'd soon be living, when she and Samuel would be thrown together to work out the confusion that single kiss had rained down upon their heads.

It was a memory that hadn't left her in the days since, and she struggled now to control a surge of blood rushing into her cheeks. To her unending amazement Samuel had admitted he was attracted to her, kissed her and then fled—leaving her with far more questions than answers and apparently precious little hope of getting any. He'd just left, leaving her to stare after him, and the *almost* accusation he'd made before he walked away had bothered her ever since.

How am I dangerous? What did he mean by that?

She simply couldn't fathom it. Those few minutes in Burton Lodge's library had left a trail of bewilderment behind and now she didn't know where she stood, Samuel's view of her apparently the very opposite of the one she'd taken as fact. Part of her didn't want to believe him, still suspicious that his confession was a lie—but for what purpose would he pretend to find her desirable if in truth he did not? There was nothing for him to gain from such a falsehood even if her good sense warned her to be careful... although surely the heat of his kiss wasn't something that could be faked, her own eagerness to return it something she hadn't

known she was capable of until an undiscovered part
had been awoken by the warmth of his lips on hers…

'Are you going to sit there all day or are you coming inside?'

Turning quickly in her seat she caught Harry's
raised eyebrow. In an uncharacteristic fit of consider-
ation Mama had allowed him to take her place as chaperone, for which Julia was very grateful indeed. With
things between her and Samuel so uncertain it was
a relief to have Harry there, his still slightly hoarse-
voiced presence a safeguard in more ways than one. If
left alone with Samuel there was the chance she might
make another questionable decision that would cause
even more confusion, and until she understood exactly
what was happening between her and the man she was
being made to wed it was better she didn't get too close.

'Of course. After you.'

With a satirical bow Harry slid across and opened
the door. He stepped down, unfurling himself from the
confines of the carriage ill suited for his height before
turning back.

'Come on, then. You don't want to keep a future
viscount waiting.'

With some reluctance she took his outstretched
hand. Her nervousness hadn't abated one bit; instead,
it grew as she set her foot down on the path leading
to the grand front door, although to her unease it was
joined by something else entirely.

A tinge of anticipation, or even eagerness…to see
Samuel again?

She tried to dismiss the feeling as she and Harry
approached the door. Her heart was beating so hard
she could hear it, and she was careful not to look at

her brother when he stood aside to let her pull the bell, sure that he would notice the tiny quake in her fingers when she reached out.

'Are you nervous?'

'Of course not,' she lied, swiftly bending down to pick up the handkerchief she'd somehow managed to drop. 'Why should I be?'

'I don't know. I just remember the last time I saw you and Samuel in the same room you didn't seem particularly happy about it.' Harry shrugged, his usual smile taking on a meaningful air. 'Things have changed, though, obviously. Clearly, you got over your objections since you're now prepared to marry him.'

Julia found herself suddenly absorbed in straightening her already straight bonnet rather than meet her brother's eye. 'Yes. Things certainly have changed.'

Only Samuel and herself knew the unfair pressure Mama had exerted to bring the match about. It was easier to pretend all parties had acted of their own free will, and Julia tamped down a pang of guilt at her deception as the door opened and a harassed-looking housekeeper invited them inside.

'Good morning, sir…ma'am. I apologise for the disarray. We're in the middle—' She broke off as a maid careened past, almost entirely hidden from view by the enormous pile of linen she carried. Another servant followed close behind bearing a heavy bucket of something, both barely pausing to curtsey before heading towards the grand staircase of carved oak that curved down into the hall.

'As I was saying. We're in the middle of opening the house again now that the master has returned home—

but of course, ma'am, you would know that better than anyone.'

Another maid approached to collect hats and coats, and Julia gazed about her as she untied her bonnet, the tumult of different emotions inside her dimming for a moment as she took in the place that would soon be her home.

If the hall was any indication of the rest of the house, she knew she need never fear the pity of her neighbours. The ceiling arched high above her, paired with panelled walls of delicate green, and the floor was so highly polished she could almost see her face. Floor-to-ceiling windows let cool sunlight stream in to illuminate every corner and make the furniture gleam, and even though the vast chandelier hanging over the staircase was covered with sacking, she still caught a glimpse of crystal glittering beneath it like fallen stars.

Craning her neck to peer up at the intricate cornicing, she didn't notice Samuel's approach until his voice at her elbow made her start.

'Good morning. It's an honour to welcome you to Larch House.'

She spun round, her heart giving a sharp jolt to find him standing so close. Dressed in a smart navy coat that complemented the deep blue of his eyes and his hair falling—as always—into a perfect wave across his brow, he was almost *too* handsome, and Julia realised her gaze had settled unconsciously on his mouth.

Immediately flustered, she dropped into a slightly lopsided curtsey. 'It was kind of you to invite me. I hope this visit hasn't come at an inconvenient time?'

The housekeeper and servants had melted away although the creak of floorboards and various thumps and thuds echoed down from the upper levels. Apparently, getting a house ready for occupation was a far bigger task than she'd thought, although Samuel shook his head.

'Not at all. It's a...a pleasure to have you here.'

He didn't sound *completely* certain but Julia could at least appreciate him trying. The scene in the library must have been just as fresh in his mind as it was in hers, and he looked quickly over at Harry, probably grateful to seize on any possible distraction.

'You've been before, of course. No such warm welcome for you.'

Harry laughed, nodding a short bow. 'Morning, Beresford. Or should I say—morning, *brother*?'

Julia's chest tightened but Samuel smiled, the trace of difficulty in it easy to miss unless the observer was paying very close attention to the shape of his lips.

'Call me whatever you like. You usually do.'

He turned back to her. The smile remained but its tautness increased, and Julia almost held her breath as their eyes met.

What is he thinking? Is he displeased to have me in his house?

Surely he must be, she decided, trying not to let her eyes stray back down to his set mouth. He'd admitted some unexpected attraction to her that had shocked her to the core, but attraction wasn't the same as *liking* a person—as she well knew, still unable to reconcile his comely exterior with the thoughtlessness she knew lurked within. It would be a mistake indeed to believe some instinct-led entanglement had changed anything between them except to make their situation even more complex.

'Would you like tea before we begin the tour?'

He waved vaguely to a door she imagined led to the parlour but she shook her head. She didn't dare hold a teacup in her present state, Samuel's presence sure to make her fingers feel like they were spread with butter, and she could only hope she could force enough composure to make it through the day.

'There's no need. We can see you're busy—we won't stay for longer than necessary.'

He nodded, again gesturing to the door to his left. 'Very good. In that case, I suppose we may as well get started. If you'd like to come this way?'

Julia had visited any number of grand houses in her life but as she followed Samuel from one room to the next—carefully, taking the time to make sure she sailed rather than stooped—she realised this one eclipsed them all. Even swathed in dustsheets the furniture managed to look stylish, each table and chair perfectly arranged with their expensive legs just peeping out from beneath their wrappings, and the curtains and wallpaper the very picture of elegant good taste. Each room was well proportioned with large windows that overlooked the manicured front drive or the landscaped gardens set behind, and more than once she stopped to admire the view over Guildbury's rooftops, the horizon dotted with trees where the edge of the town met the woods beyond.

Peering down from the long gallery at the top of the house, Julia sensed Samuel draw nearer, her skin prickling as he came to stand beside her. Somewhere behind them Harry was roaming about, stopping every now and again to chuckle at some hideous painting on the panelled walls, although it was Samuel's presence that commanded every thread of Julia's attention.

'What do you think so far? Will Larch House be to your liking?'

She nodded, careful not to look at anything other than a patinaed sundial on the patio below. 'It's beautiful. I think any woman would think herself lucky to live here.'

'Really? Even though she'd have to share the place with me?' Samuel gave what she supposed was meant to be a laugh but came out more as a harsh breath. 'I wouldn't have thought that for you any house could ever be good enough to compensate for that?'

Julia felt her heart begin to jump. He was attempting to make a joke, another spark of the humour he'd so often used as a weapon, but this time at his own expense. He hadn't attempted to deceive himself, then— he knew as well as she did that one kiss didn't mean everything had changed—and she was groping for an appropriately cool answer when Harry appeared at her other side.

'Is that your groundskeeper down there?'

He pointed to a man cutting back a dead tree and Samuel nodded, giving no clue as to whether the interruption was welcome or not.

'Hewitt, yes. Why?'

'There's a blight of some sort in Highbank's hedges. My man doesn't know what to do about it—do you mind if I ask yours?'

'Be my guest. What Hewitt doesn't know about horticulture won't be worth knowing. He worked at Rookley before coming here and my father still hasn't forgiven me for stealing him.'

Harry slapped Samuel's back in lieu of thanks and strode away, his duties as chaperone evidently less important than the state of Highbank's gardens. Still facing the window, Julia listened to his footsteps fade and then disappear completely, leaving her very much alone with her fiancé and at a loss as to what—if anything—to say to cover the silence that fell over them like a net.

Beside her, Samuel brushed an imaginary cobweb from the sill. It was the same kind of fidgeting she was trying hard to supress herself, and she wondered if he was still waiting for her to answer his question, perhaps more truth lying behind the joke than she'd previously imagined.

But she had queries of her own.

'Samuel. May I ask you something?'

He turned towards her, the sunlight glancing off his chestnut hair as he moved. He seemed cautious and Julia couldn't blame him, all too aware their conversations generally descended into antagonism. 'If you like. What is it?'

'The evening you and your parents came to dine. There was something you said…'

She watched him carefully, hoping to catch any telltale flicker that might say more than words. Her throat tightened as she took in how wariness emphasised the sharp planes of his face, hardening the jawline she had brushed with shaking fingertips…

Firmly bringing herself to heel, she pressed on. 'You called me dangerous. What did you mean by that?'

If she hadn't been specifically waiting for it she might not have seen the minute twitch of his eyebrows as he curbed a frown. He hesitated for the barest moment, perhaps thinking fast, but then any reaction was hidden behind a smooth shrug that didn't lessen her suspicions one bit.

'I hardly know. I don't really even recall saying it.'

He switched his attention back to the window. Harry was visible now, crossing the lawn towards where Hewitt was wielding his saw, and Julia didn't bother to argue as they both watched her brother bear down on his prey.

She wasn't deceived, however.

Letting her mind scroll backwards, she came to a halt at the bewildering aftermath of that heart-stopping kiss.

What else was it he said that night?

'Is that proof enough that I'm not a liar?'

He was lying now and she knew it, although why, she couldn't say. For some reason he didn't want to explain what had prompted his strange accusation, and his denial stoked her curiosity rather than dampening it, something he appeared to realise when he quickly changed the subject.

'I hadn't realised you'd been in Italy. Did you enjoy your time there?'

It was an abrupt and rather obvious attempt to distract her but Julia couldn't think how to evade it. On the night Lady Maidwell had told him they had that in common his reaction had been strange, halfway between interested and wary, and another glimmer of curiosity kindled to join the first.

'Yes. My aunt Marie was kind enough to take me. She's away again now, as it happens—Ireland this time—but Mama wouldn't let me go with her.'

'Your mama.' Samuel managed to make the two words hold a world of unspoken meaning that wasn't difficult to guess. 'She missed you too much the first time, I suppose, to part with you again?'

He had missed the mark so spectacularly that it was almost laughable, and Julia answered bluntly before she gave herself time to think. 'No. Before I went to Italy she didn't really know what to do with me. It wasn't until I came back so altered that she decided she could stand having me around. I was less of an embarrassment by then, you know—prettier, not so awkward and generally easier to bear.'

She hadn't meant to speak so freely and she caught Samuel's swift glance out of the corner of her eye. If she hadn't known better she might have thought there was something in it alongside surprise that she'd given him such an honest answer, although what, exactly, she couldn't tell.

'Ah. I see.'

Doubtless he hadn't expected her to sum up her complicated relationship with her mother in a few scant sentences, but he didn't veer off course.

'Did you learn much of the language while you were there?'

'A little. I took lessons from some friends of my aunt's, although I would have loved to learn more. There hasn't been any opportunity to pursue it since I returned home, however—Mama has kept me busy with what she considers far more important concerns than my own inclinations.'

She saw his lips press together. The smallest hint of the same thing she thought she'd glimpsed a moment before surfaced again, so puzzling that it made her heart execute a strange flip. Was it a ghost of something akin to sympathy, some acknowledgement that life with her mother had not always been easy? It was a fact he must have been starting to realise for himself, now tied to Mama more closely than he would have chosen with no way of escape.

Samuel tapped his fingers lightly on the windowsill. 'You know, there are some excellent books on language in the library here if you'd care to see them,' he offered with studied casualness, 'I don't believe we've been in there yet. Would you like to go now?'

'Oh!' Julia turned to him at once, momentarily forgetting her confusion. 'I'd like that very much. The library at Burton Lodge is one of my favourite places on earth. I can imagine the one here must be ten times as impressive.'

He made a face that might have been an attempt at modesty. 'I'm not sure about that, but if you come with me you can decide for yourself.'

He moved away from the window and Julia followed, not even pausing to glance outside for Harry or give him a second thought as she let Samuel lead her along yet another corridor, passing rooms still swathed in dustsheets and their curtains tightly drawn as they withdrew deeper into the house.

At last, he stopped by a closed door. A stack of luggage trunks stood just inside the frame, jutting out to make it difficult to pass, and Samuel studied them thoughtfully.

'These are some of the books I sent back from my travels. I thought they would have been put away, but for now I suppose we'll have to squeeze past.' He leaned forward to push open the door, stepping back again to let Julia go first. 'After you.'

She eyed the gap doubtfully. It was a tight fit and she hesitated, certain she would blunder through and tear her gown on the rough corners of the trunks. The room beyond was dark, the windows covered and the air inside cold, and she was just beginning to wonder if she'd made a mistake when a light touch at her waist made her choke back a breath.

'Would you allow me to help you?'

She didn't dare turn around, only just able to jerk a short nod as Samuel's warm palm settled on the small of her back. It filled the space there as perfectly as if it had been specifically designed to fit against the curves of her body, and she was helpless to resist the memory of the last time he'd touched her from pushing forward once again. When his arms had come around her she'd felt her blood turn to fire, every heartbeat as loud as a drum, and even this most chaste of guiding hands was enough to send a delicious shudder through her she could only pray he hadn't been able to feel. If she turned now he would be close enough to kiss her again, to bend down and make her gasp as the very tip of his tongue sought to dance with hers...

Carefully, he steered her round the trunks, her steps so clumsy she feared her hard-won elegance might abandon her entirely, and once safely inside she stumbled away from him, glad of the gloom to hide her face.

'Thank you.'

Samuel didn't reply. She heard him moving about the darkened room, his heavy boots making the floorboards creak—and then light flooded the library, cascading over the shelves and bookcases to reveal a wonderland of gleaming leather, and words failed her as she stood in the centre of the room and stared.

* * *

Samuel watched Julia's growing amazement with a strange feeling unfurling in his stomach. At first, she'd looked stunned, staring around her with her lips slightly parted, but then they stretched into a disbelieving smile that made it impossible for him to tear his eyes away.

It lit up her face, her already high cheekbones rising higher still. Astonishment made her eyes come alive, their ebony richness now shining, and as he stood beside the window, still holding the sheet he had torn from it, he had to steel himself against the desire to cross the room and catch hold of her there and then.

But you absolutely cannot. Why is it that whenever you encounter Julia Livingston in a library, you're so determined to kiss her?

The voice at the back of his mind spoke sense but it was difficult to listen. In that moment it was as if she was *made* to be kissed, so sweetly delighted that the idea of keeping his distance seemed ridiculous.

How could a woman so enchanted by a room full of books pose a threat? She'd asked him what he meant when he called her dangerous but he had refused to explain, not wanting to admit the painful lesson Lucrezia had forced him to learn. He ought to still be on his guard, watching carefully for any sign Julia could take him down the same path, although it was damnably hard to remember his suspicions when such joy illuminated her from within.

She moved to one of the shelves and ran a hand over the spines.

'What do you think?'

She spun to look at him, her eyes wide. 'It's *wonderful*! Surely not all of these can be yours?'

'They are now. I took possession of Larch House just before my eighteenth birthday and sent books back here the whole time I was away.'

Belatedly, he realised he probably sounded boastful and he grimaced internally, hoping she hadn't noticed. Some absurd part of him seemed to want to impress her, as if he was still that lad of eighteen rather than a man grown, and he was glad she was too distracted to pay him much mind.

'Really, the fifth viscount should take the credit. It was he who began the tradition of keeping the family books here rather than Rookley Manor.'

Julia nodded absently. She'd crossed to another shelf still covered by a sheet and at her enquiring glance Samuel gestured for her to pull it down.

'Please. Look at whatever you want.'

With barely concealed glee she heaved the sheet aside, sending a cloud of dust whirling into the air. Tiny motes danced in the sunlight although all Samuel could see was her enraptured face as she stood back, contemplating her newly discovered treasure with all the excitement of an adventurer stumbling across ancient ruins.

'It would take a lifetime to work through all of these,' she murmured wonderingly. 'You'd have to start as a child and then live to be one hundred, and even then I'm not sure that would be long enough.'

Cautiously, Samuel moved from the window, folding the makeshift blind he'd ripped from it over the back of a chair. He knew he ought to keep away but something drew him on, Julia's unexpected delight tempting him closer.

'I think *you* might manage it. Don't I recollect you reading a lot when we were younger?'

'Yes.'

She flicked a swift look over her shoulder at his approach, a short cut of those dark eyes before she turned them away again. 'I believe that's why you began calling me "the bookworm," which of course your friends shortened to simply "the worm."'

Samuel stopped, close enough now to see the tightening of her lips. 'Did I? Did they?'

Frowning, he cast his mind back. He'd teased her, he knew, but never mean-spiritedly; surely his young friends had been the same? There had never been any offence meant but now she was gazing at the bookshelf rather than at him, and unease began to wind through him.

'I don't remember that.'

Julia exhaled quietly. It was almost a laugh but entirely lacking in any humour, and there was an edge to her voice when she replied.

'No. I don't suppose you do.'

The glance she shot him made him take a sharp breath. Moments before there had been a joyous light in her eyes but now cynicism dulled their sparkle. The atmosphere had shifted abruptly and the discomfort wending its way through him grew worse as he watched her, trying to make sense of what that single look told him without using words.

She was intent on the embossed titles, tracing the faded letters with her fingertips. There was a new stiffness in her shoulders and a faint crease between her eyebrows that betrayed she'd revealed more than she'd meant to, perhaps mirroring his own regrets at hinting at things better left unsaid. She'd retreated from him without even having moved, turning in on herself to keep whatever bothered her inside, and something began to nag at the back of his mind.

What was the accusation she'd flung at him the last time they were together? Something about always having laughed at her flaws, and his low opinion of her being unchanged?

The words came back in a haze of understanding and he stood still as he sifted through them, attempting to shake them into order. There had been supressed hurt in her tone, he realised, unhappiness that he'd been too aggravated to notice at the time, although now the pieces of the puzzle fell into place.

'Was that what you meant the other day when you said I laughed at you? You were talking about my stupid jokes when we were children?'

He looked down at her, watching closely for her response. Colour kindled in her cheeks but she kept her focus on the books, taking one from the shelf to flip open its leather cover.

'In part.'

Clearly unwilling to meet his eye—or to give him a more detailed answer—she spoke more to the densely printed page than to him, but he heard her all the same, and Samuel hesitated, unsure whether to press further or give her the chance to escape.

He would be a hypocrite to expect further honesty when he hadn't been truthful himself. She'd asked why he regarded her as dangerous and he'd denied her the real reason, not wanting to reveal how Lucrezia had tricked him or how he suspected Julia might be capable of the same thing. By rights he should back away, allowing her to keep the secret she evidently didn't want to share, but the repressed hurt in her countenance wouldn't let him keep silent.

'Is that why, since my return—?'

'Yes.'

Abruptly, she snapped the book shut, the thump sounding far too loud in the silent room. She stared down at its cover and Samuel had the unpleasant impression she was composing herself, although when she finally turned to him it was with world-weary reluctance.

'I suppose I may as well admit it, since I've already told you too much.' She spoke quietly, as if to force out each word was against her will. 'It was indeed your past behaviour that meant I wasn't particularly pleased to see you when you appeared at Highbank. I'd had five years to reflect on the way you'd treated me previously and, after having grown in confidence and self-worth, I wasn't going to welcome you back with open arms.'

Wrong-footed, Samuel pushed a hand through his hair. He wanted to explain himself, to find some way of making her see he wasn't the villain she obviously thought him to be, but he couldn't quite find the words.

'I never meant to hurt you. The things I said were never in earnest. The silly names, the childish comments... I had no idea...'

'I know you didn't. You thought you were being amusing when you pointed out how I stumbled over my own feet and was too bashful to speak. Unfortunately for me, so did everyone else.'

Julia gazed up at him, flushing a deeper pink but not shying away from what she was now determined he heard. 'The girls that took a fancy to you were cruel to me because you paved the way for their unkind whispers. The boys that looked up to you were cruel to me because you painted a target on my back. You may not have meant for any of that to happen but it did. I was deeply unhappy for many years, thinking myself unworthy, and rightly or wrongly I have always felt you partly to blame.'

She switched her attention back to the book, looking down so the sweep of her long eyelashes concealed whatever she was thinking, and Samuel could only watch as she deliberately ran a fingertip over a crack in the leather. Her fingers seemed to be shaking a little, he noticed, that tiny tremor sending a sharp pain beneath his ribs, and he was seized by a crushing fist of guilt.

You fool. You, who think yourself so clever—and you never had a clue.

He stood silently, left with nothing to say. With immense dignity and without raising her voice Julia had shamed him, brought him face-to-face with the reality of the damage he had caused, and any thought of defending himself fled as he baldly acknowledged the truth.

It was no wonder she'd been so unhappy to see him in her brother's house the first day he'd returned and on every occasion afterwards. With unthinking cruelty he had made her life a misery, never stopping to consider the effect of his throwaway jests on a girl he now knew had already been struggling beneath the weight of her mother's disapproval, and the guilt hanging like a heavy chain around his neck grew in weight until he feared it might choke him.

Slowly, as if worried she might turn and run, Samuel reached out for the book grasped in Julia's unsteady fingers. At once, her averted eyes flew to his face, uncertainty mixing with a shadow of defiance to make his heart skip a beat, but she allowed him to take it from her, and when he came a step closer she didn't back away.

He set the book back on the shelf. Gathering his courage and without stopping to consider whether it was a good idea, he extended his hand, gathering one of Julia's much smaller ones against his palm—and a static shock lanced the full length of his arm, her slender fingers cold but the touch of them still able to set his skin on fire.

He thought he caught a soft breath escape her. They were close enough that he could have bent to kiss her again, and the desire to do so almost felled him where he stood, only stubborn resolve to make things right holding him in check.

'I'm sorry. I'm truly sorry. For everything I said and did that caused you pain—I apologise wholeheartedly.'

She blinked, a fleeting gleam of confusion and distrust passing through her eyes. Part of her wanted to pull away, he was sure, although another was willing to hear him out; and it was to the latter half of her that he appealed, his remorse so genuine surely even Julia couldn't suspect otherwise.

'I won't try to excuse myself by saying we were young. I knew better and should have done better, and I can only say I'd take it all back if I could. There was never anything wrong with you—both inside and out, you were never anything but a sweet girl I should have treated far more kindly.'

Her lips parted but she didn't speak. She searched his face as if it were one of the books on the walls, trying to read some hidden meaning in his blue gaze and the firm set of his mouth, and only after what felt like an hour did she finally gift him one brief, guarded nod.

'If that's the truth… I accept your apology.'

Relief flooded him, although why he should have felt so moved, Samuel didn't want to consider. He ought to have been pleased to have righted a wrong, felt some small satisfaction, perhaps, but not the immediate light-ness that swept over him to imagine Julia might look upon him more favourably now, or the slow beat of pleasure that she hadn't yet pulled her hand from his. Her fingers still lay in his palm, fragile but just be-ginning to feel warm, and it was a struggle to prevent himself from tracing his thumb across the pale ridges of her knuckles.

Keeping himself under tight control, Samuel offered her a solemn bow. 'Thank you. I assure you, it is most earnestly meant.'

He saw her mouth move a fraction. Whether it was to speak again or—against all odds—to smile he wasn't sure, either option agreeable in its own way; but a scuf-fling in the corridor outside followed by an audible curse made her turn away.

There was another muffled expletive and then Harry's head appeared around the barricaded doorway, pushing past the trunks to force himself inside.

'There you are. I've been looking for—'

He broke off, a grin spreading across his handsome face as he took in the sight of them standing hand in hand. 'Sorry. Am I interrupting?'

At once, Julia pulled her hand free, flattening it against her bodice, and Samuel couldn't help a strange pang of loss. 'No. Samuel was just showing me the library. It is very impressive.'

'Oh. Yes. That's the sort of thing you like, isn't it?' Harry peered around the room as if he hadn't noticed the books that filled every crevice until his sister pointed them out. 'Personally, I'm more interested in the games room. Has he shown you the billiards table?'

Julia shook her head. Out of the corner of his eye he saw her snatch a glance at him, her hand still held tightly to the front of her gown, but unless he was much mistaken there was less hostility in her gaze than he had grown used to.

'It's a beauty. Perhaps if you have the time, Beresford, we could have a game now?'

Samuel forced a laugh. Harry didn't change, even if his younger sister seemed to by the minute. In the span of one morning he had seen her innocently delighted, then unhappy and then determined to make him face the truth: all different sides of the same woman, and one he was beginning to realise he was in great peril of holding in dangerously high regard.

The sensation of her little hand in his was haunting and he realised how much he wanted to take hold of it again. Sooner or later he would have to decide which path to tread—although now he had apologised for all the hurt he had caused, was there a chance Julia's feelings towards him might begin to change?

It was a question he couldn't answer. Both Julia and Harry were waiting for him, and with another hollow laugh he gestured towards the door.

'By all means, Livingston. Lead the way.'

Chapter Seven

To Julia's wide eyes, the woman in the full-length mirror looked like an angel.

Her gown shimmered around her in a swathe of the palest dove grey, cut low and square at the neck and edged with exquisite lace barely more substantial than a spider's web. The sleeves were finished likewise with a frill at each cuff, and winter pansies embroidered in silver thread twinkled on the bodice, catching the light with every movement like a trail of fallen stars. A pearl-strewn bonnet covered her hair, its gauzy pallor only adding to the otherworldly effect, and as she stared at her reflection Julia could hardly believe she was looking at herself.

'That's all for today, ma'am. I have your measurements and will make the necessary alterations.'

The modiste waved her assistants forward to help Julia undress, drawing the curtain around them with the other hand. It took them hardly any time at all to lace her back into her own gown and the wedding dress was borne reverently away, held up by two women so the hem wouldn't touch the carpet.

Mama rose from her seat on a plush sofa as Julia reappeared from behind the curtain. Mrs Livingston's smile was contented—perhaps even bordering on pleased—and Julia wondered darkly if she ought to be pleased herself that she had finally made her mother proud.

'You looked superb. Nobody will have ever seen a lovelier bride.'

'Thank you, Mama. I'm glad you think so.'

Her mother studied herself in the long mirror for a moment, turning slightly this way and that. 'You'll need to work quickly,' she instructed the modiste, now smoothing down the ribbons on her own cloak. 'The wedding is in less than two weeks. There can be no delay.'

'We appreciate all you've done already, of course,' Julia interjected hastily, catching sight of the dressmaker's expression. 'The dress is more beautiful than I could have imagined.'

Mama's smile grew even more satisfied. 'As it should be. Only the best for the future Viscountess Maidwell.'

It seemed in poor taste to say such a thing when the *current* Viscountess was very much alive and in good health, but Julia didn't bother to argue. Their appointment had already overrun thanks to her mother's constant interruptions and demands for finer satin, and it was easier just to take her arm and steer her towards the door, only pausing for an exchange of curtsies before the bell pinged and they were outside in the cold December air.

'Mama, will Papa not be cross you ordered so much

lace to be added to the hem? It's so very expensive, and all those extra yards…'

Mrs Livingston cut her off. 'Nonsense. He wouldn't begrudge his only daughter a fitting wedding gown. What will people think if you aren't wearing the very best? I won't have anyone say we aren't a good enough match for a viscount.'

'We?'

At Julia's slightly raised eyebrows her mother gave one of her silvery laughs. 'You. Obviously, I meant you. But—oh, look.'

Her mother was peering at something a short distance away, her eyes narrowed slightly against the low sun's glare. 'Isn't that Lady Maidwell now? And with her…'

Julia turned at once.

Mama was correct. There were many people in the street, home to the most fashionable and expensive shops in Guildbury, but it was one tall, familiar figure that caught her eye. Samuel was walking beside his mother, guiding her confidently through the bustle with one hand while the other held the lead of an excitable Nelson, and Julia's heart immediately began to skip as she realised they were heading her way.

'Mrs Livingston… Julia!'

Lady Maidwell greeted them enthusiastically although Julia found it difficult to concentrate on anything other than Samuel's polite bow. She watched him as he straightened up again, the sunlight making his eyes gleam sapphire, and she almost forgot to curtsey in reply when he looked down at her, the faintest air of uncertainty hanging between them now that everything had changed.

His apology had been genuine; of that, she had no doubt. That day at Larch House had gone some way towards calming the fierce dislike for him she'd harboured for so long, and now she wasn't sure *how* she felt, years of resentment fading at the power of a single word.

Sorry.

He'd acknowledged what he'd done and made no attempt to justify it or to minimise her pain. Instead, he had listened with shame-faced acceptance and she found she respected him for not turning away, a man who could admit—and possibly even grow from—his mistakes, something that was hard to find.

The Viscountess was speaking again and Julia forced herself, with some difficulty, to pay attention.

'This is an unexpected pleasure. I had no idea of meeting you here.'

'We've just been to see Madame DuPrix.' Mama's voice was like silk, delighted to drop the name of the most exclusive modiste in town. 'Some final arrangements for Julia's wedding gown.'

'Oh! But I must hear all about it. What's been chosen?'

Lady Maidwell turned to her son. He was focused on trying to prevent Nelson from pawing at Mrs Livingston's skirts, and Julia had to hide a smile at Mama's pretence that she didn't mind the dog's attentions. 'Would you go ahead with Julia, Samuel, and leave us mamas to our whispering? There are some things a groom need not overhear, but *I* must know every detail.'

Julia just caught him glance down and she quickly busied herself with pulling up her gloves.

The sensation of his hand closing around hers was

as vivid now as on the day it had happened, when the book-laden shelves had disappeared into the background at the gentle pressure of his fingers. Surely he hadn't heard her breath catch or felt her tremble when he'd touched her, too set on making his apology to notice such trivial things? She could have been the only one whose mind had arced back to the moment he had kissed her, to wonder if a library would once again be the setting where they both lost control...

'As you wish.'

He dipped his head obligingly, although Julia thought she caught a trace of hesitance as he held out his arm. 'Will you walk with me?'

Not fully trusting herself to speak, she slipped her hand into the crook of his elbow. The instant her fingers settled on his sleeve she felt her heart turn over, already beating far too quickly for comfort, and she mustered all the composure she could manage as he began to lead her away.

She sensed her mother and the Viscountess following a few paces behind them although Samuel's towering presence overshadowed everything else. With each step she felt the muscle of his arm move beneath her fingertips, and the pleasing scent she now associated with him hung faintly in the air, cedar and shaving soap a headier combination than any cologne. With her bonnet shielding her face Julia would have to turn her head to look at him but for the moment she didn't quite dare, uncomfortably aware that some secret part of her was very much enjoying walking at Samuel's side.

He'd been the source of so much pain, but now he had tried to make things right between them, she found confusion sitting beneath her bodice instead of keen dislike. He might have been forced into their engagement just as she had, with neither of them willingly choosing the other—but did that mean the marriage would have to be as disastrous as she'd once assumed was inevitable?

If what he'd said was true then he'd actually *liked* her as she'd been before, apparently not as repulsed by her timidity and lack of grace as she'd always assumed, and to think that Samuel might one day see her real self somehow wasn't quite as worrying as she'd previously thought.

It seemed his time away had changed him, shaping him into a man of integrity instead of a thoughtless boy, and despite her attempts to block it out she couldn't help an ember of something like hope from kindling in her chest. She didn't love him, and he didn't love her, but there was more respect between them now than she would have predicted, possibly even the beginnings of regard, and surely the attraction they shared couldn't be denied. Where once there had been nothing to build on there was now at least *some* bedrock that could be the foundation for more, possibly even something worth having if Samuel was equally willing to put in the work…

'You've been to see about your gown?'

His voice seemed unexpectedly close, pulling her away from her scattered thoughts and back into the busy street.

'Yes.' Julia nodded, still not ready to look anywhere other than straight ahead. 'I'm not sure my father will be quite as pleased with it as Mama, however. I would have been content for it to be simple, but she's insisted

on more lace than I think Madame DuPrix would normally use in a year.'

'I can imagine.'

She heard the wry note loud and clear. It seemed that
any fledgling improvement in their connection didn't
extend to her mother and she could hardly blame him,
the attack on his honour Mama had used to enforce
their engagement clearly still rankling.

'Still. Simple or fine, I'm sure you'll look well in
whatever you wear. You always do.'

As far as compliments went, it wasn't the most elaborate, and yet Julia felt herself grow warmer. The other
young men who had pursued her had scattered honeyed words like confetti, but somehow the straightforward honesty of Samuel's was more gratifying than
any sonnet.

'That's very kind of you.'

For a short while they walked without speaking,
progressing slowly down the street while behind them
their mothers exchanged rapid whispers like a pair of
excited young girls. Every few yards Samuel would
have to touch his hat to some acquaintance, and Julia
find a polite smile, and she was aware of more than one
pair of eyes on her as she held on to his arm.

About one thing, at least, Mama had been right. Mrs
Heston had indeed spread her piece of gossip far and
wide, and the gazes that turned on her ranged from interested to envious as Julia and Samuel walked along.
A few of the unmarried ladies they passed looked resentful at her approach, vexed that the formerly awkward Miss Livingston—of all people!—had ensnared
the county's most eligible man; and she nodded civilly
back at them, aware of the irony that the same girls who

had made her life a misery with their scorn should look upon her with jealousy now.

For all the surrounding distractions the silence between them still lay heavily, and Julia racked her brains for the means to break it, unwilling to allow it to linger on into awkwardness.

'I see Nelson's lessons in manners haven't yet borne much fruit.'

Samuel was holding the dog's lead tightly, attempting to keep him under control as they walked, but the pointer bounced along at the end of it and, turning her head slightly so she could *just* glimpse him around the brim of her bonnet, she saw Samuel smile.

'Alas, no. Not for want of trying.'

The slight upward tick of his lips made her insides flutter like a bird in a cage. He was even more attractive when he smiled and she found herself wishing he did so more often, perhaps the new accord between them making such a thing more likely.

Realising she was in danger of staring, Julia turned her attention back to the dog. 'He's exceptionally handsome, though, for all his faults. If I'd ever been allowed a pet I think I would have chosen a dog myself, although one of the smaller kind.'

'You weren't allowed?'

'No. My mother thinks they're filthy creatures, even the pretty little ones I would have liked.'

Although she could no longer see Samuel's face, she could easily imagine his expression. 'That's a pity. In my opinion it's a dog that makes a house a home. Perhaps—'

He stopped abruptly and Julia looked up at him.

'Perhaps what?'

At the quizzical tilt of her head Samuel hesitated, seeming to consider before shrugging as if it was a matter of little importance. 'Perhaps I could get one for you…after we've taken Larch House. To make it feel more like your own home.'

He spoke as if the offer was of no consequence, but the kindness of it almost stopped her in her tracks, only the firm grip of his elbow on her fingers keeping her moving forward.

'I would like that very much. Thank you.'

She heard him say something in response but she couldn't make out what it was. The busy street suddenly seemed far away somehow, the warmth of his sleeve beneath her hand now all she could feel.

Far from being resentful of her intrusion he instead wanted to make her feel welcome, and her heart turned over to think of it, hardly daring to imagine a future where her presence wasn't a burden or something to be endured.

For most of her life she had been made to feel like a disappointment. Until her return from Italy, every day at Burton Lodge had been filled with the awareness of her failures. For the first time it seemed she had a chance at living without that shadow, and to know that *Samuel Beresford* cared about her comfort more than her own parents was hard to comprehend. Offering the gift of a dog was a small thing if taken at face value, but it was what it represented that was important: the desire for her to feel she belonged at Larch House and to make it her home, acceptance of a kind she had never known before.

The tumult of her thoughts was deafening but she

could hardly share them, instead once again falling on Nelson to prevent the silence from returning.

'Well… If I'm to have one of my own it occurs to me that I have much to learn. Perhaps I could take Nelson's lead for a moment, to understand the method?'

'I don't think that's a good idea. He's strong and could easily pull you over.'

Julia hesitated. The middle of the street was *not* the place to confront the feelings Samuel's kindness had stirred in her, so at odds with everything she'd so recently believed. What she needed was a distraction, both from her own mind and from the way the sunlight picked out the grey highlights in his eyes, and with renewed resolve she tried again.

'I'm sturdier than I look. I'm sure I can manage.'

He turned to her, the grey flecks glowing almost silver, and she could have sworn she saw a ghost of amusement.

'Are you?'

'Why, yes. At least I'd certainly like to think so.'

She watched him consider, wondering whether he was recalling the fumbling ineptitude of her youth, but then he held out his other hand.

'Very well. If you insist.'

Eagerly, Julia took hold of the lead, unable to prevent a secret thrill when her fingers brushed Samuel's palm. Nelson leapt forward at once, doubtless sensing a lighter touch on his restraints, and she hurriedly let go of Samuel's arm to clamp both hands around the leather loop.

'He *is* strong, isn't he?'

'Shall I take him back?'

'No, no. I can do it.'

She hauled on the lead, only just managing to keep her balance as Nelson towed her along. He seemed to be walking her rather than the other way round, and she felt the beginnings of alarm to find herself moving faster.

'Are you sure you don't want me to have him back?'

Samuel's voice came from slightly behind her now and she had to turn her head to speak over her shoulder. 'I'm fine, really. I just need to find the right grip…'

Suddenly, the lead slackened. Nelson stood perfectly still, his tail slowing from a frantic wag to a cautious wave, and she was about to feel relieved when instead horror broke over her as she realised what had caught his eye.

'No, Nelson. No—!'

But it was already too late.

The cat sunning itself outside the milliner's shop looked up. In a flash it was fleeing away down the street in a blur of orange and white, and Julia had no choice but to break into a run as Nelson dragged her after it, almost pulling her arm from her shoulder as she clung to the lead. Passers-by skipped hastily out of the way but she couldn't stop to apologise, the dog so intent on his prey that he was more like a charging bull than a pointer with a pink-tongued grin.

'Wait! Stop!'

She tried to yank him back but he was too strong. Her presence on the other end of the lead hampered him slightly but couldn't halt his chase altogether, and if she let go he might run under a carriage or be trampled by one of the many horses trotting past. All she could do was hang on desperately and hope he would choose to stop, although as the cat disappeared around a corner Nelson showed no sign of slowing down.

Together they barrelled onto a quiet side street lined with houses, Julia's bonnet flying off as the chill wind ripped it from her head. A large tree stood in the middle of one front lawn and she saw the cat make a beeline for it, throwing itself desperately onto the trunk and then climbing for the safety of the higher branches. Still Nelson didn't slow, hurtling towards the tree with no sign of reducing his speed, and Julia was certain he would dash her against it when she felt a pair of strong arms close around her waist.

They anchored her to the spot, bringing the dog to an abrupt standstill, but it wasn't the wrench of her shoulder that made her snatch a sharp breath. She could feel the long, lean length of her rescuer's body pressed to hers, her back to his chest with not an inch in between, and she had to fight the urge to lean against him as sensation licked from her nape to the base of her spine.

It had to be Samuel: no other man smelled as good or had such strength in his arms, holding her upright with no effort at all. For the second time in barely a few weeks he'd come sailing in to save her from some catastrophe of his dog's making, and she had just enough time to wonder at how their connection had improved since the first incident when he leaned down, speaking so close to her ear that she felt his breath on her neck.

'You can let go now. He won't run anymore.'

She dropped the lead. Nelson immediately raced to the foot of the tree and stood staring up at the branches, but Julia hardly noticed. All her attention was on the press of Samuel's firm chest and his palm flat against her bodice, still holding her steady, and she found herself reluctant to break free.

Her legs were shaking, she realised belatedly, although whether from running or the heat of his touch she wasn't sure. Her heart was pounding and her breath coming short, and for a split second she thought she felt Samuel trembling likewise until she realised the truth.

'Are you—are you *laughing*?'

The quaking behind her grew more pronounced. 'I'm sorry. I really am.' He sounded as if he was trying to collect himself with little success. 'It's just how you took off into the distance…'

Julia turned sharply. With her legs still wobbly she staggered slightly, and Samuel redoubled his grip, helping her keep her balance as she looked up into his face.

He glanced down at her, his merriment fading as he met her eye. 'I am, of course, deeply relieved you weren't harmed. If you had been, I would never…' He tailed off, looking unsure.

Julia watched his smile dwindle and uncertainty creep in to replace it—but it returned full force when she heard herself begin to laugh.

She couldn't control it. Something about his amusement sparked her own, the gleam in his eye so comical she couldn't help but join in, and her heart leapt when his much deeper laughter combined with hers. His hands still steadied her but now she felt weak for a different reason, and she thought she might have carried on laughing for ever if she hadn't felt a sudden burst of heat as Samuel bent to claim her mouth.

Her eyes flew wide but fluttered closed as sensation

overcame her, surprise turning rapidly to bliss with the movement of his lips. They traced the contours of hers, drawing her in with every deft stroke until the world around them fell away, and the only thing that existed was the scalding desire for him never to stop.

With her bonnet lying somewhere on the grass she felt his hand stray to cup the back of her bare head, his fingers pushing into her hair and sending spikes of delicious longing through every nerve. His other hand had slipped down to her waist and she mirrored its blazing grip, her own palm sliding round to feel the hard muscle of his back and count the ridges of his spine. He shuddered beneath her wandering fingers, his now bunching into a fist amidst her curls, and when she lightly grazed his lower lip with her teeth she triumphed at hearing him swallow a groan.

His breathing was harsh and hers little better, coming in ragged gasps that were all she could manage to snatch. To breathe more easily she would have to break the kiss and that was impossible, everything in her rising to the point where she couldn't let him go.

If he hadn't moved, Julia knew she would have stayed there, entangled in broad daylight so scandalously that even a wedding might not have been enough to save her good name—but all the same it was a wrench to feel him step away, his eyes glazed and his reluctance clear as he released her from his hold.

'I'm sorry.' Samuel took a shuddering breath, although Julia saw his eyes stray at once back down to her mouth. 'I couldn't help myself. It just sounds so wonderful when you laugh.'

She blinked, trying to rein in the wild racing of her heart. It railed against her ribs as though it wanted to break free and his words only made it pound harder, so sweet that she could taste them on her tongue.

'You—you needn't apologise. I can't pretend any offence.'

He smiled, a shaky thing clearly masking something else he was too much of a gentleman to voice. His eyes were intent on her, however, a dark glitter in them suggesting his blood ran just as hotly as hers, and there was a good chance he might have pulled her to him once again if an ill-timed interruption hadn't sent them stepping hastily apart.

'Julia? Is this *your* bonnet?'

Her mother sounded disapproving as she came towards her, carrying the bonnet as carefully as one might a small child. Lady Maidwell's face was creased with concern, and Julia turned quickly back to Samuel before they got close enough to hear her speak.

'Will you be at Sir William's house tomorrow?' she murmured, aware their mothers were swiftly gaining ground. 'For his Yuletide card party?'

Samuel gazed down at her and Julia felt herself flush. Perhaps she should have pretended she wasn't bothered whether he'd be there or not, but the memory of his laughter in harmony with hers was too affecting to resist. His humour was a pleasure when she knew there was no malice in it, and for it to be something they could share made fresh hope for the future leap within her chest.

'An evening of whist and festive favourites? Of course. I can hardly wait.'

Samuel's light chuckle stirred the embers in her stomach—embers that glowed hotter when the smile faded to be replaced by something far more serious.

'It's your presence that holds the appeal, however. If you'll be in attendance, I shall make sure I don't arrive late.'

Samuel held true to his word.

He was among the first to arrive at Sir William's vast yet welcoming house, and for half an hour he found himself trapped in a corner with one of his host's old army friends, only half listening to the tales of glorious victory while he kept one eye on the door. It opened and closed what felt like a hundred times and with every turn of the handle his hopes rose, only to be dashed again when some other lady or gentleman entered the room.

It wasn't until he had almost given up and abandoned himself to the mercy of the elderly major's war stories that *at last* she appeared.

Julia came in on Harry's arm, resplendent in the same Christmas-green gown she'd worn at Lady Fitzgerald's ball, and it seemed to Samuel that the whole atmosphere changed. The buzz of conversation around him retreated and the light from the many candles seemed to concentrate on Julia's face, illuminating it as though her countenance was the centrepiece of the entire room. Major Latimer was still talking but Samuel hardly heard him, too intent on curbing the urge to immediately go to stand by her side, and he couldn't look away as she greeted Sir William, her smile so dazzling it could have eclipsed even the sun.

'Don't you agree, Beresford?'

At the sound of his name, Samuel reluctantly turned back to the Major. 'Yes. Absolutely. Just as you say.'

What he'd just agreed to he had no idea. Every sense

was trained on Julia and he could have laughed at himself, almost amused to be behaving more like a moonstruck lad than a grown man—but a faint twinge low in his gut warned some caution should still remain.

Yesterday he'd seen yet another side to her, another facet to add to the growing collection of different faces she could present to the world, and the latest was perhaps his favourite of them all. Standing with the cool sunlight glancing off her uncovered hair, Julia's laugh had been the sweetest he'd ever heard and it echoed inside his mind like the peal of a golden bell, high and pure and so wonderful he hadn't been able to resist kissing the lips that produced it. Then, of course, his mind had strayed onto other things—but for a precious moment she'd seemed happy in his arms, actually *enjoying* his company where once she'd made no secret of her vehement dislike, and he still hadn't managed to untangle exactly how that made him feel.

His heartfelt apology had been the key to unlocking this new version of the woman who was to become his wife, and despite her gracious acceptance of it some guilt remained. She might have been good enough to grant him forgiveness but that didn't mean he had yet forgiven himself for behaving so poorly towards her, aware as he was that his feelings towards her were in danger of slowly beginning to change.

But you ought not to allow it. Would you really revisit the pain Lucrezia wrought?

The colour of Julia's dress paired beautifully with the holly boughs draped over every possible surface. Christmas was fast approaching and with it his wedding day, an event that despite his attempts to control it now filled him with wary anticipation rather than stark dread.

He watched Harry draw her farther into the room, both Livingstons smiling and nodding at the many others who came to greet them. Julia curtseyed prettily but it seemed she was looking for someone, her glossy head turning this way and that to peer around the parlour, and his pulse quickened to wonder if she was searching for him.

Doubtless it was safer to keep his emotions in check, at least until he could be certain what lay behind her gleaming smile. Lucrezia had the face of an angel but not the nature to match, and her deception had taught him caution in the cruellest way…although every sensible thought vanished as Julia finally saw him, the immediate colour that rose in her cheeks when their eyes met making any hope of keeping his distance frankly impossible.

'Would you excuse me, Major?'

With a brief bow he managed to extract himself before the old veteran plunged into yet another story of past triumphs. Julia still held her brother's arm but the usual cluster of young ladies had begun to gather around him, and she looked faintly relieved when Samuel reached her, letting go of Harry to dip an elegant curtsey.

'Good evening.'

'Good evening. I was beginning to think perhaps…'

He abandoned the end of his sentence. He'd been about to tell her he'd feared she wasn't coming and he almost winced at his own eagerness, the very opposite of the nonchalance he'd meant to adopt. Apparently, just the sight of her was enough to make him forget himself and he straightened his cravat, deliberately busying hands that longed to place even a single finger on her bare arm.

'Are you parents not in attendance?'

Julia's lips folded as though she was hiding a smile. 'No. Papa rarely leaves his study, even for the parties of old friends, and Mama thinks she may have caught a chill when we were in town yesterday. My only chaperone for the evening is Harry…if one can call him that.'

He followed her amused glance to see her brother had already drifted away, surrounded by a veritable harem of debutantes who looked to be hanging on his every word. Until very recently he'd experienced the same thing himself, but word of his engagement had largely put a stop to it, only the most determined now bothering to flutter her eyelashes in his direction.

News of their match hadn't necessarily discouraged Julia's suitors, however, he saw with a prickle of unease. The moment she'd entered the room Sydenham had turned his beady eyes upon her, and even now Ollerton was watching more closely than Samuel liked; men who had been his friends when they were boys now clearly wishing he had stayed in Italy and left Miss Livingston alone.

Trying to ignore their scrutiny, Samuel attempted a sympathetic frown.

'What a shame. I should hate to think of your mother being unwell.'

'Terrible, isn't it?' Julia replied brightly. 'Now I'll have to get through an entire card party without her telling me where to sit and what hand to play. I don't know how I'll manage.'

Her high spirits were infectious and Samuel only

just managed to supress a smile of his own as she fanned her rosy cheeks with one gloved hand.

'It's warm in here. Perhaps we might stand a little closer to the door? Every time it opens there's a draught of cold air. I believe the only reason we ventured this far into the room was so Harry could show himself to his best advantage.'

Privately thinking back to the last time she had declared a parlour too hot, Samuel offered his arm, his already swift pulse skipping faster when she laid her hand—slightly shyly?—on his sleeve. That had been the evening he'd first kissed her, had learned how soft her lips were as they moved under his, and the desire to repeat the experience now pierced him like the tip of a blade.

They strolled leisurely across the room, Julia blazing like an uncut emerald as her gown caught the light. Some young lady had taken command of the pianoforte and Christmas carols filled the air, the music and merry chatter combining in a pleasant din that made it difficult for Samuel to hear himself think.

There was, however, something that managed to hold his attention in spite of the noise. In his breast pocket he carried a small parcel and it felt as though it was growing heavier by the minute, his uncertainty rising with every step until Julia was installed comfortably beside the door.

'Is that better?'

'Much, thank you. It's far cooler standing here.'

At her smile his apprehension leapt upwards. He was being ridiculous and yet he couldn't quite shake it off as he reached into his pocket and drew out the package tied with striped twine.

He held it out to her, feeling absurdly self-conscious. 'Here. This is for you.'

'Oh?' Surprised, she took the parcel from him, turning it over in her hands. 'What is it? An early Christmas gift?'

'Just a small thing. Nothing of any importance.'

She glanced at him, puzzled, and he tried not to let his apprehension show as she carefully peeled back the paper.

Her eyes widened. 'A book of Italian grammar?'

'I recalled you saying you wanted to learn more of the language. It won't be as good as having lessons, but I thought perhaps you might find it useful.'

Samuel smoothed the back of his hair, suddenly overly aware of his limbs. It was like being a child again, uncomfortably similar to showing his mother a drawing he had made for her and hoping she'd like it, and he realised his voice had roughened with unease. 'As I said. Just a small thing. You needn't use it if you'd rather not.'

'No, it's… Thank you. This is very thoughtful.'

He felt his shoulders relax. To an onlooker it might have been a small gift but to Julia it meant something— just as he'd intended, in the unwise part of himself that wanted to draw her further in.

The warning voice in the back of his mind held up a restraining hand but he realised he was finding it more and more difficult to heed it. The more time he spent with his unlikely fiancée the warmer his feelings for her became, and she did nothing to discourage them when she smiled up at him like a flower in bloom.

'I can begin my studies again with this. In no time at all we'll be able to speak Italian together at home.'

Samuel stilled, the clamour of the parlour around him receding.

Home came from her lips so naturally it conjured a picture of warmth and comfort the likes of which he hadn't thought possible, of a place so much more than a mere house. Julia spoke as though she would belong there and he along with her, perhaps hinting the future could be brighter than he'd believed—which made the second thought that flitted through his mind even harder to bear.

Italian would indeed have been spoken for much of the time if he'd married Lucrezia, and he felt himself tense again as an unwanted reminder of the parallels between the two women pushed forward with renewed force. When he'd learned that Julia had spent time in the country where he'd left his heart, it had seemed an uncanny coincidence, the link tenuous but a link all the same. What he wanted was to focus on the differences between them, not the similarities, the fear that Julia could turn out to possess the same dishonest core still worrying at him like a wolf would a sheep. He no longer believed she'd played a part in contriving their engagement—her reasons for disliking him had been so genuine there was surely no chance she had entered into it willingly—but her vibrancy was entrancing and her face beguiling, and as much as he tried not to he couldn't completely prevent the spectre of Signora Bianchi shadowing Miss Livingston's step.

Thankfully, Julia seemed unaware of the battle raging inside his head. She had flicked open the book and was immersed in one of the pages, only looking up when Sir William appeared at Samuel's elbow.

'I'm sorry to intrude, Beresford, but I'm hoping to steal Miss Livingston away from you.'

He laughed heartily and Samuel copied, although the accidental voicing of his secret fear made it difficult to raise a smile.

'Did you need me, Sir William?'

At Julia's polite curiosity the old knight leaned closer, first glancing around to ensure he couldn't be overheard. 'Will you come with me and make up a table? Lady Carstairs has just sat down to whist and—strictly between ourselves—she is neither a good winner nor loser. I'd rather my little Christmas party wasn't the scene for some petty scandal and I doubt she'd try anything under your shrewd eye.'

'Ah.' Her knowing nod suggested she was already aware of the dangers posed by the dowager baroness. 'Of course. I'm pleased to help where I can.'

With old-fashioned courtesy Sir William offered his arm and Julia took it, sliding Samuel a smile as she was steered away. He inclined his head in reply and watched her glide across the room, almost as tall as Sir William, and the straight-backed grandeur of her posture equal to that of any princess.

He wasn't the only one to admire it, however. Ollerton followed her progress with far too much interest, his head turning to keep pace with her, and Sydenham had already pulled a chair out for her at the table he was standing beside. Captain Jacobs was somewhere near about, the flash of his red coat persistently catching the eye, and Samuel's discomfort grew to imagine himself surrounded on all sides.

And they all want Julia.

She'd reached the whist table and taken the seat Mr

Sydenham had so thoughtfully arranged. The moment she sat down he was bending to speak to her, so close he was all but whispering in her ear, and Samuel realised he was holding his breath.

Is that how it would be even once they were married? A constant procession of men fighting for his wife's attention, perhaps hoping to steal her away from beneath his very nose? The situation with Lucrezia had been hauntingly similar, almost re-created now like a portrait of the past, but of course in those days he'd been hopelessly naive. *Then* he had smiled when the gentlemen gathered around her, understanding their fascination but secure in the knowledge that she wanted only him, and to find out—*just* before it was too late— that he had been entirely wrong...

Captain Jacobs with his damned scarlet coat was standing at her other shoulder now, and Sydenham straightened up, casting his rival a narrow glance. Julia didn't seem to have noticed the raising of hackles going on behind her but Samuel couldn't look away, aware that any action on his part was likely to make an embarrassing scene, but his hand somehow balling into a fist nonetheless.

He didn't want to possess her. She wasn't a trophy or some prize to be won. Julia was her own person and he respected that absolutely, but the idea of again attaching himself to a much-desired woman left a bitter taste in his mouth. He'd placed his faith once before and been burned for it, and to have the same thing seemingly unfolding again before his eyes was torture he wasn't sure he could bear.

Julia might dislike him less now, even be starting to consider him a friend of sorts, but love him she did not. There was scant reason for her to cleave to him when she had so many options elsewhere, and the pain-filled words she'd flung at him on the day of their engagement came back to him now like a knife plunged into his gut.

'I could have had my choice of men but instead I waited. I wanted a man who would love me, value me for myself instead of what was on the outside…and instead, I get you.'

On that day he'd been too focused on his own panic and rage to hear the despair in her voice, but he heard it now as loudly and clearly as if she'd been shouting in his ear. Surely things between them had improved since then, however; surely since he had tried to make amends things weren't now quite so bleak. He might be doing her a disservice in comparing her to the woman he'd loved before, and there had to be a chance she wouldn't turn on him in the same way…but he couldn't *know*. Only time would tell if Julia was likewise going to shatter his trust, and he had no choice but to balance on a tightrope of uncertainty until he could be sure.

Entirely unaware of Samuel's confusion, Julia looked serene. Her face didn't change as she took up her cards, glancing down at her hand—and then carefully, deliberately, she placed the book he had given her down beside her on the table.

She touched the leather cover lightly, just brushing it with a fingertip, but apparently that was enough. With a small smile she sat up straighter in her chair, glanced once more at the little book beside her as if it would bring her luck, and then she began to play, keeping her eyes on her cards and the smile in place… And

Samuel had no idea what thoughts were going on behind it, his own fears buzzing loud enough to silence the rest of the room.

Chapter Eight

Julia hadn't realised how tightly she was holding her father's arm until she heard his sharp intake of breath above the echoing notes of the church organ. Her hand clutched his sleeve in a frozen grip and she stared straight ahead, the faces of those turning to watch her walk up the aisle nothing but blurs glimpsed from the corner of her eye. There was only one thing she could see clearly and that was Samuel waiting for her at the altar, and when he turned around she thought her legs might give way there and then.

The deep blue of his richly embroidered waistcoat made his eyes shine sapphire in the light pouring through the church's stained-glass windows, and he didn't look away as she came towards him, her heart beating louder with every step. In a matter of moments they would be standing together, prepared to throw themselves into the other's keeping for the rest of their lives, and the same dazed trepidation that had overwhelmed her since she'd woken at dawn came again to make her wonder how it had come to *this*.

Not, of course, that she was as unhappy at the prospect of taking Samuel as her husband as she would have been only weeks before. Then the very idea would have made her run for the hills, but now, by some miracle, things were different. Quite what the relationship between them had become she wasn't sure—perhaps something like a friendship with an edge of physical attraction thrown in to complicate things further, although of one thing at least she harboured no doubts.

I always hoped for a husband who loved me. I wanted a man who married me by choice—and however far we might have come together, I know Samuel wouldn't be wedding me now if Mama hadn't forced his hand.

That stark truth followed her as she reached the end of the aisle, Samuel still never taking his eyes from her. It was difficult to know what thoughts he might be hiding behind that blue gaze but he offered her a smile nonetheless, that hint of reassurance more welcome than he ever could have guessed.

She came to a halt beside him, looking to the vicar but keenly aware of Samuel's tall presence at her shoulder. Carefully, her father prised her hand off his sleeve and with an unexpectedly warm squeeze of her fingers stepped back, leaving her to stand unaided and pray her nerves wouldn't bring her to her knees.

The organ's final note blared out and then died away, a silence settling over the watching congregation. The time had come for both her and Samuel to face their fate, and Julia tried to tamp down the rising apprehension that made her windpipe feel like it was closing over with every breath.

Any chance to back out was long gone. Her closest family were watching, with the exception of Aunt

Marie and Uncle Cecil, who had sent congratulations from Dublin, and Samuel's parents beamed from the front pew. Mama's triumph was almost complete and it seemed to Julia that the two people most affected by the match were the two who'd had the least say in it, irony that faded slightly when Samuel's arm accidentally brushed against hers. Even standing in the austere surroundings of a church his slightest touch could light a taper in her, and she tried not to flush as the vicar began to speak, watching him but every nerve alert to the other man standing at her side.

Somehow, she managed to maintain her composure throughout the clergyman's droning monologue. It wasn't until Samuel turned to her, reaching to take her hand in his, that the agitation circling inside her almost broke free, and she felt her heart turn over as her fingers slipped into his palm.

He looked down at her, the handsome planes of his face like sculpted stone. Once again, it was impossible to guess what he was feeling, and Julia realised she was hoping it wasn't resentment, his lips now set in an unsmiling line. If he hadn't agreed to marry her, Mama would have seen to it that his honour was tarnished beyond repair, and she hated that he was a casualty of her mother's ambition, their marriage tainted before it had even begun. Her regard for him might be blossoming day by day but there seemed less chance of his doing the same, and she swallowed down sudden sorrow at the knowledge she was about to bind herself for life to a man who didn't love her and probably never would.

Samuel was speaking now, his voice low and so intimate that Julia had to supress a shiver. She couldn't help but watch the movement of his mouth as he framed each word, and the blush she was trying to restrain rose again to recall how he had kissed her with those very same lips, the ones now delivering the vows that would make him hers. She couldn't look away, not while he was swearing to have her and hold her and cherish her 'til death them did part, and only when it came time for her to make the same promise did she realise a lump had risen in her dry throat that made it all but impossible to force out the words.

'I, Julia Marie Livingston, take thee, Samuel Edward Beresford...'

Stumblingly she repeated the vows, Samuel's right hand now grasped in hers. It felt large and reassuringly strong and she wondered if it would be enough to save her if she fell, her head beginning to spin as the full magnitude of what they were doing hit her like a runaway cart. She was almost his wife and he was almost her husband, and all that remained was for him to slip a ring on her quaking finger and to sign their names in the register that would mean neither of them would ever be free again.

Cousin Eliza grinned at her in a not entirely genteel fashion as Samuel guided Julia back down the aisle, her wedding ring gleaming on her numb hand. Harry's smile was scarcely any less broad, and Mama looked as though Christmas had come four days early, seizing her daughter by the elbow the moment the newlyweds reached the church's porch.

'Come here, dearest. Let me kiss the bride!'

She drew Julia away from Samuel and he let her go slightly unwillingly, although his attention was at once claimed by his own mother and her lace handkerchief-stifled tears. His parents glowed with excitement and Julia just had time to feel pleased *somebody* was innocently thrilled about the match before Mama pulled her into a theatrical embrace.

'You've done it. You've finally done it.'

There was a tremor in her lowered voice but Julia wasn't naive enough to mistake it for happiness. It was triumph, not joy, that made Mrs Livingston so emotional, and she had to steel herself not to pull away.

'I confess there were times I feared you might never wed, but now look. The future Viscountess Maidwell! Come outside at once. Half the town is waiting to congratulate you, and I must have you admired in that gown. The extra lace was worth it after all, don't you think?'

The implication was that Mama deserved the credit for the bride's ethereal splendour but Julia was too distracted to oblige. Samuel had handed the sniffling viscountess to Harry and was coming towards her with the delightfully intent expression of a man who intended to reclaim his wife, and when he stood beside her she had to fight the urge to lean closer to his broad chest.

'Is something amiss?'

'No indeed.' Mama smiled up at her new son-in-law although Julia could tell his interruption wasn't wholly welcome. 'I was just telling Julia she needs to come out and be admired. Now's hardly the time for her to revert to a wallflower, when she's wearing a king's ransom of lace and silk!'

Mrs Livingston gave one of her tinkling laughs and Julia felt discomfort nip beneath her bodice. It was the same feeling as when her mother used to insist she play the pianoforte in company and she shook her head quickly, aware Samuel had seemed to draw a little nearer to her side.

'I'd really rather not be stared at, Mama. You know it isn't something I enjoy.'

The light of battle flared in her mother's eye. 'Nonsense! On today of all days you *must* be seen. All you need do is linger outside the church for an hour until everybody has had a chance to observe you. I'm sure Samuel agrees with me.'

Samuel's eyebrows rose. 'On the contrary, madam. If Julia would rather proceed straight to Burton Lodge for the wedding breakfast as planned, I would be happy to acquiesce to her wishes.'

He shrugged politely and then Julia felt a delicious tingle spread through her as his fingers brushed her hand. 'I would always have her do whatever makes her feel the most comfortable. My wife's happiness is, of course, now my foremost concern.'

His fingers traced over hers again and this time Julia took them, her heart beginning to skip as Samuel gently placed her hand into the crook of his arm. He looked down at her, an entire ocean captured in his sea-blue eyes, and she looked back, the embers his proximity always lit in her beginning to smoulder again at the frank honesty she saw in his face.

Where once Samuel had been her very least favourite person in all the world, now he was beginning to become the opposite: a man whom she regarded more highly than she ever would have dreamed. To have him hold her hand and call her *wife* with such calm certainty sent a warm sensation to pool at the base of her spine. She couldn't be sure what he felt in turn, doubtless nothing like the unformed emotion he had started to inspire in her, but there was respect there now, and plenty of marriages had been built on far worse. At the very least, she knew he was attracted to her, she thought now with another of those curious thrills; although what that would mean for their wedding night she would still have to wait hours to find out.

'But—but the lace! And the silver embroidered pansies...'

Mrs Livingston was frowning and Julia hurriedly curbed the unladylike direction of her mind. What came after their bedroom door was closed was something that had to be done to cement their marriage and was not to be dwelt upon, no matter what Eliza had whispered to the contrary. Her cousin had audaciously claimed that the act wasn't necessarily the *duty* Mama had discreetly hinted, although the very idea was enough to make Julia's skin feel like a furnace, and she tried to turn her attention back to her mother's annoyance.

She felt the muscle of Samuel's forearm tense. For a moment she wondered if he was going to enter the fray to defend her, but the approach of Lady Maidwell broke the tension beginning to fill the church's cold porch.

'Shall we go to Burton Lodge now? I imagine poor Julia must be famished. On my own wedding day I was so nervous that I couldn't eat so much as a crumb before the service!'

The Viscountess beamed mistily, now holding her husband's arm instead of Harry's, and Mrs Livingston found a smile like one chewing a lemon.

'Oh, of course. I was just saying the same thing myself.'

In front of Samuel's parents Mama was powerless to argue. She would rather have eaten her own bonnet than lose her composure before a peer of the realm, and she could do nothing but follow as Samuel led Julia out into the crisp, clear sunlight, the bells pealing overhead and a sea of smiling faces waiting to congratulate them.

It was past midnight by the time Samuel climbed Larch House's shadowy staircase, his footsteps echoing in the darkness. The rest of the household had already retired after the long and busy day, the afternoon and evening following the wedding breakfast taken up with the bustle of installing Julia and her belongings in her new home, although as he reached the landing sleep was the furthest thing from his mind.

Since the first moment he'd glimpsed her as she walked down the aisle he hadn't been able to help wondering what would happen when they were finally alone. Her dress had shimmered around her in a silvery haze and her pearl-strewn bonnet had framed her face like a painting, her expression slightly hesitant but characteristically resolute, and it had been all he could do not to let his mouth hang open. If there was a more beautiful woman in Guildbury he'd certainly never seen her—or perhaps there wasn't even in the whole world, every other pretty countenance paling in comparison with the determined set of Julia's jaw and the way her gaze had held his as she'd come to stand at his side. It had been exquisite torture to sit next to her at Burton Lodge's long dining table and be unable to touch, her lips curving as she smiled and talked with the family and friends that had gathered to celebrate their marriage; lips he'd longed to kiss again since the last time she'd granted him that honour.

The candle he held cast strange shapes on the walls

as he moved towards his rooms, and he realised his hand wasn't entirely steady. Julia had gone up before him, the trace of a blush across her cheekbones suggesting her thoughts had turned in the same direction as his own, and he felt his breath hitch at the question of what might be awaiting him when he opened his bedroom door. She may have been unwed until that morning but she was no fool: she knew as well as he did what was supposed to happen the first time they shared a bed, and he took a second to gather himself before he turned the handle and stepped inside.

For a moment he couldn't see much at all. The curtains were drawn over the tall windows, preventing any moonlight from spilling into the room, and the fire in the grate had begun to die down to embers. The single flame of his candle was the only real light and he hesitated, peering through the almost darkness with apprehension now climbing his backbone.

Was she already sleeping? No sound came from the direction of the bed, the closed hangings around the magnificently carved four-poster gleaming dully in the low light. If she was, he could hardly blame her; it had been a taxing day, and doubtless the last thing she would want was for him to disturb her, even if society and indeed the law expected him to set the seal on their union at once. He had no intention of pushing in where he wasn't welcome, however, no matter how the more untamed part of his mind had imagined this moment, and he was about to retreat as quietly as he had entered when a voice made every hair on the back of his neck stir like reeds in a breeze.

'You needn't leave. I'm not asleep.'

He turned back towards the bed. There was a small

gap in the hangings that he hadn't noticed in his first brief study, and he felt his stomach clench when he saw something glitter in the slice of darkness beyond, Julia's almost black eyes reflecting the candlelight like an ebony mirror.

His pulse began to quicken. 'Ah. I thought you were. It's been a busy day and I imagined you must be fatigued.'

A soft sound came from behind the hangings as if Julia had shifted a little in the great island of his bed. 'I ought to be…but somehow I find myself not tired at all.'

It was difficult to tell what she meant by that, and Samuel didn't trust himself to guess. It could simply be the excitement of the wedding that had left her so wakeful, unable to relax while the events of the day were so fresh in her mind…or perhaps her sleeplessness was caused by the same thing as his own, the thought of sharing a bed with him keeping her on high alert in the best possible way…?

Without a word he crossed to his armoire, setting the candle down on the polished washstand beside it. He had dismissed his valet hours ago, on this particular evening preferring to attend to his own nighttime rituals, although his hands felt almost too unsteady to unbutton his shirt as he reached for his collar. With his back to the bed he couldn't see whether Julia still watched him, and a crackle of excitement ran through him, the thought of her eyes on him as he undressed so sharply arousing he had to hold back a harsh breath. For all he knew she was staring as he slipped off his shirt, his bare skin illuminated by the candle's guttering flame, and he fumbled slightly at the fastening at his waist. It wouldn't be the first time he'd shucked off his breeches in front of a woman but he couldn't recall his pulse racing so lightning fast before, something about Julia's unspeaking presence behind him more affecting than any other. All he had to do was slide them *off* and pull his nightshirt *on*, but with every inch of his skin prickling he couldn't seem to manage even those two simple tasks, and he rolled his shoulders, the tension in them making the firm muscles of his back contract—

A whisper of sound behind him made him turn.

The gap in the hangings abruptly fluttered shut again. Apparently, he'd had an audience after all—one that hadn't wanted to be caught looking—and his throat felt tighter than ever as he finally stepped out of his breeches and pulled his nightshirt on over his head, leaving the top few buttons open. No other noise came from the bed and he wondered if Julia could hear how hard his heart was flinging itself against his ribs, the rush of blood loud in his ears as he blew out the candle and approached the now-closed hangings.

'May I come in?'

'Of course. It is your bed.'

Julia's voice was quiet but something in it made him clench his jaw: slightly strangled and sounding every bit as winded as he felt, and he could have sworn he heard a bitten-off breath as he carefully parted the curtains and—before he could do anything as stupid as change his mind—slid beneath the covers.

At once, every nerve blazed with the knowledge Julia was beside him, lying barely a hand's breadth away and wearing nothing but the thinnest of shifts. The warmth of her body had already invaded his half of the bed and for a moment he lay still, revelling in the intimacy of her heat and the faint floral scent of her hair on his pillows. It had been well over a year since he'd had a woman in his bed, not since before he'd first seen Lucrezia—but he didn't want to think of *her* now. She had no place intruding into his wedding night and he firmly set her aside, determinedly ignoring the ever-present gnaw of doubt as to whether Julia might turn out to be the same...

'You don't have to stay over there. I know what we're to do.'

He knew what she was referring to. How could he not? It was the same thing he had been trying not to focus on all day, and another ripple of anticipation ran through him. Surely most men would feel something similar at having a woman like Julia willing and waiting in his bed—but with difficulty he reined himself back.

Go gently. You only have one chance to get this right.

Carefully, he rolled onto his side. Peering through the gloom he could just make out the shape of her face above the coverlet, a pale moon crowned with that abundance of curls, and again he restrained the urge to touch her.

'I make no demands of you. I hope you know I would never have you act against your own inclinations.'

He tried to keep his tone light but at the first word he knew he had failed. His voice was hoarse with suppressed longing and he heard Julia move slightly in response—although with a sharp squeeze of his heart he realised it wasn't to increase the distance between them.

Her reply was a delicious murmur near to his ear. 'I appreciate that. All the same…'

She tailed off and Samuel closed his eyes, summoning the strength to stay calm. He could feel her breath on his face, coming as quickly as if she'd been running, and it would have taken the smallest shift to bring himself close enough to claim her mouth. Even in the darkness he knew exactly what she'd look like: her lips slightly parted and her eyes wide, the dusky-pink flush of her cheeks so pretty she could have melted a heart of stone. He almost wished it were daylight so he could drink in the sight of her in nothing but her nightgown, although something in having to rely on senses other than sight raised his awareness of every move she made, the blind tension between them beginning to crackle like a freshly lit fire.

He heard her take a breath, swallow and then stumble on. 'I understand it needn't be a burden. My cousin Eliza explained that what happens between a husband and wife can even be enjoyable…if he knows what he's doing.'

Samuel's eyes snapped open again.

Hellfire. Is she trying to unman me?

To lie there and listen to Julia talk of such things was more than he could bear. There was innocence bound up with her boldness and the combination did something strange, heating his blood until he feared it might boil over. If he didn't act soon he might lose his wits and yet still he made himself hold back, only the gravel in his voice betraying how badly he wanted to catch her up then and there.

'Cousin Eliza is a wise woman. If you would allow me… I could show you that she was right.'

Julia's tiny inhale was music to his ears. That minute breath was answer enough—although the sound of her hair brushing the pillow as she nodded finally gave him the unmistakable permission he'd been waiting for.

He could feel the warmth of her skin through her shift as he took her in his arms, sliding one hand between her and the mattress so he could pull her against his chest. She came willingly, her mouth seeking his, and her kiss was like a benediction when she tilted her head back and allowed him to capture her lips. She was neither hesitant nor shyly obliging as might have been expected for one so inexperienced: instead she pushed herself forward, curving against him as if some compulsion drove her on, and when he felt her hand tighten in his hair, Samuel thought he'd found heaven on earth.

He deepened the kiss, relishing Julia's half sigh when the tip of his tongue found hers and ventured into the blistering heat of her mouth. Their legs were twining together, the bedclothes beginning to tangle around them, and with sudden impatience Samuel kicked them away, delighting in another stifled gasp as Julia found herself uncovered. He needed space to go about his work and the sheets were too constricting, although he hardly had time to consider it before a static shock lanced through to his core.

Julia's hand had found the open neck of his nightshirt and her palm slid over the taut muscle of his chest, the scattering of darker hair there stirring at her touch. Her fingers left a scalding trail and it was his turn to choke back a breath as her hand explored that burning terrain, drifting higher until she lightly traced the dip at his throat. It hardly seemed fair that she should be able to touch his bare skin while hers was still covered by her flimsy nightgown, and he lifted himself onto one elbow, propping himself so he could just make out her face looking up at him through the gloom.

He could hear the ragged cadence of her breathing and knew his own was no slower. Desire pulsed through him like the beat of a drum, something primal pushing out all rational thought, and he could hardly stop himself from groaning aloud when she reached out again to try to pull his mouth back down to hers.

Deftly he moved out of reach, Julia's little cry of protest piercing through his innards like a knife. She wanted what was about to happen just as much as he did and knowing it made it hard for him to concentrate, determined as he was that Cousin Eliza's wisdom wouldn't be proven wrong.

He pushed himself up to sit beside her, staying her with a firm hand when she tried to follow. Under other circumstances he doubted she'd be so obedient but for now she was content to do as he asked, settling back down again with her eyes *just* catching the flicker of the dying fire through a gap in the hangings to glitter like black stars. In that dim light her chest rose and fell as quickly as a rabbit's, and when Samuel ran one finger from her chin to the ribbons at the neck of her gown he felt even that instinctive movement shudder to a halt, her entire being focused on him and awaiting the next delicious touch of his hand.

With aching slowness he undid the ribbons, parting the linen so her pale throat glowed in the darkness. She twitched but didn't try to sit up, and he smiled as he leaned down to place his lips just below her jaw, the tiniest moan falling from her lips as he teased the sensitive spot where her pulse leapt so wildly. Leisurely he trailed his mouth downwards, dropping soft kisses as he went until he reached the flat plane of her breastbone; and then he held his breath as carefully, gently, he pushed her gown farther open, slipping it past her shoulders to pool behind her on the bed.

At once she arched upwards, her spine curving as he continued his unhurried progress south. Her hands were in his hair and the harsh staccato of her breath was loud in his ear but he didn't stop, savouring the velvet of her skin against his mouth even as he wondered if her heat might burn down the house around them. She bucked in his hold, squirming against his mouth as he brushed first over one perfect mound and then the other, his tongue tracing scalding patterns across her and leaving her wanting more. His own body was more than ready, his arousal rising so sharply it was almost painful, but he didn't intend to rush. He would take his time to show his unlikely bride exactly how good it could be if indeed a husband knew what he was doing and when he at last ran a hand over the slender length of her legs, silently worshipping their pearlescent lines as he drew the hem of her nightgown upwards her head, he wished he could bottle the sound she made that told him everything he needed to know.

Something else seemed to be making his decisions for him now—something far less civilised, and he felt another shudder of helpless want course through him as he gazed down at his wife. The light was too low to see her clearly but even the fair haze of her was opaline, the lush curves and angles of her body against his mattress maddening in their half-hidden beauty and calling out for him to cover her with his own. She didn't try to avoid his blazing scrutiny, doubtless able to feel the intensity of his stare even if she couldn't see it, and when he moved to kneel between her thighs he could have sworn he saw the pale gleam of her smile.

Her head jerked up when he drew his nightshirt over his head, the barely visible pools of her eyes widening. This time her attempts to reach him were successful and she looped her arms around his neck as she sat up, dragging him down into a kiss so passionate it was almost bruising. Her tongue danced with his and the conflagration in his blood blazed hotter as he ran a thumb over each of her ribs, his throat raw as her hand found his naked thigh and began to wander closer to where he hoped he had the strength to withstand her—

'Lie back.'

He ground out the words against her lips, gently taking her wrist so she couldn't explore any higher. His need was too great to bear her touching him, and he felt half-crazed as she swallowed audibly, the sound unnaturally loud in the midnight quiet.

'You'll be gentle? I hear the first time can sometimes hurt…'

'I will.'

He nodded, his nose softly brushing against hers. With only the barest hesitation she dropped back onto the mattress, and he felt heat roar up to engulf him when she lay still, waiting breathlessly for his approach and so willing he could easily have skipped straight to the part she was clearly expecting.

But he hadn't finished yet. Her enjoyment was every bit as important as his own, and he gritted his teeth as a procession of possibilities—each more enticing than the last—flooded his mind.

She shivered when he ran his fingers over her inner

thigh, instinctively curving closer, and Samuel bit down on a smile of his own. She was the most intoxicating mix of naive and sensual and it set him on fire, the pent-up longing for her he'd worked so hard to control now nearly ready to be released. They might not have chosen each other but at least on this one level they seemed a good match, and he loved the sound she made when he bent over her to kiss her once again.

'I swear I'll never hurt you…but *that* will come later. I've much more proving myself to do first and the night is still young.'

Chapter Nine

Christmas Day dawned crisp and bright and Julia's step was light as she descended Larch House's staircase, a new gown of berry red rustling about her as she moved. Great boughs of greenery were threaded through the banisters, and holly gleamed from every available shelf and crevice, the mistletoe kissing balls she'd been busy making every day since the wedding swaying gently on their ribbons. The air was filled with the scent of oranges and spices and roasting meat drifting enticingly up from the kitchen, and as she reached the hall she couldn't help but gaze around her with hesitant pride.

My first Christmas as a wife and first in my own home. To think that once I was convinced this would never happen—but look at me now.

Samuel had given her free rein when it came to the decorations and had even attempted to join her in her favourite task of making the bay and laurel wreaths that hung from every door. His endeavours were a little on the misshapen side but she'd appreciated his enthusiasm, his face so intent as he'd tried to bend the twigs it had been difficult not to cup his set chin in her palm. Since the molten wonder of their wedding night she found she wanted to touch him all the time, her fingers constantly itching to trace the strong line of his profile or skim the firm planes of his back, and just the memory of his skilled exploration of her body made her have to steady herself against the carved newel post at the bottom of the stairs.

But that wasn't what she ought to be thinking of at that particular moment. As a married woman she was to take up the mantle of festive hostess for the very first time, and her nerves fluttered as she cast her mind over the preparations she'd worked on so tirelessly, sure there was something she'd forgotten. Samuel's parents would be arriving after church along with Mama, Papa and Harry, all of them expecting a lavish Yuletide feast, and for a moment she wavered, wondering whether she ought to go down to the kitchen to check on the goose in its spiced plum sauce...

'You were up early this morning. Were you too excited to sleep?'

Samuel was looking down at her from the top of the stairs. The sunlight from the landing windows made his hair shine bronze, and as always she felt herself warm as he came towards her, lightly gripping the banister with the same hand he had so recently run over her burning skin. The passion that so consumed their nights was restrained during the daytime, Samuel maintaining a respectful distance that in truth Julia found more frustrating than she cared to admit, although once or twice she'd caught him watching her with an unguarded expression that made her shiver. It was a look that spoke of desire and temptation and a hundred things besides, and as he drew nearer she wished he would forget his gentlemanly convictions and seize hold of her the way he did in their bed.

'Terrified rather than excited. I suddenly had the most overwhelming fear I'd forgotten to ask Hewitt to bring in some grapes from the hothouse.'

Samuel laughed, the same deep note that she was growing so fond of. 'Aha. Pre-hosting jitters?'

'Of course. My mother's standards are incredibly high. How will she boast about my arrangements to her friends if I get something wrong?'

She saw his eyebrow twitch as if he was having trouble preventing it from rising. Instead, he settled on pushing a stray tendril of ivy behind a picture frame, turning briefly to the wall so she couldn't see his face.

'You won't get anything wrong, but even if you did, you needn't seek her approval any longer. You are your own woman now and nobody gets to tell you what to do.'

He stepped back to admire his handiwork and Julia realised she was worrying at her lower lip. What he said was true: she was indeed out from under Mama's thumb, even outranking her now where society was concerned, but it would take time for old habits to break. With Samuel's encouragement, however, she was coming to believe it could be done, and she felt a flicker of warmth to know she had his support, at one point the most unlikely ally now the one on whom she was beginning to depend.

'Nobody can tell me? Not even you, my lawful husband?'

Samuel glanced over his shoulder, his lips curling into that all too handsome smile.

'*Especially* not me. Do you think I'd dare?'

Julia tried not to flush but it was impossible. Surely few women could have resisted that wolfish grin, and she was about to excuse herself for the kitchen when he laid a hand on her wrist, heat streaking at once from his ungloved palm.

'I was thinking, before I came down this morning... Could I give you your Christmas gift now? While it's just the two of us?'

He surveyed her closely, his eyes seeming especially blue. In all honesty she probably would have agreed to anything while his warm fingers strayed so close to her pulse, and Julia found herself nodding.

'Why, yes, if you prefer. I'm sure I'd be grateful for anything you were kind enough to get for me.'

Another grin was her reward for being so obliging. 'I was hoping you'd say that. Would you wait here? I'll be back in a moment.'

He let go of her wrist and strode back towards the staircase, only pausing when Julia called after him.

'Here? Can't I wait in the parlour instead?'

'Oh. Yes. In fact, that would be better.'

She watched him climb the stairs two at a time, taking a moment to admire the toned length of his legs in their slim-cut breeches before she moved for one of the doors leading from the hall. She settled herself on one of the sofas beside the fireplace where the Yule log blazed cheerfully, her curiosity beginning to rise.

What had he imagined she'd like as a Christmas gift? Did he know her well enough yet to judge? They'd been acquainted since they were children and yet it was only over the past few weeks she felt she was starting to see the real Samuel Beresford, the man be-

hind the charming mask far more likeable than she'd
ever believed. The kindness in him had wiped away
her long-held loathing, and sometimes she suspected
his feelings for her were growing likewise, although
surely the notion of him ever coming to love her would
be a step too far…?

Footsteps on the floorboards outside gave her no
chance to answer that question. Perhaps it wouldn't do
to consider it too closely, the truth doubtless one that
wouldn't bring her much happiness, and she tried to set
it aside as she looked towards the doorway.

It creaked open an inch or two—and then stopped.

'Close your eyes.'

Samuel's unseen voice issued from the corridor,
and instinctively Julia tried to peer through the barely
open door.

'Why?'

'Because… Just close your eyes and keep them
closed until I tell you to open them.'

Her curiosity well and truly piqued, Julia shut her
eyes, holding her hands over them for good measure.
She heard the door creak wider and Samuel crossing
the room, and then a thrill skittered down her back at
the gentle touch of his hand on her shoulder, careful
not to make her jump.

'You can look now.'

She lowered her hands to find him standing beside
her, looking down with such apprehensive anticipation that she almost reached out to reclaim his hand.
For an instant she merely gazed up at him, wondering
what could possibly make him seem so unsure; but
then a wriggling movement in the middle of the carpet caught her attention.

'Oh!'

At her gasp the black-and-white puppy trying to climb out from a wicker basket set down on the floor squirmed harder. Its tail was little more than a blur and its enormous, fringed ears seemed too big for its head, two bright eyes fixed on her like a pair of shiny jet buttons. It hopped and squeaked and flapped its miniature pink tongue, and when she dropped to her knees and scooped it up it leapt to lick her face.

She held it to her chest, too delighted even to speak. Out of the corner of her eye she saw Samuel was watching her, and still on her knees she turned towards him, the puppy nestling beneath her chin.

There was a half second of hesitation, and then Samuel joined her on the carpet, his shoulder brushing hers as he knelt closer. 'He's a papillon. A continental toy spaniel. He won't grow much bigger than a cat.'

Carefully, he reached out to stroke the white blaze between the black patches over each of the puppy's eyes. His fingertip *just* caught the skin of Julia's neck and she shivered instinctively, the smile she hadn't realised she wore flickering at the rush of sensation.

'Do you like him?'

'Of course! He's the sweetest thing I've ever seen.'

She moved the puppy from beneath her chin to her lap, spreading her skirts to create a nest. Clearly, all the excitement was too much for him as he let out a minuscule yawn and fell asleep at once, a little heap of fur that even after only two minutes Julia knew she would love.

She watched the soft pink belly rise and fall, unable to tear herself away. Surprise and happiness glowed inside her, and when she finally glanced up she knew

Samuel must have seen the joy in her face, a smile coming to his lips that mirrored the one on hers.

'Thank you. He's the most wonderful Christmas gift I've ever had.'

Samuel inclined his head, suddenly endearingly self-conscious. 'I said I wanted you to feel at home here. This ferocious beast is the first step.'

Julia nodded, looking back down at the scrap of dog she cradled in her lap although now she could barely see anything but a black-and-white blur.

He remembered.

What he'd said the day of their chance meeting in town hadn't just been a throwaway comment, then. He had meant it: that Larch House was to be her *home* rather than just a place for her to live, as much hers as it was his, and to her alarm she felt an unexpected prickling behind her eyes. For as long as she could remember she had wanted somewhere to belong, somewhere she could be herself without people watching or judging or pointing out her flaws, and although he didn't know it, Samuel had given her two precious gifts instead of the single one he had intended.

'Thank you.' Her voice was scratchy and she tried again, hoping he hadn't noticed it catch. 'I'm touched that you would want me to be happy here.'

'I do. There's nothing I want more.'

Surprised, she looked up at him. He had no time to turn away and she saw the honesty in his face, not so much as a hint he was telling anything but the truth. There was no resentment, she realised with dawning wonder, no hidden bitterness she might have expected from a man forced into marriage against his will, and despite her good sense warning her to be cautious, a budding hope began to bloom in her chest.

Against all odds he cared for her now, she knew for sure, and wasn't there only a small leap from caring to love?

She set the puppy back down in his bed as tenderly as one might a newborn baby. He stirred a little in his sleep but didn't wake and Julia tried not to make a sound as she slowly stood up, turning to see Samuel already leaning against the door.

'I shall have to think up a name for him. I won't be able to concentrate in church now and it's all your fault.'

Samuel's lips twitched. 'I'll be sure to give the good rector my apologies.'

He shouldered himself away from the door as she came towards him, standing aside to let her pass— although at the very last minute he glanced up.

'Oh, look. Mistletoe.'

Following the direction of his upturned eyes, Julia saw the little ball of greenery hanging from the door frame, the leaves studded with white berries. She had the sneaking suspicion he'd known it was there all along but the rush that swept through her still almost knocked her off her feet, already off balance from his thoughtful gift and her tentative hopes. He was standing close enough for her to smell the sharp tang of his soap…and when he came a half step nearer still, she was the one who closed the final distance and reached up on tiptoe to bring her mouth to his.

His hands immediately settled on the smooth sweep of her waist and she relished the brush of his thumbs over her lowermost ribs as he held her, his grip so tight she felt its warmth through her gown. It was a sweeter kiss than those they traded in the darkness of their bed. Nighttime roused passion that strayed into urgency, but under the mistletoe they twined together more slowly, Julia's hands running over Samuel's shoulders until she could slide her arms around his neck. Rising higher on her toes she leaned against him, the full length of her body pressed shamelessly against his, and she felt him shudder as he dropped one palm to her lower back, holding her to him as the air around them began to simmer with unspoken desire. Gathering her courage she ventured her tongue to dance with his, triumphant when she heard his breathing become ragged, and everything else seemed to fall away as they swayed together, drinking each other in as though they had thirsted for a week rather than having sated themselves only a few hours before.

When Samuel stepped back his eyes were almost as dark as Julia's, his pupils dilated until there was hardly any blue left at all. She half thought he would pull her to him again but he let her go, pushing a flatteringly unsteady hand through his tousled hair.

'We should get ready. We'll be late for church otherwise, and then what would your mama say?'

Her mother wasn't really the person she wanted to think about while her heart slammed so forcefully against the bodice of her gown, but Julia nodded all the same, reaching up to pat her own hair back into shape. He was right. If they were late it wouldn't go unnoticed and she would die of mortification if anyone were to guess why two newlyweds might not have left the house on time.

'What about my new friend?'

She looked over her shoulder at the basket, where the puppy was still contentedly fast asleep.

'I don't want to leave him. Do you suppose the rector would notice…?'

'If you sneaked him into chapel in your reticule?' Samuel's laugh was warm and Julia felt the pleasure of it right down to her toes. 'I'm afraid so. I'll call a couple of the younger maids. They'll be delighted to keep him company until we get back.'

He stood aside and this time she was able to leave the parlour without being waylaid. Fenshaw would have to fix a handful of curls that had come loose from her stylish chignon, and there was little time left before they had to leave the house—and yet Julia couldn't seem to make herself move quickly, too consumed by both her husband's gift and his kiss to think about anything else as she wandered—still smiling—towards the stairs.

By the time everybody had finished eating, the sun had set and Larch House's magnificent chandeliers blazed with candles, throwing their cheerful light over the male members of the party as they entered the drawing room. The ladies were already there, having retired to drink tea after the lengthy feast, although it took Samuel a beat to locate his wife as he looked around the room.

Julia wasn't arranged elegantly on one of the sofas as her mother was or even reclining comfortably like his own. Instead, she was sitting on the floor beside the fireplace, trailing a length of ribbon across the carpet for her little dog to chase, and he had to hide his amusement at her mama's poorly concealed disapproval. Evi-

dently, Mrs Livingston didn't care much for the puppy
or for her daughter's choice of seat, but there was nothing she could say while Lady Maidwell watched so in-
dulgently, the Viscountess possessing several lapdogs
herself and clearly enjoying the puppy's clumsy game.
His father often joked in turn that he loved his hounds
almost as much as he did his son—or at least, Samuel
thought he was joking—and the Viscount chuckled as
he sat down beside his wife, gently poking the puppy
with the very toe of his boot.

'I see you're pleased with your present. He was hidden with us at Rookley Manor until late last night—
Nelson will miss having a playmate now the secret's
out.'

Harry dropped into an armchair, leaning forward
to study the playfully growling scrap on the other end
of the ribbon. 'What's one supposed to call it, though?
It's too small to be a real dog. What name have you
given it?'

'*Him*, not *it*,' Julia corrected her brother firmly. 'And
I thought Pirate. Doesn't it fit him, with the patches
over his eyes? Although I suppose a real pirate only
has one...'

Samuel heard Mr Livingston snort what might have
been a laugh, although the cold turn of Mrs Livingston's eye cut it short.

'And what did you give dear Samuel in return? In
exchange for such a...thoughtful...gift?'

Julia glanced up at her mother's question, the tips
of her ears reddening slightly. 'I've yet to present it.'

'Why not do so now? We'll wait while you run and
fetch it.'

Samuel felt irritation prickle through him. Couldn't

Mrs Livingston keep her opinions to herself for once, if only for Christmas Day? He didn't need Julia to bring forth a gift for him—the joy that had radiated from her as she whisked the red satin about for Pirate was a present in itself and he needed no other, simple happiness softening the strong angles of her face and making her look for once as though she wasn't wearing a stiff mask of propriety. Now that joy had dimmed, her mother's interfering spoiling a moment he had wanted to commit to memory, and if Harry hadn't chosen that moment to intervene, Samuel wasn't sure he'd have been able to keep his cool.

'Perhaps Julia would prefer not to have everyone staring at her? She might want some privacy to give her new husband his first Christmas gift as a married woman.'

Julia cast her brother a small sideways smile but she didn't lift her eyes to meet Samuel's. Still toying with the ribbon she kept them trained on the carpet, and he wished everyone in the room would disappear for a moment so he could kiss away the hesitancy that had replaced her delight.

'It isn't anything anywhere near as perfect as Pirate. I don't know of any present I could give that would come close.'

The puppy bounced towards her and she gathered him up, holding him closely to the bodice of her gown. He didn't struggle to free himself, snuggling closer against his mistress as though there was nowhere he'd rather be, and Samuel's chest tightened when she bent her head to drop a kiss on the tiny button nose. It was only a small action unconsciously done but it touched him all the same, unthinking proof of the sweet nature he once hadn't realised she still possessed, and he found his lips moving before he'd given them leave to speak.

'Even the smallest token would be kept close to my heart if it was from you.'

An unspoken ripple spread around the room. His mother looked thrilled, doubtless amazed her son could manage such romanticism, and his father's eyebrows rose, mirroring the surprised amusement that crossed Harry's face. Mr and Mrs Livingston merely appeared mildly uncomfortable at talk of hearts in mixed company, but it was only Julia's reaction he cared about, the wordless parting of her lips followed closely behind by a blush as pretty as a poppy in a field.

He hadn't meant for such sentiment to slip out but even as he felt himself grow warm with embarrassment, he knew it was true. Everyone was looking at him and he might have wished he'd kept silent if not for the slow flush of shy pleasure that had stolen over Julia's face. Perhaps she was thinking he was just being polite in front of their guests but he knew better. He meant every word and the weight of them settled over him like a heavy blanket, having admitted the truth out loud before he'd even acknowledged it to himself.

I've grown to care for her, and even more dangerous than that—I think I might be falling in love.

A dart of something close to fear skewered him where he sat. Was that really what had happened? He had let himself fall into the same trap he'd vowed never to be caught in again? After the pain he'd left behind in Italy he hadn't wanted to give his heart away again, and certainly never to a woman like the one who had come before, her lovely face and inner spark a siren

call to men for miles around. From the moment Julia
had re-entered his life, he'd suspected she was dangerous and now he was at her mercy, her power over him
something he didn't think he could fight.

An awkward silence threatened to fall over the
drawing room and it was a relief when the Viscountess came to the rescue.

'Why don't we all exchange presents now? Nobody
need feel on display if we're all giving gifts at the same
time, and I'm sure it's much more fun.'

Mrs Livingston was, of course, in immediate agreement. 'That's just my opinion, too. Mr Livingston, will
you ask the butler what he did with the bag we brought
with us?'

Under cover of the fetching and passing round of
parcels, Samuel watched Julia get quietly to her feet,
depositing Pirate in Harry's lap before she left the
room. She didn't look back and he had to curb the
urge to follow, wishing he knew what she was thinking as she slipped away.

Was she pleased with what had come tumbling out
of his unwary mouth? He'd thought she seemed so,
but who was he to judge? If Lucrezia had taught him
anything it was how poor he was at understanding the
working of a woman's mind, and it wouldn't surprise
him if he'd made a mistake. Julia's eagerness for him
in the bedroom was born of instinctive attraction, not
love, and just because she sighed his name in the night
that didn't necessarily reflect her feelings for him during the day. The only way to know for sure would be
to ask her...but to his shame he realised he didn't dare.

He had already been rejected once. When Lucrezia's regard had proven false he had at least been able

to walk away, but Julia was different. They were married, bound together now for the rest of their lives, and if he tried to force her into saying something she didn't feel then neither of them could escape whatever came next. Probably anything so risky was better left unsaid, and yet he couldn't stop a gnawing ache beneath his shirt, beginning in his stomach and then reaching up to worry at his heart—

'I had no idea you were such a poet.'

Harry's grin was infectious and even with discomfort lodged in his chest, Samuel was tempted to return it. 'What? You mock me for being civil to your own sister? What kind of brother are you to object to that?'

'I don't object. I just know you aren't a natural romantic. From which of your many hundreds of books did you steal that line?'

Harry smirked again but this time Samuel didn't see it. Julia had reappeared in the doorway and seemed as if she intended to come to sit beside him, glancing at the empty space on the sofa, and he hastily shuffled up to make room. He knew both sets of parents were watching keenly—while pretending not to—and he felt a stab of gratitude when Harry casually stood up from his armchair, affecting to cradle Pirate like a baby, but in fact stepping forward to partly shield them from the rest of the room.

'I think this is the most privacy we're likely to get.' Julia smiled although Samuel was certain he caught a hint of trepidation in the tilt of her lips. 'I'm beginning to wish I'd given you this before we left for church this morning instead of waiting 'til now.'

She drew out a parcel from behind her, prettily wrapped in striped paper. For a moment she hesitated, flicking a swift glance up to see whether they were still being observed, but between Harry's broad back and their parents now focused on opening their own gifts, she evidently judged it safe to place the package in his hand.

'I hope you haven't built your hopes too high. It's really nothing grand...'

She didn't finish, allowing her sentence to fade away as she looked down at her hands. For one fleeting breath he caught another glimpse of the side of her she still tried to conceal, shy and uncertain, and the knowledge that he had once played a part in making her so drove a dagger between his ribs.

'I'm sure I'll like it.' He picked at the twine holding the paper closed, weighing the parcel in his hands. It was light and pliant and he wondered briefly what it could be, although he had already made up his mind to pretend delight whatever was inside. He refused to ever upset her again, and if that meant feigning joy at some ugly scarf or too-small shirt he would do so, anything to prevent her from turning away from him with unhappiness in her eyes...

But as it happened, no pretence was needed.

Samuel stilled as he gazed down at the waistcoat in his hands, the paper lying discarded on the floor. It shimmered blue as the Mediterranean Sea between his fingers, tiny pearl buttons studding the front and the collar cut so sharply he could have used it to shave. Delicate embroidery picked out in the finest silver thread followed every hem and seam, an exquisite pattern of winter pansies he was certain he'd seen somewhere before, and at the inside nape his initials were worked in a subtle font. As a wealthy man he was used to wearing the very best clothes, but Julia's gift was on another plane entirely, and he knew he must have looked amazed when he heard her sigh of relief.

'Oh, good. You like it?'

He turned to her. She wore a tentative smile, but her hands were clasped in her lap as if she was still nervous and he longed to take one in his, only the presence of their families so close by making him hold back.

'It's extraordinary. Where on earth did you get it? This silk, and the embroidery... I've never seen anything like it before.'

To his surprise Julia frowned. 'You're teasing me. Surely you know I made it?'

'*You* made this?'

'Yes. The silk I brought back from Italy, and the pansy design...'

She looked down at the waistcoat, lowering her voice so he could hardly hear her. 'It's the same one that was on my bridal gown, if you recall. I thought perhaps it might be a pleasant reminder of our wedding day.'

Samuel's heart lurched against his breastbone. It wasn't an unpleasant sensation, however; it was a sudden surge of emotion that sent it crashing forward and he found he couldn't speak.

She made this? It would have taken hours, days, and she did it all for me...?

He traced a fragile petal with one fingertip, admiring the countless stitches that formed it. She had sewn each one while thinking of him, and the idea was too much to believe, so sweet and so pure it could scarcely be true. Surely a woman wouldn't spend so much time on a gift for a man she had no regard for? Surely a connection that existed solely in the bedroom wouldn't warrant such work on his behalf?

Beside him Julia toyed uncertainly with the lace on one of her sleeves. Clearly his silence unnerved her but while his thoughts raced so dizzyingly he wasn't able to offer any relief, her voice still little more than a murmur. 'I began it after you showed me your library. Your apology... I wanted you to see that I accepted it fully and wanted us to begin our marriage with a clean slate.'

He nodded, still not trusting himself to open his mouth. If he spoke he had no idea what might come spilling out: perhaps a declaration of his feelings or— even worse—a question about hers that he ought not ask. It wasn't the time or the place, not while the drawing room was filled with people, but even their presence couldn't stop his mind in its wild dance.

Lucrezia had been beautiful and enchanting, but not kind. There was a brittle edge to her, he realised now, lacking softness, and her dazzling charm was diamond-hard. The similarities he'd thought stretched between her and Julia only went so far before his wife outstripped her entirely, the kindness of Julia's nature more valuable than all of Lucrezia's allure, and the fear Julia might hurt him in the same way suddenly began to lose its sting.

She'd done nothing to deserve his mistrust. If anyone should have difficulty placing their faith it should be her, and yet she had declared her forgiveness and desire to move on with their lives...together. It seemed she was optimistic for their future and that gave him hope, too, and his throat was tight as he gently took her hand.

'Thank you. That hardly seems like enough in the

face of such a special gift, but I don't know what else to say.'

She coloured, the blush he always seemed able to conjure in her rushing once again to the fore, and if Harry hadn't discreetly coughed to remind them of his presence, Samuel would have kissed her without hesitation.

As it was, all he could do at present was hold her hand, and so he did, not surrendering it despite the scandalised glance his mother-in-law shot him when Harry returned to his seat.

Mrs Livingston could stare all she liked. Julia was his wife now, not merely just a sad, neglected daughter, and as Christmas Day drew to a close he swore he would never give her cause to regret it.

Chapter Ten

Eyes slightly narrowed, Julia surveyed the small mountain of boxes piled up on the dining table. One of them was missing a tag and she frowned as she scanned the paper in her hand, the names on it not yet familiar, but she was determined that by the end of the morning she'd be able to put a face to each one.

'Who haven't I accounted for?' she asked Pirate, although the puppy was too busy chasing his tail somewhere behind her to be of much use. 'Are all of the footmen there?'

It was tradition on St Stephen's Day to give Yuletide gifts to the servants, and just because she had been at Larch House for less than a week didn't mean she intended to shirk her responsibilities. She'd tasked Samuel with drawing up a list of everyone who worked for him from the potboy to the gravely respectful butler, and she unthinkingly sucked in her lower lip as she checked each label, hardly aware her husband had entered the room until she heard Pirate bark.

'You've been busy.'

Samuel's deep voice sent a pleasant current through

her and she turned to look back at him, his smile prompting one of her own.

'I wanted to make a good impression as the new mistress of the house. I thought I'd hand out the boxes and then give the servants the rest of the day off. That's the usual thing, I believe?'

'Yes. For at least one day out of an entire year I think we can fend for ourselves.'

He came to stand beside her as Julia pointed at the anonymous parcel. 'I forgot to label that one, however. I'm trying to see who I missed, but there are so many names…'

She glanced down at the list he'd given her again, about to resume checking it against the tags when Samuel stepped round her.

'Allow me.'

He took a swift tally of the labelled boxes, nodding to himself when he came to the last one.

'It's Dawlish. One of the grooms. Used to work for my father at Rookley but, much like my groundskeeper, I stole him away when I took my own house.'

Surprised, Julia's eyebrows rose. 'You know your servants so well you can pick out one missing name? Among this many?'

'Of course. Wouldn't I be a poor employer if I couldn't?'

He shrugged, the movement of his shoulders effortlessly catching her attention. They were covered in a well-cut black coat that emphasised the golden undertones of his skin, the Italian sun deserving credit for making his handsome face even more comely—if such a thing were possible. Even after so much time had passed there were still moments when Julia was tempted to simply stare at him instead of speaking, and now might have been one of them if he hadn't asked her a question that required a considered reply.

'I'm not sure. I don't know that many gentlemen would take the time to memorise every last employee, right down to the stable hands, and be able to tell in a moment who wasn't there.'

She leaned forward to write on the final blank label, tying it onto the parcel with a neat loop of twine. She could sense Samuel behind her, each nerve trained on him as happened every time they were in the same room, and she heard the floorboards creak as he shifted his weight from one foot to the other.

'It's my duty to know. Every servant, tenant, farmer on our estates… When I take over from my father I'll have even more people that look to me for their livelihoods. I may as well start as I mean to go on.'

Still with her back to him, Julia ran her hand over the pile of boxes, tweaking a knot here and a fold of paper there. She didn't want him to see her face while she was thinking, sure her thoughts were written too clear to remain hidden.

It shouldn't have surprised her he knew every name by heart. It was that same decency that had been the net that caught her, his good looks perhaps the bait initially, but something deeper drawing her in to stay. Now there was little hope of breaking free again even if she'd wanted to, their first Christmas together more enjoyable than she'd dared dream, and his genuine appreciation for the present she'd given him imprinted on her mind for ever. He'd seemed moved by the work she'd put into making the waistcoat and had refused to surrender hold of her hand afterwards, even while

Mama fussed and tutted, and she knew it would soon be time for her to broach a subject with him that the very idea of made her insides flutter.

But maybe not today.

She brushed a nonexistent crumb from the tabletop, cursing herself for a coward but still not quite ready to take the leap.

With her face carefully blank she turned around, giving the list an apologetic glance.

'Well. I barely recognise any of these names. It'll be embarrassing to give the boxes out when I don't know who's standing in front of me, even if I *have* only been here a few days.'

Samuel lifted his shoulders again in another motion no less eye catching than the first. 'Not necessarily. If it'll save your blushes, I could stand beside you and whisper each name as they come forward.'

The thought of him leaning close enough to murmur into her ear was extremely tempting, and Julia almost accepted there and then, although for the sake of her dignity she attempted to pretend at least *some* restraint.

'But you won't be here. Aren't you going on today's hunt? Almost all the other men of our circle are—the day after Christmas is always when they ride out with the hounds.'

There was a fine gilded clock on the mantel and Samuel strolled over to it, checking his pocket watch against it for the time. Julia watched as he opened the clock's glass front and nudged the minute hand a fraction to the right.

'Tormenting some poor creature by chasing it for miles has never been my idea of fun. At least after a shoot one eats the pheasants. I've never heard of anyone enjoying roasted fox.'

He snapped the clock face closed again, rechecked his pocket watch with a satisfied nod and then looked directly at her, one eyebrow raised so appealingly that Julia felt her pulse pick up speed. 'And had you not considered I might simply prefer to stay here with you instead?'

She swallowed, her pulse flickering faster still when she saw his eyes flit at once to her throat. 'I—No. I hadn't.'

'Perhaps you should.'

He spoke simply but his eyes were now fixed on hers, their bottomless blue holding her captive like a pair of strong arms. 'I find more and more often these days that wherever *you* are is where I want to be myself.'

Julia took a steadying breath, the unexpected turn catching her off guard. Was now the time to tell him she felt the same way, too? It was the truth, after all. No matter where Samuel was in the house she found herself drawn there. Countless times she had entered a room only to find him already in it as well as the reverse, the two constantly pulled together like a pair of opposing magnets too powerful to be wrenched apart. It made her heart sing to think he wanted to be near her, and it was on the tip of her tongue to tell him so, all her caution sent flying by his intense stare—but then he came closer and every word died in her mouth.

Fenshaw had worked her usual magic on Julia's hair that morning, her unruly curls tamed into a crown on the top of her head, but they were too determined to behave for long. A couple of coils had sprung free and it was these that Samuel twirled around his fingers, his hand straying to the nape of her neck as he came near enough to look down into her face. The feeling stirred her, his soft fingertips trailing across the achingly sensitive skin, and she gave an involuntary sigh as he gently ghosted his other hand over her collarbone, coming to rest just above where her heart was pounding in her chest.

She gazed up at him, her mouth drying as she saw the darkness in his smile. He had the look of one with things on his mind and she wanted nothing more than to find out what they were, her lips parting on instinct as she rose up on her toes to press them to his—

A discreet tap on the door sent her stepping smartly away, her hand flying guiltily to tidy the back of her hair. Dimly, she heard Samuel mutter something that didn't sound fit for the ears of a lady, but when he called out he was every bit his usual affable self.

'Come in.'

Julia glanced at him as the door opened, holding back a shiver when she caught his eye. For all the good humour in his voice, the look he gave her was shadowed with barely restrained desire and she quickly turned her attention to the butler.

'Are all the servants assembled, Mirren?'

'Yes, ma'am. They're awaiting your instructions.'

The butler waited as she considered, although a good part of her hesitation was caused by trying to wrestle her heart rate back under control.

'Would you have them form a line in the corridor, please? They can file through here and out by the adjoining door, after which they're free to spend the rest of the day as they choose.'

'Very good, ma'am.'

Mirren bowed and left the room, his footsteps barely making a sound. It would only be a few moments before the first of the servants came in, and Julia didn't trust herself to look over at Samuel as they waited, no longer standing close enough to touch but the tension in the drawing room growing with every second that ticked by.

Belatedly, she realised she was still holding the list of names and she quickly laid it aside as a young girl came into the drawing room, her hands clasped nervously in front of her. The maid dropped into a curtsey, giving Samuel the chance to move closer again and bend his head to mutter into Julia's ear, and she had to steel herself not to wilt as his warm breath caressed her skin.

'Margaret Keyes. Scullery maid.'

Mutely, Julia nodded, forcing a smile as the girl came forward.

'Miss Keyes. Please accept this as a token of our thanks for your service this year.'

She turned to pick out the right box from the heaped table but Samuel got there first. He passed the package to her, his fingers brushing hers as he handed it over, and she gritted her teeth when she saw him bite back a smile of his own.

Scheming wretch. He did that on purpose!

Her knuckles tingled where he had grazed them but she could do nothing while they were so closely observed. Instead, she presented the box to the scullery maid, curtseying as she accepted Margaret's thanks, and the next maid appeared too swiftly for Julia to say anything to her husband as he again murmured a name into her ear. He seemed to be enjoying himself, however, his smile turning to more of a poorly concealed grin, and as the procession of servants filed through the drawing room Julia feared his 'helpful' intentions were slightly less than pure.

She was right.

The next hour was unrelenting torture. With every unfamiliar face that appeared round the door, Samuel whispered to her and the rapid tempo of her heart never dropped the whole time she was forced to stand and smile and pass out presents as though she wasn't burning from the inside out. Every time she reached behind her for a gift Samuel was already holding it, determined to touch her with every pass, and by the time the final footman had bowed and left the dining room Julia ached from the effort of holding herself upright.

Once she was certain the last servant had gone, she turned to face her tormentor.

'You...!'

Samuel frowned innocently, although the gleam in his eye was anything but. 'Me, what? I said I'd help you, so I did.'

'Oh? And I suppose helping *yourself* never crossed your mind?'

She tried to sound indignant but she knew she'd failed the moment she opened her mouth. Her voice was too strained and the rise of her chin none too convincing, and she didn't even attempt to move back when Samuel came towards her, the glint in those blue depths now more of a smoulder.

'Of course not. My thoughts were all for you.'

Exactly what those thoughts were wasn't difficult to guess, and Julia felt herself grow hot as he slipped a hand around her waist, tugging her towards him as though she weighed nothing at all. He pulled her closer, his free hand coming up to tilt her lifted chin higher still, and it was a blistering combination of relief and yearning when finally, after an hour of agonising restraint, he brought his mouth down to meet hers.

He tasted of honey from the sweet cakes they had eaten for breakfast, and Julia wanted to devour him in turn as she wrapped her arms around his neck, revelling in the approving rumble in his throat when she pressed herself against him. His clever fingers had rediscovered the loose curls at her nape and she swayed as sensation glittered down her spine, his touch on her neck so delicious it was almost unbearable. She tunnelled her hands through his hair, wanting to keep him in exactly that position, but Samuel had other plans and she gasped as he kissed a blazing path from her mouth to her ear, nibbling at the lobe and sending want spiking right through to her core.

'You gave all the servants the day off, didn't you?'

His murmur was hoarse, and Julia shuddered at the naked desire in it. 'Yes, but—'

'Good. This time, then, there's nobody to interrupt.'

He nipped the shell of her ear and she clung to his shoulders for fear her legs might give way beneath her. The hard muscle hidden by his shirt was warm under her palms, and she gripped tighter as she tipped her head back, allowing him greater freedom to trail his burning lips down towards the low neckline of her gown. Without her realising he had coaxed her backwards and the edge of the dining table dug into the backs of her thighs, encouraging her to abandon all elegance and sit down on the polished top, and as Samuel's mouth reached the creamy mounds pressing at the top of her bodice she felt her well-bred sensibilities slipping away.

'Shall we go upstairs?'

Those four little words all but growled against her flushed skin nearly made her burst into flames. Every sinew in her body was alive and trembling and her breathing had lost all rhythm, coming in ragged snatches as if she'd run a mile. Her hands were still in Samuel's hair and when the very tip of his tongue dipped below the neckline of her dress her eyes flared wide, seeing nothing as stars scattered before her and wild longing robbed her of all thoughts…except one.

'I can't.'

She exhaled heavily as Samuel stilled, his face hidden in the curve of her neck.

'You don't want to?'

'Oh, I want to…'

She gave a shaky laugh, her heart still railing against her rib cage. How could he ask that question when she'd very nearly disgraced herself in broad daylight, and in her own dining room, no less? Her whole body ached to fit against his with no layers of silk and linen in between but an annoying little voice nagged at the back of her mind and with unending regret she gently pushed him away.

'I have another engagement this morning…one I'm almost sorry I committed to now, thanks to your bad influence, but I gave my word.'

Samuel's breathing was no steadier than hers as he looked down at her. His hair was in disarray from her exploring fingers and his colour high, and Julia almost smiled with the quiet triumph of knowing that this time it was he who was left wanting more.

'Gave your word? Who to?'

'Mrs Gladstone. She's a patroness of the Guildbury School for Impoverished Young Ladies and this year I promised I would send my St Stephen's Day charity contributions to her. I was supposed to call on her this morning and if I allowed you to distract me any longer I'd be unforgivably late.'

She moved away from the table, half wondering if Samuel would try to stop her escape. He watched her closely, that dangerous glint still in his eye, and she was almost certain he was plotting something, his mouth beginning to lift again into the smile that turned her bones to water.

Preempting whatever he was planning she held up a warning finger. 'You can come with me if you like—*if* you promise to behave.'

'I'm not certain I can make that vow.'

His response didn't help her to regain the composure his kisses had stolen. Instead, it set her pulse fluttering faster and it was only by crossing determinedly to the door that she stopped herself from falling back into his arms.

On the threshold she paused, peering back at him over her shoulder. His smile was still intact and he made no attempt to hide it as he leaned against the table, so handsome in his mischief that she felt her own mouth lift in reply.

'Well. I suppose you can come with me all the same. After all—with the footmen gone, I'll need somebody to carry the parcels.'

* * *

Sitting politely as he drank his third cup of tea, Samuel wondered if Julia was taking her revenge for his game with the servants' gifts. She'd changed into a particularly pretty walking dress for their visit to Mrs Gladstone—one of those pale trimmed confections that made her look like a Grecian goddess—and she must have been aware how the cut flattered her silhouette as she talked with their hostess, safe in the knowledge her husband could do nothing but watch.

If that's the only option open to me, I'll still take it. How could anyone with eyes resist?

He rested his teacup on his knee, attempting to turn his attention to whatever Mrs Gladstone was saying rather than the sweep of Julia's neck. Barely two hours previously he'd been kissing it, and the memory wasn't one to revisit while in someone else's parlour—especially not one belonging to a genteel lady he'd known since he was a boy and who would probably be scandalised by the direction of his thoughts.

'I must thank you again for your generosity. The young ladies in our care will be so grateful for your kindness.'

Julia shook her head, jet earrings the same colour as her curls clicking as she moved. 'Not at all. It's always a pleasure to help those who need it. I was glad of the opportunity.'

Samuel took another sip to cover the twitch of his lips. To hear Julia now she might have been a nun—prim and pious and not at all like the woman who had pressed herself against him in their dining room not long before.

For all his amusement, however, he knew what she

said was true. She wasn't playing at being charitable as some Society ladies did, making a show of giving but secretly scorning those who received it. Julia had a good heart and it did her credit, and now he had come to realise he was ashamed he had ever harboured doubts.

Under cover of Mrs Gladstone taking another little cake, Julia slid him a sideways glance. At the slight rise of his eyebrow, however, she looked quickly away again, busying herself with preventing Pirate from leaping from her lap directly onto the tea tray set out in front of them.

'Such a pretty little dog. Where did you say you got him?'

Their hostess held out a crumb for the puppy and he took it eagerly, his tiny tail wagging furiously. She seemed very taken with him although her own dog, a greying spaniel sitting at her feet, appeared distinctly less impressed, and Samuel sympathetically scratched its head.

'I bought him to help my wife feel more at home at Larch House. It would be an adjustment for anybody but so far I think he's been a success.'

This time Julia was careful not to look at him. 'He certainly has. I'm already beginning to feel I belong there, even after such a short time.'

Samuel smoothed the spaniel's soft ears but he had grown suddenly warm. It was the first time she'd voiced her opinion of having come to live with him, and to hear her speak so glowingly echoed his own thoughts. She'd been a fixture in his home for hardly any time at all, and yet somehow it felt as though she'd always been there, her presence so natural he wasn't sure now how he'd ever intended to live alone.

I wonder if it's just the house she feels she belongs with, though...or if she means me as well?

It was a question that followed him from Mrs Gladstone's parlour and into the street when they left, the cold air a jarring contrast to the comfort of her fireside. Julia hugged Pirate to her with one hand and slipped the other into the crook of Samuel's elbow and he felt the most absurd pang of pleasure that she didn't think twice about placing her little glove on his arm. It seemed so strange that when he'd first returned to Guildbury she hadn't even wanted to look him in the eye, but now she was happy to allow him to escort her down the chilly street, walking beside him as if they had never been anything other than a perfect match, and again the unanswered question pushed itself forward.

Is she happy at Larch House because it's an improvement on life with her parents or is it my being there, too, that holds the appeal?

She certainly seemed far more relaxed in his company now, even allowing her facade of ladylike exactness to slip occasionally into the more believable behaviour of a real human being. He'd caught her sitting with less than ideal posture once or twice, hunching slightly as she curled up in an armchair with a book, and sometimes she spilled a little when pouring out their tea. In the grand scheme of things they were tiny instances of her letting down her guard, but he noticed each one, gathering up the evidence that she was emerging from her false shell.

He could just ask her how she felt, he mused as they

walked past manicured gardens and the houses beyond them, each stretching tall and white against the sky. There was no need for him to confuse himself trying to second-guess her every word and deed when he could so easily know for sure what she was thinking—but the same old hesitation still held him back.

They had been married only a matter of days and she might feel pressured if he began asking difficult questions or making impassioned declarations she could feel obliged to return. There was no rush; whatever was growing between them ought to be given time to flourish rather than be forced, and he would have to swallow his impatience, doing nothing to make Julia feel she was being held to anybody's schedule but her own…

Consumed by his thoughts he almost missed the polite nod of a vague acquaintance, only just in time managing a nod of his own. The man was one he knew slightly from his school days, and Samuel saw him look at Julia with frank admiration as he passed by, his eyes lingering on her face for a moment too long. It wasn't quite a stare but it was close enough for Samuel to feel mildly uneasy, and he couldn't help but glance down to see her response, for a split second afraid of what he might find.

But there wasn't one.

She hadn't even noticed, he realised. She hadn't registered the other man's interest at all, focused instead on keeping Pirate tucked warmly beneath her cloak, and Samuel frowned to himself, displeased by his instinctive flare of concern.

It was natural for a beautiful woman to draw the eye, and Julia could no more help that than she could have flown to the moon. She was more than worthy of every flattering word and glance, and Samuel never wanted to dim her light, her hard-won confidence among the things that had impressed him the most. His wife might draw attention but she didn't court it—a crucial difference from the first woman who had captured his heart and he tightened his jaw, disappointed in himself for his momentary lapse.

Julia had done nothing to make him distrust her and he owed her the courtesy of stopping any comparisons with Lucrezia. If they were to have any chance at a happy future together, he would have to move on and to do that he would have to try harder, pushing back his fears every time they tried to creep in. If he allowed the past to dictate his behaviour in the present he'd be an idiot, ridiculous to be so influenced by a woman he would never see again, and as he and Julia drew nearer to Larch House, he determined once and for all that he would never think of Signora Bianchi again.

Once they were past their own gate Julia placed Pirate on the ground, laughing when he raced ahead towards the front door.

'Look. Isn't he clever? He knows where he lives already.'

'Clearly. I hope he won't turn out to be more intelligent than us.'

Julia laughed again, letting go of Samuel's arm to chase the puppy up the path. At the front step she scooped him up again, peeping back over her shoulder as she pushed open the door, and the discomfort circling in Samuel's gut evaporated at the sunlit happiness of her rosy, smiling face—as well as the deliberate sway of her hips as she disappeared into the house, his insides shifting for a very different reason as he lengthened his stride.

By the time he entered the hall, however, she was nowhere to be seen. The less noble part of him wondered if she had gone up to their bedroom, perhaps waiting for him to finish what they'd started that morning, although that particular hope was dashed when he heard her voice from the parlour. By the sounds of it she was instructing Pirate to lie beside the fire so he might get warm, and Samuel was about to go offer some moral support when a letter lying on the hall sideboard caught his eye.

Mirren must have placed it there before he disappeared, Samuel thought absently. The address scrawled on the front was in an unfamiliar hand, and with automatic swiftness he broke the letter open, surprised when something small and oval fell into his palm.

He looked down at the miniature portrait gazing back at him from its gilded frame. The handwriting of the address hadn't been one he recognised, but the identity of the woman in the painting most certainly was—and he felt his heart shudder to a halt as he stared into a set of painted eyes he'd so recently thought he would never see again.

Chapter Eleven

Samuel sat quietly, staring into his glass of port as rain lashed against the windows of his study. Lucrezia's letter lay on the desk in front of him with her portrait just peeping out from beneath it, but he didn't look at either reminder of the woman he had once loved. In the two days since he had received them he'd studied both so many times he now knew them by heart, the words and the painted face looming large every time he closed his eyes, and he tipped his head back as he rubbed his aching brow.

He'd barely been sleeping and it wouldn't be long before Julia asked what was amiss. Already she'd started casting him sideways looks as if trying to work out what was on his clearly preoccupied mind, and it was only by avoiding her as much as possible that he'd so far managed to escape any questions. He didn't want to put distance between them, the new closeness that had grown since their wedding day more precious than he dared admit, but now the spectre of Lucrezia had returned he didn't know how else to calm the turmoil in his mind. Memories he'd been so determined never to think of again wouldn't leave him alone—both the good times and the bad came at him in a relentless flood, and he couldn't deny that even now, with months and hundreds of miles separating them, Signora Bianchi still had the power to command his attention.

He glanced at the letter. She'd taken the precaution of having someone else write the address, just in case one glimpse of her hand was enough to make Samuel throw her missive into the fire without bothering to read it, and he couldn't help a bitter smile.

If he hadn't already known her true nature, that alone might have been enough to make him suspect it; and yet he hadn't cast the letter into the flames after he'd realised its author. He'd read it, with his stomach feeling as if it was in a vise, and for reasons he didn't fully understand he had taken the letter and the portrait up to his study and shut them in his desk drawer.

Grimacing, he pulled another sip of port through his teeth, for the umpteenth time wishing he had never broken that accursed wax seal and let Lucrezia's lies come spilling free.

Nothing in the flowing sentences that covered the page was new. They spelled out the same falsehoods she'd claimed the final time he'd seen her, when tears had rained from her beautiful eyes and she'd held her hands up like some actress in a tragic scene; but he wasn't fooled then and he wouldn't be now, either. She might write that she loved him, missed him, wanted nobody else but him, but he knew it wasn't true. What she wanted was the same thing she'd always wanted: his money and eventual title and the admiration that came from holding his arm, all the while encouraging the attention of other men and revelling in their pursuit of her favour—until they were successful in obtaining it, and then her game would begin all over again, selecting some new victim but keeping Samuel as a safe haven behind whose back she could play…

He tossed back the rest of his drink and set the glass down on his desk so forcefully his inkstand rattled. Shame writhed inside him, the knowledge he had taken so long to realise the truth mocking him mercilessly, and he wondered when he would have found out if fate hadn't intervened. If the doctor hadn't let slip his flyaway comment, Samuel would have been trapped, in his ignorance taking a woman to wife who would betray him the very first chance she got.

The portrait was smiling up at him, the painted eyes so wide and innocent it could only have been created by one who didn't know the *real* Lucrezia. 'Something to remind you of me,' the letter had said as if they'd parted on fond terms instead of in a storm of weeping and regret, and he felt his jaw clench involuntarily as he picked it up, turning the gilded frame over to look at the back where two words were written in a curling script.

Ti amo

He stood up, dropping the portrait back onto the desk and turning to pace to the window. Rain hammered against the glass, the wind howling around Larch House's chimneys, and the gardens gleaming wet and rippling beneath the iron sky. It was a day for staying in beside the fire but nothing could warm the chill in his chest conjured by Lucrezia's ghostly presence, the frank truth behind his unhappiness one he didn't want to face.

In that little oval painting the resemblance between Lucrezia and Julia was unmistakable—and it disturbed him in a way he just couldn't seem to shake, the worries he'd had before he and Julia found their common ground once again attempting to break through.

'But I won't let them.'

His tense face was mirrored dimly in the rain-spattered glass and he held its transparent gaze, staring steadily into his own eyes. 'I won't allow the past to ruin the present. Julia is not Lucrezia and never will be—and she deserves better than any comparison.'

They were words he was determined to abide by and he nodded grimly at his reflection, both the real Samuel and his ghostly twin resolved not to be beaten. His trust might have been shattered once, but Julia had helped to rebuild it and he owed it to her not to be influenced by the one who had come before...even if the idea of being hurt again lurked at the very back of his mind, an unwanted guest that had long since outstayed its welcome but still refused to leave...

The rain was hammering so hard against the window that he almost didn't hear the tentative knock on the study's closed door.

'Samuel? Are you in there?'

His heart executed an unpleasant flip. Julia's voice was uncertain—and coming from just outside. She could turn the handle at any moment and he strode back to the desk, hurriedly sweeping the letter and the portrait back into the top drawer and closing it tight before moving to stand by the fireplace.

'Yes. You can come in if you wish.'

He tried to look casual as the door opened and Julia appeared round it, a flash of white showing Pirate following close behind. On seeing his second favourite person, the puppy raced over and Samuel was glad of an excuse to hide his face as he bent down to pick the little dog up, certain Julia would see his unease.

'There you are. I was wondering where you'd been hiding.'

She sounded happy enough but he caught a note of something just beneath the surface. Evidently, he'd been right to think she had suspicions. She was too sharp not to notice his distance of late, and his conscience gave a guilty tweak when she continued with determined cheer.

'What have you been doing all morning?'

Glancing up from ruffling Pirate's comically large ears, Samuel attempted a smile, finally making himself meet Julia's eye. She had a basket over one arm, he noticed for the first time, although what was in it he couldn't guess.

'Just sitting by the fire. I like listening to the rain rage outside when I'm warm and comfortable indoors.'

His conscience gave another twinge but Julia nodded. 'So do I. When I was a little girl I loved hearing storms at night while I was in bed. I'd draw the covers up over my head and pretend I was an adventurer sleeping in a cave.'

She shot him a smile, the slight edge of shyness in it more endearing than she could possibly know. 'Just between you and me, I might still do that even now.'

Pirate was wriggling and Samuel crouched to set him carefully on the rug before the hearth, once again grateful to have a reason to look away. The upward tick of Julia's mouth was so like Lucrezia's in the miniature portrait that he suddenly found it hard to breathe, the shape almost identical in its pink softness and crying out to be kissed. Confusion coursed through him, in his mind the two women beginning to merge into one, although some of the clamour quietened when he looked up to see Julia watching him with an expression he had never seen in the face of his previous love.

Her strong eyebrows were drawn together in unmistakable concern. There was genuine worry written across her countenance, and Samuel felt the knot inside him loosen a fraction to see it, something so unlike Lucrezia that the merging of their faces ground to a halt.

'I wanted to ask you… Is there something wrong?'

Julia peered down at him as he knelt on the floor, still smoothing Pirate's silky ears. The puppy had begun to fall asleep and Samuel slowly straightened up again, half wishing she would look away from him with those big, dark eyes.

'You haven't seemed yourself for the past few days. Is there something on your mind? Something that troubles you?'

She studied him, reading his face for an honest answer, and he had to work hard not to let anything show. It was the question he'd been hoping to avoid and he could hardly reply with the truth. He needed a way to distract her from her line of questioning and he seized on the first thing that came to mind, his eye falling on the basket still hooked over her arm.

'What do you have in there?'

His apprehension rose as he watched her eyes narrow, his deflection not clever enough to deceive even a child, but to his relief she didn't push back.

'Oh. This?'

She swung the basket down onto the arm of one of the chairs beside the fire, whisking a cloth off the top to reveal what was inside.

'You were so busy listening to the rain that you forgot to come down for luncheon, so I asked for it to be packed in here instead. I thought perhaps we could have a picnic of sorts—indoors, of course.'

Samuel's eyebrows rose as he took in the sandwiches piled into the basket, cakes and buns winking at him with currants like eyes. Julia was busy extracting a set of napkins but he was sure he saw satisfaction in her downturned face, his surprise evidently the reaction she'd been hoping for.

'You brought all of this up for me?'

'Obviously. I didn't want you to go hungry.'

A slight blush crept up on her cheekbones and Samuel found he could only stare as she unpacked her wares and laid them out on the hearthrug, plate after plate of little delicacies she'd ordered with him in mind. It was true that in his preoccupied state he had missed a meal and as if to underline the fact his stomach felt suddenly hollow, although a glimmer of warmth in the very pit of it took the edge off any discomfort.

She did this for me. If actions speak louder than words, surely this is proof that she truly cares?

He didn't know what to say as she placed the final dish and settled herself near it, abandoning elegance to sit on the floor. Tucking her skirts neatly around herself she peeped up at him, patting the rug beside her with the first trace of hesitance.

'Will you join me?'

At once, he found himself bending down, trying to

maintain his dignity while arranging himself on the floor. 'Of course. I would never let a lady eat alone, especially when she'd gone to such trouble on my behalf.'

Julia nodded approvingly. With a dainty pair of tongs she placed a couple of sandwiches on a plate alongside some cold meat and passed it to him before taking a caraway bun for herself, bringing it to her mouth with one hand cupped beneath it to catch any stray crumbs.

For a while neither spoke as they ate, but the quiet that fell wasn't awkward. There was something comfortable in the silence and Samuel was glad of the chance to work through his thoughts, picking them apart like a length of knotted string until he realised—with a growing sense of relief—he was coming close to the end.

He turned to Julia. She was nibbling at a handful of grapes and for a beat he was able to watch her without being seen, fleetingly admiring the arresting lines of her face before she could notice.

Pretty was too flimsy a word to describe her. Her father's strong jaw gave her an air of determination while her mother's wide-set eyes tempered that power with softness reminiscent of a deer. Her face was made up of features lent by other people but the result was entirely herself, owned by no one and somehow, despite the resemblance to Lucrezia, like nobody he had ever seen before—and he had been a simpleton to have ever thought anything else.

As if feeling his eyes on her, she glanced over at him. 'What is it? What are you looking at?'

He shook his head quickly. 'Nothing. I was just going to say this was very thoughtful. Thank you.'

'Well.' Julia popped another grape into her mouth, looking at him with such straightforward openness that he suddenly longed to taste the sweetness on her lips. 'We *should* think of each other now…don't you agree?'

'Yes. I do.'

She smiled and he couldn't help but return it, his inner turmoil finally dying down until soon barely a whisper would remain.

Lucrezia didn't care that she'd hurt him. Her letter might have pretended remorse, but the truth was different. He had escaped her, that was all; been the one who got away from the control she exerted with her allure, and her pride couldn't bear the loss. She had never truly cared about him and he knew it now—but Julia *did*.

Every day she showed him with some word or deed that her feelings for him were real, not rooted in greed or kept alive through manipulation and deceit. Despite their shaky beginning they were on the way to finding something *real* and he wanted to seize it with both hands, starting by taking one of Julia's in his.

First chance I get, I'll destroy that letter and the portrait along with it. I don't want their shadow hanging over us anymore.

Julia coloured slightly when he brushed his thumb over her knuckles, and he had to hold himself back from leaning in to kiss her, determined to at last give her the answer she deserved.

'You asked if something was troubling me, but there's nothing. Not anymore.'

Mrs Livingston settled herself into the best seat in Larch House's parlour. Samuel had gone to see one of his tenants following the storm the previous day, and

Julia had deliberately invited her mother to call while he was away, still not entirely comfortable when the two of them were in the same room. Mama might be all smiles now but the aspersions she'd cast on his honour were difficult to forget, and as she poured a cup of tea Julia reflected it was probably best to keep them separate where—and for as long as—she could.

She passed the full teacup to her guest. 'How is Papa today? Is his cough improving?'

'I hardly know. What I can be certain of, however, is how it makes my ears ring to hear him.' Mrs Livingston took a sip, pursed her lips and set the cup back on its saucer. 'He doesn't seem to realise what a hardship it is for me when he's unwell.'

'I don't suppose he gets these winter chills on purpose, Mama.'

'Perhaps not, but he could always try harder not to catch them.'

Julia poured herself a cup, attempting to relax her shoulders. Her mother had been at Larch House less than ten minutes but already she could feel herself tense, just waiting for the next disapproving comment. It was uncomfortably like the atmosphere at Burton Lodge, where for years she had crept from room to room trying not to draw a critical eye, and she had to use all her willpower to sit straight in her chair. She'd escaped that unpleasantness and had no desire to experience it in her own home, for the first time wishing that Samuel was there to keep his mother-in-law at bay.

'And are you well? No ill health has befallen you?'

'Nothing I care to mention.' Mama sniffed bravely, deigning to try again to drink her apparently disappointing tea. 'You know I never complain.'

'No. Of course you don't.'

Julia dropped a fragment of sugar into her cup and watched it dissolve. As a hostess it would probably be considered rude to laugh at one's guest, but her mouth wanted to curve, grimly amused by the barefaced lie.

Acting quickly before she could betray herself she waved towards the little table set out near the sofa. 'Will you take a cake? Or a sweet biscuit? They have lemon in them from Viscount Maidwell's hothouse.'

At the mention of the Viscount her mother took one at once, although she didn't lift it to her lips. 'His Lordship's? I thought you'd have a glasshouse of your own?'

'It isn't fully established. Our trees aren't ready to bear fruit yet but by next summer Hewitt hopes to have a favourable yield.'

'I see.'

Mrs Livingston nibbled daintily at her biscuit. It must have been more acceptable than the tea as when it was gone she took another, perhaps the knowledge it was a peer of the realm's lemons that gave it such zest making it more appealing. No lesser fruit would have tasted as good and again Julia had to clamp down on a smile, her shoulders still tense but now able to find humour where once she'd felt nothing but unease.

I have Samuel to thank for that.

Before they had wed she'd been at the mercy of her mother's whims rather than amused by them—but she didn't have time to think of that now. Mama had finished her second biscuit and was regarding her in a way that put Julia immediately on her guard, such close scrutiny not something she enjoyed.

'I must say that married life evidently agrees with you. Clearly, you're glad to have finally taken your place among the grown women—you're positively glowing.'

Mama smiled complacently and Julia forced herself not to react, although she couldn't stop her hackles from rising.

I hadn't realised it took a man's intervention to make a woman fully formed. What was I, then, in the time between coming of age and Samuel returning home?

'Yes. I'm finding being married to Samuel more agreeable than I'd anticipated.'

That was as far as she was willing to bring her mother into her confidence, but she probably didn't need to say anything more. If even her mother could see the change in her then it must be obvious indeed, and Julia realised she was blushing slightly.

Samuel had given her some brief worry during the few days when he'd seemed to withdraw from her, but it hadn't lasted long. For that short interlude she'd been uneasy, the happiness their growing closeness inspired dimming as she wondered what could be wrong, but whatever had bothered him was clearly now resolved, and since their impromptu picnic he had been as attentive as ever, perhaps even more...

With some difficulty she forced aside the memory of last night. It wasn't a thought to linger over while her mother sat in front of her, and Julia hoped her cheeks weren't *too* flushed as she sipped her tea, attempting to look more demure than she currently felt.

Fortunately, she wasn't required to say anything more. Mama was still smiling with more than a touch of self-satisfaction, and Julia could have predicted what she was about to say right down to the last letter.

'I'm not one to claim credit, as you know, but I do

think you might remember who brought your match about in the first place. Not, of course, that I'd ever look for recognition.'

Julia held herself still as another ripple of irritation ran over her. Despite Mama's insincere modesty, her meaning was clear. She truly believed she deserved thanks for the unexpected joy her daughter had stumbled upon after being forced into a marriage neither the bride nor groom had wanted, her only motivation in pushing for it being the pursuit of position and wealth. Julia's happiness hadn't entered into her mother's plans, and it rankled to hear Mama talk now as if she'd given a damn.

At one time Julia would have let such blatant provocation go, too afraid of stirring up yet more disapproval to voice her disagreement, but now things were different. With every day Samuel's acceptance and support strengthened her, bolstering her confidence until she cared for nobody's good opinion but her own, and it was a strange kind of thrill to shake her head.

'It's just as well you don't claim the credit, Mama. I thought I compromised myself into the match by behaving so poorly? Or it was Samuel's unsavoury intentions towards me that left us no choice but to wed? Either way, I distinctly recall you saying it had nothing to do with you.'

Mrs Livingston's mouth opened and then closed again without a word, and Julia watched as for the first time in her life she rendered her mother speechless. It didn't last long, perhaps only a few ticks of the mantelpiece clock, but the sweetness of the moment was like honey for one used to bitterness for as long as she could remember.

Mama sat up straighter in her chair, a frown creasing the unlined brow of which she was so proud. 'You might show a little more gratitude. If I hadn't intervened, thinking only of your happiness, who knows what would have become of you?'

Deaf to having just contradicted herself with such a brazen lie, Mrs Livingston paused, clearly allowing space for her daughter to jump in with the apology she was owed, but she was to be disappointed.

'That isn't true.'

Julia spoke quietly, hardly able to believe what she was doing but somehow unable to stop herself. 'You never considered what I wanted for so much as a moment. All that mattered to you was that I married a rich, important man and you would have done anything to make sure that happened.'

Mrs Livingston's eyes widened. Julia saw the shock in them and felt her own heart begin to jump faster, the act of arguing with her mother both frightening and freeing in almost equal measure. Somehow, the lid seemed to have come off Pandora's box and the truth was pouring forth, the confidence in herself Samuel had helped her find driving her on, and she refused to be cowed when Mama deployed her most chilling glare.

'How can you be so rude? I can't think what's come over you. I barely recognise you at all!'

There seemed to be more admonishments to come, although at that moment the sound of the front door opening and slamming shut again echoed through the house, immediately redirecting her mother's focus.

'Is that dear Samuel returned? I haven't seen him in an age. He never seems to be here when I call.'

She set down her teacup and spread out her skirts to

show off the expensive material, as always aiming to appear to her best advantage. In her vanity she seemed to have forgotten what they had been discussing—but Julia had no intention of doing the same.

Calmly, she placed her own cup down, folding her hands neatly in her lap. She could hear footsteps now, her heart beating faster still at recognising that heavy tread, but she made sure not to betray herself as she summoned the courage to strike.

'I'm always surprised when you call him *dear* Samuel, Mama. It wasn't long ago that you thought something very different.'

Behind her she heard the parlour door open and watched her mother half turn towards it, although she herself made no attempt to move. She knew it had to be Samuel who stood on the threshold, and she wasn't sure she'd be able to finish what she'd started if she caught his eye, her attention fixed on her mother as Mrs Livingston's expression segued into alarm.

'Julia—'

With delightful irony Julia cut her off with the same flick of a hand she so often used herself. 'I don't recall you thinking there was anything *dear* about him when you were questioning his honour. You said hurtful things that you knew very well weren't true, and you've never apologised for them. He's far from being the kind of man you accused him of. Indeed, he's one of the best, most decent gentlemen I've ever known.'

She kept her voice steady, not allowing it to rise even as Mama turned horrified eyes towards the doorway. Mrs Livingston would rather have gone without a dress allowance for a year than be embarrassed before witnesses, and there was no need for Julia to make an undignified scene in order to hammer home her point.

'I wonder if you've ever thought about the effect of the things you do and say. Words can be more powerful than you know and I've been wounded by them more times than I can count.'

The faintest creak of a floorboard behind her was all the evidence she needed that Samuel was still there. He hadn't spoken, probably caught between feeling he should withdraw and curiosity about what he had stumbled into, and she felt her skin prickle to know he was watching her. He must have heard her defend him and she wondered what he would make of it, his feelings more important to her now than any lash of Mama's tongue.

Carefully, she leaned forward, giving her mother nowhere to turn. Mrs Livingston looked supremely uncomfortable but while Samuel was present, there was nothing she could do aside from sit with her usual rigid propriety and wait to be released.

'Did you realise that when you heard I'd been pulled from the river, your first thought was how to turn it to your own advantage? You never even asked if I was hurt—your own daughter, soaked to the bone by freezing water, and you didn't seem to care.'

Mrs Livingston bridled at the accusation—but then to Julia's everlasting amazement she saw something flit over her mother's face she had never seen there before.

Was that...? Could that possibly have been...guilt?

She blinked, unsure whether she had imagined that remorseful flash. Mama was usually so convinced of her own rightness that she never felt the need to regret anything, let alone reproach herself, and Julia could scarcely comprehend that her words had succeeded in hitting a nerve.

Glancing—yet again—towards the door, her mother dropped her voice into a tight murmur. 'Well. Of course I cared. Perhaps…perhaps I could have made that more clear. And as for your husband… I suppose, on that one occasion, I may have misspoken.'

Mrs Livingston looked away, apparently finding something particularly fascinating in the hearth, and Julia felt herself buoyed by a sudden wave of incredulous triumph. She had forced *her mother* into admitting she'd been at fault—and Samuel had heard it all, his unspeaking presence behind her no doubt giving her the courage she'd needed to take a stand.

There was grace to be found in victory, however, and Julia knew better than to push too far. Mama was still the only mother she would ever have, and to mortify her further would be unkind, even if her sharp words over the years now made retaliation tempting indeed.

Picking up the teapot Julia poured herself another cup, pleased when none of it dribbled onto the table-cloth beneath. Her mother slid her a wary glance, holding her own cup forward slightly hesitantly, and Julia made sure to make herself speak lightly when she delivered the final crushing blow.

'You attempted to cast doubt on Samuel's morals but I think perhaps it was your own that were at fault that day, Mama. That might be something for you to consider…although of course, it isn't my place to say.'

From somewhere behind her she heard the door click shut, and she fought to keep a smile from her lips as she filled the second cup. Samuel had decided to exercise admirable tact in withdrawing but not before he'd shared in her conquest. There was no coming back from it. Still respectful yet blunt enough to make the desired point, and Julia sensed her mother's disquiet as she straightened her jade necklace, clearly intending to change the subject as quickly as she possibly could.

'Well.'

Mama's gaze roamed the room, taking in the fire and Pirate sleeping soundly in front of it, although evidently he wasn't worthy of comment. A few more seconds passed in which Mrs Livingston's unease clearly grew, until at last she seized on the perfect escape.

'Well… Have you chosen what you'll wear to Lady Donaghue's Twelfth Night ball?'

Despite the tension that had flared to envelop the room, Julia almost laughed. When in doubt there was always one topic her mother could be relied upon to return to: the latest fashions, and woe betide any lady who wasn't up to date…including her own daughter.

'Yes, Mama. Have you?'

'Of course. I ordered my gown in August to be sure Madame DuPrix had it ready in time.' Mrs Livingston eyed Julia with sudden suspicion. 'What did *you* decide on?'

'White with blue satin sleeves. I believe Fenshaw has some new ostrich feathers for my hair as well.'

'Good. That's very good.' She nodded authoritatively, her once unshakeable self-assurance slowly but steadily creeping back. 'I always said that was the most flattering colour on you.'

It was difficult not to roll her eyes, but Julia managed to restrain herself just in time. It would have been a miracle if one conversation was enough to change her mother entirely, and she settled instead on watching how the firelight made the black of Pirate's ears gleam like silk.

Mama could swipe and criticise now as much as she liked. She would never again possess the power she'd once had, her judgement no longer a thing of any importance. While she'd lived at Burton Lodge, Julia had been under a shadow, conscious of the many ways in which she fell short of the bar Mrs Livingston had set so high, but now...

Now I'm the mistress of my own house, living by my own rules—and I have a husband who gives me no reason to doubt my worth.

The knowledge sat inside her like a smouldering coal, warming her to the core. It was the most precious secret, admitted to nobody but herself, and she found she wasn't listening to her mother's talk of embroidered hems as the hidden truth came again to murmur in her ear.

There were some things in life one had to accept, and her weakness for Samuel was one of them. The feelings he inspired had taken root and now they flourished, turning the once barren plain of her soul into a garden bursting with new life. With him at her side she could begin to truly live, and the word she hadn't even whispered to *herself* yet urged her to speak it out loud for Samuel to hear.

Love.

Mama's voice was a distant hum in the background and Julia gave the occasional nod, wondering vaguely if she seemed like she was listening. Those four little letters ran riot, however, taking up all her attention, and she found herself staring down into her empty teacup as she tried not to smile.

She'd tell him soon.

There were signs he felt the same, after all. The dislike he'd seemed to feel once upon a time had disappeared completely, replaced by soft words and kisses that made her melt in the dark, and surely she'd be a fool indeed if she'd managed to misread the affection in his face every time her gaze locked with his. The men who had chased her before had valued her outer beauty, but Samuel looked deeper, bothering to peel back the layers to discover who really lived beneath, and as Julia sat beside the fire she knew she was glad indeed that he had.

Chapter Twelve

Julia muttered under her breath as she pawed through the contents of her desk drawer. The new quill she was certain she'd put there had disappeared, and she frowned as she sat back in her chair, the pretty writing table Samuel had set up for her in the library giving no clue where it could be. Aunt Marie's latest letter lay on the leather top and she'd intended to answer it while Samuel was out shooting with Harry, although if she couldn't find her quill...

'Was it you? Did you run off with it?'

Pirate gazed back at her with round, innocent eyes. He might look as though butter wouldn't melt but he had stolen a stocking and a glove that morning alone and Julia picked him up, imprisoning him in her lap like the tiny felon he was.

'How am I supposed to manage my correspondence? It's already taken me longer than it should to reply to Aunt Marie, trying to draft a letter in Italian. She'll think I'm ignoring her and it's all your doing.'

She ruffled the puppy's fur, glancing at the various half-finished missives that littered her desk. The book of Italian grammar Samuel had given her before Christmas sat open beside them, some passages carefully underlined in pencil, and she felt a small measure of satisfaction. Her grasp of the language was coming on in leaps and bounds and soon she'd be able to hold a conversation, perhaps still stumbling over some words, but thanks to Samuel's thoughtful gift her progress undeniable. Aunt Marie was already fluent and would be delighted to receive a letter that showed her niece's improvement—if, of course, Julia was ever able to finish writing it.

One last look in the drawer and under the table still produced no result. The quill had well and truly vanished and with a sigh she stood up, letting Pirate hop back down onto the floor.

'I'll have to find another one. I wonder…'

She placed her scribbled draft between the open book's pages and closed it, tucking it under her arm. Samuel's study was only a few steps farther up the corridor and he'd be sure to have spare quills she could use. If he'd been in the house she would have asked first, but he wouldn't be back until later in the afternoon and she wanted to send her letter as soon as possible. He wouldn't mind her borrowing his things, she was sure, and without another thought she left the library and made for the closed door of his study, the little dog scurrying at her heels.

Despite knowing it was empty she still paused to knock before turning the handle. Papa's study had always been strictly out of bounds and it felt faintly taboo to set foot inside this one without express permission. The ghost of her time at Burton Lodge still lingered, those sad days determined not to be forgotten, but Julia was just as resolved to set them aside. Life with Samuel was so happy she had no use for thoughts of the past, and she moved purposefully towards his desk, laying the book down with an air of finality as she pulled out the chair. There was nowhere in this house she didn't feel welcome, in large part due to her husband's efforts, and she smiled as she settled herself in his seat.

For all his other admirable qualities, Samuel did *not* keep a tidy desk. There were screwed up sheets of paper scattered around, and the place on his inkstand where his quill should have been held a letter opener speckled with wax, and Julia wrinkled her nose.

'Where—don't tell me *his* is missing, too?'

Cautiously, she lifted a torn bit of paper overhanging the edge of the desk. There was no quill underneath—but in moving it she caught sight of a slim drawer tucked away to one side, so inconspicuous she might otherwise have missed it. It was exactly the right size and shape to hold a quill and she pulled it open, fully expecting a large white feather to meet her eye…

For one confused moment she thought she was staring down at a picture of herself.

A small oval frame sat inside the drawer on top of what looked to be a letter, the portrait within so uncannily familiar it was almost like seeing her own reflection. The young woman's hair and eyes were nearly identical to her own, dark and shining like polished jet, and her skin the same olive that came from long days spent in the sun. She was smiling as though she knew something interesting, her full lips set in a gentle curve, and Julia felt a chill ripple through her as if she'd been plunged back into the icy waters from which Samuel had saved her all those weeks before.

*Who is that? And why does Samuel have a minia-
ture of her in his drawer?*

Trying to ignore the slow creep of uncertainty, Julia
hesitated. There could be a hundred reasons for him
to keep a painting of another woman—couldn't there?
She might be his cousin, or some other relation he was
especially close to…although he'd never mentioned
such a person so far…

She didn't move, uneasy curiosity warring with the
urge to slam the drawer shut and try to forget what
she'd seen. Part of her argued it was none of her business what Samuel kept in his own desk, but another
insisted she find out, murmuring to her like a devil on
her shoulder. He was her husband, after all, and if he
was hiding things from her she had the right to know,
although all the justification in the world couldn't stop
her hand from shaking slightly as she drew the miniature out.

The painted woman gazed up at her serenely. She
was beautiful: even if the artist had flattered his subject
she must still have been handsome, her jawline pristine
and her brow smooth beneath a crown of curls. The
more Julia looked at her the less likely it seemed the
stranger could be related to Samuel, their colouring and
features nothing alike, although the same couldn't be
said for herself. It could have been her twin sister captured in oils, and Julia's throat felt tight as she turned
the picture over in her unsteady hand, already afraid
of what she might find.

The two words written on the back of the portrait
hit her like a punch to the stomach.

Ti amo

She stared at the unfamiliar handwriting, right in front of her and yet somehow as if she was seeing it through a haze, the coldness moving over her now sitting like ice in her gut.

Even somebody with the scantest grasp of Italian knew what that phrase meant. Samuel had a painting of a beautiful woman and on the back of it she had written that she loved him, and Julia found that for one heartbeat she couldn't move.

She breathed slowly, forcing herself to remain calm. Perhaps it was an old picture. It would be hopelessly naive of her to imagine he hadn't had a life before they wed, his time abroad something they had never really discussed. If he'd formed a connection while in Italy then he'd done nothing wrong, his actions as a single man entirely separate from his new role as a husband. Probably she was worrying about nothing, only having found a relic from his past, and she was trying to cling to that reasoning when the letter lying in the bottom of the drawer caught her eye.

It was written in the same hand as on the back of the miniature, the ink suspiciously fresh. The paper looked too crisp to be some long-forgotten memento, and Julia felt the ice inside her grow colder still, sending out icicles that pierced between her ribs.

The portrait was still in her palm and unthinkingly she closed her fingers around it, holding it in her fist as she tried to set aside the nausea rising in her gullet. The letter peeped up at her, tempting her to read it, but she couldn't seem to lift her arm to pick it up. At the very top of the page a date was written, just below the sender's address, and Julia sat very still as her whole world shifted sideways.

The tenth of December. But... By then we were engaged...

She stared at the neatly written date, a strange numbness spreading through each limb. Pirate was rolling around somewhere by her feet but she could no longer hear his playful growls, the room around her shrinking until pen strokes on paper were all she could see.

They were still declaring their love for one another even after Samuel was engaged to me. The whole time we've been married, when I thought something was blossoming between us, he was wishing I was someone else.

Fresh bile rose and she almost choked on it, its bitterness spreading over her tongue. She didn't want to believe what she had seen, her mind racing to find another way to explain it, but she couldn't ignore what she had read with her own eyes. When she had entered the study she'd been happy, looking forward to whatever the future held with the husband she was coming to love, but now those hopes had been torn down and she could do nothing but sit among the wreckage like a broken china doll.

The edge of the miniature's frame was biting into her palm and she loosened her grip, looking down to meet the painted eyes. The woman's smile seemed more of a smirk now, as if amused by her rival's foolishness, and Julia couldn't bring herself to glance at it again as she dropped the portrait back into the drawer and blindly slid it closed.

For a moment she stared at nothing, unable to move. She just couldn't. Misery and confusion held her immobile and she barely had the strength to lift her head, too stunned to do anything as her thoughts swirled in a dizzying carousel.

He never cared for me after all. How could he, when his heart already belonged to someone else?

Was that how he had managed to be so convincingly attentive? Because she resembled the woman he *actually* loved? He might have been forced into marrying her but at least he could take some solace in the familiarity of her features, possibly even able to pretend his new wife was someone else in the darkness of their bedroom...

Julia's stomach churned and she took a deep breath, trying to steady herself as a sickening wave swept over her. There was a stinging behind her eyes now and she clamped her mouth shut, only aware a tear had escaped when she felt it slip down her cheek.

All the things she'd been planning to say to him seemed so stupid now that she knew the truth. She'd been on the cusp of revealing the depth of her feelings for him, believing that he felt the same...but now the blindfold had been ripped from her eyes. She had almost made the most humiliating error, confessing her love to a man who would certainly have turned away from it, and burning shame enveloped her to think how easily she had been tricked. Samuel hadn't changed since he was that arrogant, careless boy she'd once known. All that had happened was the passing of a few years and he hadn't altered one bit, still capable of inflicting harm without a second thought.

The intensity of her unhappiness blunted her senses. A distant sound at the front door echoed through the house but she barely heard it, only the realisation of who it would be making her struggle up from her chair.

Samuel and Harry must have returned early from their shoot, she thought as she stood for a second, wishing her head would stop spinning. In a few moments they would come upstairs in search of her, and she would be damned if they found her crying, suddenly unable to bear the idea of Samuel seeing her so vulnerable. She'd have to face him, of course, but not with red, swollen eyes, and from somewhere deep within her she summoned all the resolve she had left.

He was the one who had been dishonest. *He* was the one who had led her to believe a lie. It should be he who felt shame, not she, and if she didn't make him look her in the eye and tell the whole truth, then she would be a coward indeed.

Hearing his confession would be painful, perhaps the most painful thing she would ever have to endure… but if she had any pride then endure it she must. Even if her heart was breaking she had to hear the words directly from Samuel's lips, and her chest felt as though it would burst as she unsteadily crossed the room, pausing only to rub her cheek dry before she pulled open the study door.

The moment Samuel saw her, he knew something was wrong.

He was unbuttoning his coat while laughing at something Harry had said, but he saw the smile fade from his brother-in-law's face and he turned to look behind him. Julia was standing at the foot of the stairs, her steps so quiet he hadn't heard her approach, and the flicker of pleasure he always felt at seeing her turned rapidly to concern.

'Julia? Are you unwell?'

She was indeed pale but she shook her head, turning her curiously blank eyes to her brother.

'Did you have a good time?'

Harry frowned. 'Yes, but…is something amiss? You look—'

She cut him off with the same wave of a hand Samuel had seen her mother deploy so expertly, although Julia didn't quite manage to summon her mama's authority. Her fingers gripped the newel post so tightly he saw her knuckles had turned white, and her voice had the almost metallic edge of one fighting to stay in control.

'I'm fine. You must be chilled, however. Will you come into the drawing room for some tea?'

The formality of her phrasing was the final straw. She'd never normally speak to her brother so rigidly, and as Harry walked ahead of them Samuel placed his hand on her arm, bending so he could mutter into her ear.

'You're not fine. What's wrong? Did something happen while I was away?'

To his surprise she shrugged him off, still refusing to meet his eye. 'Yes. But I won't speak of it now.'

'Why not?' He let his hand drop, confusion growing by the second. 'What is it? What have I done?'

At last, she allowed him a glance, the coldness of it almost making him stop dead in his tracks. 'This isn't the time. Not while we have company.'

She tried to outpace him, attempting to catch up with Harry as he opened the drawing room door, but Samuel barred her way.

'No. If something's upset you this much then I want to know about it.'

Julia's face tightened but he didn't give her the chance to argue, and striding ahead he put his head around the door frame.

'Harry, I need to speak to Julia for a moment. Would you mind?'

'Not at all.' Harry flopped onto one of the sofas, folding his hands behind his head as he stretched his legs towards the fire. 'Feel free to make yourselves at home.'

Samuel withdrew, carefully closing the door behind him. Julia hadn't moved, still standing in the corridor as if she didn't want to come any closer, and he felt another stab of bewilderment when she stiffened at his approach. He tried to take her hand but again she pulled away, her expression as fixed as a porcelain mask.

'I don't understand. When I left this morning, everything seemed well. What can have happened since to earn me your displeasure?'

'You truly can't guess?'

A memory edged into the forefront of his mind. The first time they had danced together, at Lady Fitzgerald's St Nicholas's Day ball, he had asked a similar question and received a similar reply; and it made his stomach twist to wonder why they were re-creating such a moment now. He'd thought they had left all that unpleasantness behind, the final gulf between them having closed when he'd heard her defend him to her thoroughly unpleasant mother, but evidently he had been wrong. Something had abruptly transformed her back into the ice queen he'd encountered all those weeks ago, and he couldn't fathom what, only that the Julia standing in front of him now was not the same one he had kissed before he left the house.

'Please just tell me. I'm sure neither of us enjoys these games.'

The lift of her chin was sharp and immediate. *'Games?'*

She raised her ink-spotted hand as if to make some gesture but stopped herself, curling it into a fist at her side. 'The only person who has been playing a game is you. Making me believe—' She abandoned the end of her sentence and looked away, whatever she'd been about to say lost between clenched teeth.

'Believe what?'

She didn't answer and Samuel raked his fingers through his hair, unease and confusion now running unchecked.

Why was she being so cold? It felt unnatural to stand so close to her and not be allowed to touch, still able to recall with perfect clarity how her lips had brushed his when he'd left their bed only hours before. Her rejection stung and he disliked the fear that circled through his innards, apprehension lending an edge to his voice.

'Damn it, Julia. Won't you speak plainly? What *is* it?'

As soon as the words left his mouth he knew he should have softened them, and he wished he could cram them back inside when she took a half step away from him, the shutters on her face slamming down like those on a vacant house.

'You want me to speak plainly? That's really what you want?'

He saw her chest rise as she took a deep breath but she didn't break, still keeping that terrible composure. 'Very well. I know what you have hidden in that drawer in your study. And what's more, I understand why.'

Samuel felt all the air leave his body.

No.

How could I have forgotten to destroy...?

Dimly, he watched her pull herself up to stand taller, perhaps trying to preserve her dignity, although it was like seeing her through a fogged window. Blank dread gripped him as he realised what she must be thinking and he tried to interrupt, only for her to silence him with a harsh shake of her head.

'I know you didn't marry me for love. I know you were pushed into it against your will. But for you to have been unfaithful the entire time, when I thought we had come so far...'

'It isn't like that.'

Immediately, he stepped forward but she drew back just as fast, holding a palm out to prevent him from getting any closer.

'You have a portrait of her inscribed with a declaration of love, and a letter written after we were engaged! Do you take me for a fool?'

The emptiness in her countenance had been replaced by cold anger although she couldn't hide the pain beneath it. Her pitch had risen and she looked to be working hard not to cry, and he wanted more than anything to fold her in his arms, her unhappiness like a knife slicing through to his heart.

'I would never. Surely you know that?'

She glared up at him. Another man might have shrunk from the power of that single glance but Samuel stood his ground. 'It's true I received the letter and miniature but I didn't reply. There's only one woman I care for now and that is you.'

He'd hoped she would be swayed by such heartfelt

sentiment but she didn't soften. Instead she exhaled a mirthless laugh that almost made him flinch.

'If you have any feeling for me it's only because I remind you of her. How can it be otherwise? I saw how alike we look. I'm but a poor imitation of the person you'd prefer, am I not?'

There was a tiny quake in her voice and the blade in Samuel's heart twisted cruelly. How could she think *she* was the one lacking? That of the two women who had ever captured him *she* was the consolation prize? She completely eclipsed Lucrezia in every way and he cursed himself for not telling her so from the very beginning, the misplaced worries that had caused him to hold his tongue now making him pay the price.

He dipped his head to look directly into her eyes, leaving himself nowhere to hide. 'There may be some physical resemblance but your natures are like night and day. I was engaged to her, yes, but in truth, there was never the connection between us that I now feel with you. You are no imitation—only ever yourself, and that is more than enough for me.'

He saw something flit over her face, an expression passing through as fleeting as lightning. It would have been impossible to interpret even if it had lingered, although this time when he edged forward she didn't immediately back away, still holding herself ready but allowing him that one precious inch.

'Why didn't you just tell me you'd been engaged? You could have been open from the start. Instead, I had to find out by accident, which makes me wonder what else you might have hidden—and why.'

She regarded him with all the fierce distrust of a

feral cat, and the hope that had leapt inside him at her allowing him closer was snuffed out like a candle.

Whatever he said now would be viewed with suspicion, and he only had himself to blame. He should have been honest from the beginning, giving her the opportunity to see the vulnerability inside him he had been so determined to hide, and knowing his actions were the sole cause of her misery now cut him to the bone.

Samuel ran a hand over his eyes, suddenly overwhelmingly tired. 'I never told anyone about Lucrezia, not even my parents. It ended badly and I had no desire to drag the past into the present, which I realise now happened anyway.'

He looked down at her, watching the way the light moved over her face when she turned her head. Once she would have smiled to catch him staring, perhaps a trace of that ready blush rising along her cheekbones, but he had no right to expect that now. In one morning he had taken everything they'd built together and smashed it into pieces, and there was nothing to say that her trust, now shaken, could ever be repaired.

'Please don't pull away from me now. Not when we were doing so well together.'

The muscle in her jaw contracted again. She wasn't looking at him any longer, her eyes fixed on the floor, and some cowardly part of him was almost glad he couldn't see the emotion in them when she replied.

'We were doing well, weren't we? And yet, now I don't know what to believe. I thought we were trying to make this marriage work together, in spite of its unfortunate start, but now I wonder if I've been in it alone.'

She didn't sound angry anymore, and Samuel's torment raged harder to hear the quiet thread of pain in her voice. Although they were standing barely an arm's length from each other, there was a gaping chasm between them now, all of it his making, and he found he had no idea what to say to make things better.

Julia twined her fingers together, still not meeting his eye. 'I need some time. I think... I think I'll go to stay with Harry for a while. It would be best for both of us.'

At once Samuel started forward, his heart leaping up into his throat.

'There's no need for you to go. Surely you know by now that your place is here? At Larch House with Pirate...and with me?'

The previous time he'd approached she hadn't drawn back but now she turned away, his final glimpse of her face sending a dagger beneath his ribs. Her lips were pressed together and her jaw set like marble, but there was no mistaking the glitter that had settled on her down-swept lashes as she began to walk away.

'For a while I was coming to think that—but now I'm not so sure.'

Chapter Thirteen

If anyone had asked her a few days ago whether she was looking forward to Lady Donaghue's Twelfth Night ball, Julia would have said yes without hesitation. Her gown was hanging up and her new silk slippers standing by, waiting to be broken in by dancing 'til dawn, but now it was one of Harry's guest bedrooms in which she was getting ready, not her own at Larch House, and as she waited for Fenshaw to give the feathers in her hair a final curl Julia felt nothing but dread. For the sake of appearances she had accepted Samuel's plea to be allowed to collect her in his carriage rather than arrive separately, and she couldn't stop herself from fidgeting as she sat in front of the dressing table in her borrowed rooms.

Taking a deep breath she attempted—yet again—to quell the rising apprehension that was trying to take her by the throat.

She hadn't seen her husband since the day her world had fallen so spectacularly apart, and the prospect of spending an evening with him now made her insides feel as though they had been passed through a mangle. He'd sent notes asking to call on her but she hadn't dared receive him in her current state, still too confused and upset by the secrets he had finally seen fit to reveal to risk meeting him face-to-face. She missed him so much she might have run into his arms at the first sight of him and that would be a mistake, knowing she had to set her mind in order before she could choose how to proceed, although it was difficult to be rational while emotion insisted on crowding out everything else. Memories of the portrait she'd found haunted her, the painted eyes of his former fiancée watching her every move, and no matter how hard she tried she couldn't seem to forget the two words now burned into her consciousness.

Ti amo.

With Fenshaw still fussing with her hair adornments Julia couldn't drop her face into her hands, but the desire to do so was strong as the hideous scene replayed itself once again.

How was she supposed to decide what to do when she couldn't think straight? Samuel had assured her the phrase on the back of the miniature meant nothing, written by a woman he no longer loved, but could she believe him? She wanted to so badly it hurt, a constant ache that sat miserably inside her, and yet she couldn't quite take that leap. A lifetime of thinking she was lacking, not good enough first for Mama's high opinion and then those of her peers, made it so damnably difficult to believe she could be anyone's first choice. The woman in the painting was far more beautiful and Samuel had evidently cared for her once, and the question of whether he still did was ringing in her ears when a quiet tap sounded at her bedroom door.

'Are you nearly ready?'

Harry's voice came from the landing and Julia almost found a pained smile at his uncharacteristic hesitance. He hadn't asked for details when she'd requested to stay at Highbank and she was glad of it, the barely restrained tears she'd been fighting at the time probably telling him everything he needed to know. He'd carried her hastily packed bags down Larch House's front steps, and if he'd spoken to Samuel about what was happening he hadn't given any indication, only having her usual rooms readied and then leaving her to lick her wounds in peace.

Nobody but the three of them knew she was staying there and that was how she wanted it. If their wider acquaintance heard of an estrangement—and so soon after the wedding—gossip would run rife. Arriving at Lady Donaghue's house alongside her husband was the only way to avoid whispers and as Harry knocked again Julia knew what he was about to say.

'Your—Samuel's—carriage is here. It's time to come down.'

Her stomach lurched and she held on to the edge of the dressing table to steady herself. It was too late to change her mind now. Samuel was waiting outside and she had no choice but to go to him, and she felt her heart pick up speed as she rose from her chair.

Harry was in the hall when she descended the staircase, the front door slightly ajar. Beyond it she caught a glimpse of Samuel's moonlit carriage standing out on the drive and she almost stumbled, only her brother's hand on her arm stopping her from tripping over her own feet.

'Steady. If you must break your head, please don't do it in my house. You know Mother would blame me.'

Julia tried to laugh but her lips were too tight to move. Instead, she stood mute as her cloak was draped around her, barely feeling its fur lining against her skin. All she could think of was what would come next, when she'd step outside and see Samuel at last, and the combination of anticipation and anxiety sat inside her like a lead weight.

Somehow, she found the resolve to walk to the door and was about to pass through it when once again she felt Harry's hand on her arm.

'I'll be following behind you in my carriage. Just so you know.'

He let go, looking slightly uncomfortable. Stuck between his sister and his friend, his position couldn't have been easy, and Julia tried again for a smile as she slipped past him, the chill night air rushing to help disguise the quaking of her hands as cold instead of nerves.

Hold your head up. You can do this.

Her limbs felt heavy as she approached the carriage, the gravelled drive crunching underfoot. Countless stars were strewn overhead but she didn't stop to look up at them, her attention fixed on the landau with its gleaming, black-painted sides, and she just had time to notice a movement at one of the windows before the door swung open and a tall figure stepped out.

'Good evening, Julia.'

Just the sound of Samuel's lowered voice sent a rush through her. It stirred the butterflies already fluttering and she had to battle not to quicken her stride, every fibre of her being yearning to bury her face in his neck, but her pride *just* managing to hold her back. He didn't move as he watched her come closer, perhaps not wanting to frighten her away, although his eyes never left her, and after the first glance she didn't dare look into them again.

'Good evening.'

He stood to one side so she could step up into the carriage's shadowy belly. Out of the corner of her eye she saw his hand twitch as if he meant to offer it, but she hauled herself up before he could take the chance, settling into the farthest corner and pulling her cloak around herself like a shield. Samuel followed her inside, closing the door behind him, and then with a creak of the wheels they were moving, and Julia didn't know whether to be joyful or nervous to find herself alone again with the man who, despite her uncertainties, still set her heart racing.

The clip of the horses' hooves rang out in the darkness, but inside the carriage there was silence until Samuel finally spoke.

'You look beautiful. As always.'

Julia tightened her fingers in the folds of her cloak, pressing her nails into her palms in a reminder to stay calm. 'Thank you.'

She gazed determinedly out the window, watching the silvery streets pass by. She could *feel* him watching her and knew if she looked at him she would be lost. His presence filled the whole space and she was aware of every tiny shift he made, able to tell he was about to speak again before he'd even opened his mouth.

'How's Pirate? It feels strange not having him getting under my feet all the time.'

Still with her eyes averted, she inclined her head. 'He's

fine. Keeping in practice by getting under Harry's feet instead.'

'Good. I'm glad some things are still the same.'

He seemed to be trying to speak normally although he hadn't succeeded. His tone was as unnatural as hers, and Julia bit her lip on a crackle of pain, the knot in her stomach pulling tighter.

Samuel sat quietly for a moment, allowing the pause to stretch out until it seemed he couldn't take any more.

'When are you coming home?'

The question was delivered so bluntly Julia couldn't curb the reflex to turn towards him, although as soon as their eyes met she wished she hadn't.

There was such longing in his face that she almost gasped, unprepared for the depth of feeling he could express with a single glance, the eyes looking back at her clouded with unhappiness that cut her to the quick.

She stared at him, feeling her heart hammering. Was he really missing her? Enough for her absence to have had such an effect?

'I don't know. I still need to think.'

Samuel nodded, dropping his gaze to fix on his hat as he held it in his lap. If he was disappointed he hid it well, although Julia was sure she saw the smallest slump of his shoulders.

'I won't try to pressure you. Only know that I hope very much you won't stay away much longer.'

It was fortunate that at that moment the horses began to slow. What would have happened otherwise was impossible to guess, but Julia was relieved when Lady Donaghue's grand house loomed up out of the darkness, and there was no chance for either of them to say anything more before the carriage rolled to a halt and the footman opened the door.

The servant handed Julia out and she gave him a vague smile of thanks as she looked around, trying to steady her nerves. The air was cold and she took a deep, calming breath, feeling it burn in her lungs—until the lightest touch on her elbow made her flinch.

'Sorry. I didn't mean—' Samuel started back half a pace. 'I was just going to ask if I might escort you inside? The steps are steep and there's frost on the ground already.'

'Oh. Yes. Thank you.'

He held his arm out—slightly hesitantly—and she took it, knowing as she placed her palm on his sleeve that it was probably a mistake.

The instant she felt the muscle of his forearm under her fingertips she knew she didn't want to let go. A rush of something like relief washed over her and it was all she could do to put one foot in front of the other as he helped her up the slippery steps, hardly able to focus on anything but the strength in that firm arm. He felt so solid and dependable, and she was just teetering on the brink of abandoning all restraint and telling him so when they reached the front door and he carefully disengaged her hand, giving a respectful bow as he moved away.

'There. Safe and sound.'

She gave him a hollow smile, keenly feeling the loss of his touch. 'Thank you.'

Together they entered the hall, the darkness immediately replaced by the glare of a hundred candles. Great swathes of greenery hung from the ceiling, and wreaths of holly and laurel festooned every wall, the combination of rich red and green more striking than any other. The next day every single leaf would be taken down and burned and Lady Donaghue's Twelfth Night ball was her last chance to show off her tasteful decorations before next Christmas, her party known throughout Guildbury as heralding the end of the festive period for another year.

Handing her cloak to a waiting servant Julia looked around, momentarily distracted by the splendour and press of bodies all around. It seemed everyone had accepted their invitations this year. A swift scan of the crowds showed a dozen faces she knew, and she'd turned to see if Samuel was still behind her when a glimpse of Mediterranean blue brought her up short.

He's wearing the waistcoat I made him.

Beneath the magnificent chandelier the silver embroidery that had taken her so many hours to complete sparkled like sunlight on water, the design of winter pansies subtle against azure silk. It had been too dark in the carriage to notice, and in any case, she hadn't dared look close enough to see, but now he stood in the flame-lit entrance hall she didn't know what to say.

He looked back at her, his expression unreadable but for the slightest trace of uncertainty about his mouth. He didn't move and she didn't, either, although the crowd was too dense to stand still for long. There was a queue of people waiting to go into the ballroom and she had no choice but to be borne along with them, forced to walk on without having said a word.

Does it mean something that he's wearing it?

She couldn't think of anything else as she was funnelled through the double doors to where the dancing was taking place, trying to find civil nods and smiles for everyone who greeted her. In truth, each face barely registered, Samuel's the only one she really wanted to see, although no sooner had he appeared at her shoulder than he was turning away once more.

'Your cousin is coming over. I won't intrude.'

'You needn't—'

Instinctively, she put out a hand to stop him but it was too late. With a polite bow he was moving away from her, withdrawing into the throng, and she felt a heavy blow of confusion and disappointment fall over her as she watched him go.

'Julia. Thank heaven you're here.'

Eliza sounded short of breath above the din of the orchestra and buzz of raised voices, the mound beneath her skirts more pronounced than ever. Strictly speaking, she probably should have stayed at home but Julia knew she could never resist a party.

'You shouldn't be jostling about in your condition. Have you been here long?'

'Long enough to know your mama is looking for you. Will you be slinking off to hide again? As, I recall, you did last time we met at a ball?'

Julia exhaled a dry laugh at the frank but accurate summation of past events.

'She can't force me into any more marriages, that much is true…but I confess I'm not in a frenzy to see her.'

'No? Is something wrong?'

Eliza's eyebrows rose. Doubtless some of her curiosity was rooted in boredom, her condition leaving her unable to dance, but in large part it was genuine interest that made her take Julia's arm. 'Come with me.

I'm sure we can find a shadowy corner where you can tell me all about it.'

At once, Julia shook her head. 'There's nothing, really. I'm perfectly well.'

'You've never been a good liar. You blush too easily.'

There seemed scant point in trying to argue. Ever since they were children Eliza had taken the lead and she did so now, her grip surprisingly firm as she towed Julia towards the edge of the room. There were no curtains to hide behind this time, but there was an alcove furnished with two chairs and a table, and by the winsome fluttering of her eyelashes Eliza was able to make the gentlemen occupying them graciously depart.

She settled into one of the chairs with a sigh, laying a protective hand over her middle. 'That's better. I can hardly bear to stand for long.'

Reluctantly, Julia took the other, quickly glancing around before she sat. If Samuel was watching her she didn't want to seem as if she was searching for him... although she couldn't seem to stop herself from peering into the crowd, hoping to catch another flash of that distinctive blue or the chestnut gleam of his hair...

'So. What's amiss between you and Samuel?'

Julia looked round to find Eliza's hawk-like eye fixed on her. 'Why should something be amiss?'

'Don't be tedious. I can read your countenance as if it was a book.' Losing the stern edge, Eliza's face softened and she leaned forward, resting her chin in her palm. 'You don't seem happy. I don't like to see that.'

Her green gaze was unwavering and the real kindness in it made Julia feel suddenly vulnerable. She'd been so unhappy and not told a soul what was going on in her head, not wanting to burden Harry, and the idea of confiding in her mother out of the question. Eliza had always been a friend as well as a cousin and could be relied upon to keep her council, her heart in the right place even if her opinions sometimes were not.

'Could I trust you not to speak of it to anyone else?'

'Of course. Anything you choose to tell me will be taken to the grave.'

Julia risked another glance around the ballroom. There was still no sign of Samuel or even Harry and Mama, her brother probably already somewhere surrounded by debutantes and her mother busy telling all and sundry about Viscount Maidwell's wonderful lemons. Nobody seemed to be watching and she drew her chair closer to the table, dropping her voice to little more than a barely audible murmur.

'I found a love letter in his desk, dated after we were engaged. There was a miniature, too, and on the back of it she'd written that she loved him.'

Her lips felt dry and she paused, wishing she had a glass of punch to give her courage. It was hard to put her situation into words and saying it out loud didn't bring her much comfort, forcing her to confront the upsetting truth with no way of softening the blow.

'When I asked him about it he told me he'd been engaged before and that he no longer cared for her, but…'

'But you don't know if you take his word?' Eliza's keen eyes were narrowed now, sharpening further at Julia's shaky nod.

'Yes. I know he didn't marry me for love. I never thought otherwise. But I believed something was growing between us, and to think he might have been pining after another woman the whole time, perhaps still telling her he loved her, hurts more than I ever thought it could.'

She stopped, closing her mouth before her voice could become even more unsteady. There was a quiver in it as if she was about to cry and she tensed her jaw, refusing to embarrass herself where everyone could see, although the unhappy combination of feelings running riot inside her was increasingly difficult to contain.

Eliza frowned, her pretty face creased in thought. 'Why did they part?'

'I don't know.'

'You didn't ask him?'

'No.'

This time the fold of her brows was more incredulous than thoughtful. 'Why on earth not? It might make all the difference. How can you reach a conclusion when you don't have all the facts?'

Eliza shook her head as if it was the most exasperatingly obvious thing in the world, and Julia blinked at her, feeling as if she was trailing a few steps behind.

'Do you think I ought to?'

'Yes! Of course I do!'

Eliza couldn't have sounded more frustrated if she'd tried. Clearly despairing of her cousin's dim-wittedness, she leaned forward, looking into Julia's face with the careful patience one might use when explaining something to a child.

'If you want my opinion, he's in love with you, not this other woman, and if it was me I wouldn't let another moment go by without knowing the truth.'

She sat back again, folding her hands over her bump with a finality that suggested there was nothing more to be said. Julia's mouth opened, unsure herself what she was going to say, but Eliza's sharply raised finger was firm.

'You heard me. That's what you should do and I believe deep down you know it—so why are you wasting time sitting here with me?'

Samuel only realised he hadn't been paying attention to what Captain Jacobs was saying when the rest of the group around him laughed and he found he had no idea of the joke. The music was loud and the heat stifling, but it was the contents of his own mind that made it impossible to fix on anything else, the din of the ballroom no match for the cacophony inside his head.

Was she pleased I wore the waistcoat? It was meant as a tribute to her, but now I wonder if it was a step too far...

He hadn't seen Julia since he'd left her with her cousin, and a scan around the packed room gave no clue where she might be. He hadn't wanted to part from her—the moment he'd seen her coming down Highbank's front steps he had wanted to burst out from the carriage and catch her up in his arms, but he had to wait. If he pushed her too hard he might spoil things more than he already had, although giving her the space she needed in which to think was a torture like nothing he'd ever known. Larch House felt empty without her, the rooms quiet and lacking warmth even the biggest fire couldn't provide, and the thought he might have chased her away for ever made his heart sink down into his boots.

Captain Jacobs had evidently made another witty remark. The ladies were laughing again and this time

Samuel forced himself to join in, oblivious to what was supposed to have amused him. Until Julia returned he had nothing real to smile about, and his face felt stiff with the effort of holding up the pretence, the muscles of his cheeks just beginning to ache when he heard a soft voice just behind him.

'Samuel? I wonder…might I speak with you a moment?'

He turned at once, his heart catapulting from his boots up into his mouth.

Julia was sucking in her lower lip as she stood behind him, her hands laced over the bodice of her shimmering gown. He recognised the anxious action immediately and a rush swept through him to wonder what could have caused it—and whether it should give him room to hope.

'Of course. Where…?'

'I thought on the terrace. It's too loud to talk in here unless you shout, and I… I don't wish us to be overheard.'

She gave him an almost shy glance and turned away, the feathers in her hair swaying as she moved, and he followed without hesitation. If she wanted to speak to him privately there must be a good reason, he thought with a rise of fresh apprehension that he tried to rein back, his mind already darting ahead as he made his way through the masses towards the doors at the other end of the room. She wouldn't have sought him out unless she had something to say, and he wasn't sure whether to be worried or pleased that she wanted a private audience.

The air on the shadowy terrace was cold but after the heat of the ballroom the chill was a welcome relief. Julia seemed to feel the same, closing her eyes briefly as she laid the back of her hand against one cheek, and for a split second Samuel was able to study her unobserved.

She looked tired. There were smudges below her eyes and her skin had lost some of its fresh bloom, but to him that hardly mattered. She was still the most beautiful woman he had ever seen, and he wished he could watch her for ever, drinking in the sight of her in case he was never given another opportunity. Depending on what she had brought him outside to talk about he might have missed his chance at making amends and the thought of having made her so unhappy was like an icy dagger to the heart, his longing to hold her in his arms burning stronger than ever, and the effort of keeping himself in check wearing him down.

Opening her eyes, Julia gave him another of those shy glances that made him catch a breath. 'Thank you for coming. I thought perhaps we might talk... That we could perhaps speak about...'

Her sentence faded into uncertainty and he saw the twine of her fingers tighten. She looked back at the doors leading into the ballroom, the chatter and music floating out still loud in the night, and Samuel took a cautious step towards her.

'There's a bench a little farther out. We could sit there if you'd prefer some more privacy.'

The moonlight made her curls gleam ebony as she nodded. 'Yes. I think that might be best.'

At a respectful distance he followed her along the patio towards a stone bench set against the back wall of the house. The noise from the ballroom faded the farther they walked until it was reduced to an indistinct hum, the stirring of the ivy that covered the wall a far more relaxing sound than the bray of voices and scrape of violins.

Julia settled herself carefully on the bench, hesitating for a beat before gesturing for him to sit beside her.

'Please. You needn't stand.'

He thought she stiffened slightly when he sat down next to her but she didn't draw away. The seat was too small to leave much of a gap between them, and he steeled himself against the scent of rose water he caught on her hair, mingling with the warmth from her body that made him want to lean closer still.

But you can't. If there's to be any hope of her returning, you'll have to let her set the pace.

She was looking down at her gloved hands, her moonlit side profile showing a frown. Clearly, whatever she'd brought him outside to discuss was difficult to put into words, and Samuel weighed up whether he ought to speak first. The suspense was uncomfortable, caught between curiosity and dread, and he couldn't balance on that tightrope for long.

'I think there must be something you want to ask me.'

He kept his voice gentle and low as if it was a wild bird sitting next to him rather than his wife. 'It can be anything. I'll keep nothing back from you—not now.'

There was a sigh, a tiny sound he only just caught above the whisper of the leaves. Unless he was mistaken it was one of relief that he had broached the subject, and Julia turned slightly more towards him, still studying her hands but her face now easier for him to see.

'Yes. In fact, there is.'

Samuel felt a sensation like a cold finger slip down the back of his neck as she at last lifted her eyes to his, the rich darkness of them allowing for no escape.

'I've been thinking about what you told me of your previous engagement and how your feelings for the woman in the painting have changed. You said you care for me now, not her, and I…'

For a moment she faltered, but gathered her nerve and went on. 'I would like to believe you. There's nothing I want more. But before I can know for certain I think I need to know the circumstances in which you parted and why your attachment to her came to an end.'

With an unsteady hand she tucked a stray tendril of hair back behind her ear, her colour now much higher, and Samuel watched her in silence.

It was something he'd hoped to avoid. The last thing he wanted was to bring Lucrezia back again, invoking her presence where it was least welcome…but if it would help Julia to forgive him then that was what he would do. The story wouldn't reflect well on him, but to win back his wife he would try anything. Once she'd heard the tale, Julia would know everything, not a single secret left for him to conceal, and he would have laid himself bare before her judgement and only able to pray for the best.

'I understand. I think, if the situation was reversed, I would want to know the same.'

It was his turn to look down at his hands. It would be easier to speak if he couldn't see her watching him, and he didn't raise his head when he sensed her gaze fix on him, the same rich darkness once again holding him a willing prisoner.

'It isn't something I've spoken of to anyone. Not

my parents, not my friends here… But I see why you need to know. If it'll help repair the damage my secrecy has done to our marriage then I'll tell you, and I won't leave anything out.'

He sighed wearily, wondering where to start. Should it be with the first time he saw Lucrezia, or the moment he'd learned who she really was inside? Both choices brought back memories he had no desire to revisit, and he realised he was frowning, only Julia's silent presence beside him forcing him to begin.

'I'd heard about Signora Lucrezia Bianchi before I encountered her. I'd been told she was beautiful and charming and when I eventually met her I saw it was true. She was everything I'd expected and it didn't take long before I believed myself in love with her and thought she felt the same way about me in return.'

A fleeting image flickered through his mind—a captivating young woman alighting from a gondola, the sun lighting up her laughing face—and forcefully he brushed it aside. Julia was sitting like a statue, hardly seeming to breathe, and he made himself continue against every instinct screaming at him to turn back.

'There were always other men surrounding her but she quickly persuaded me I had no cause for concern. She liked the attention they gave her but she assured me I was the only one she cared for and I took her at her word, sure the woman I loved must be telling me the truth. When I proposed she agreed without hesitation, and I was excited to write to my parents to tell them I'd found the bride they had been so anxious for me to take.

'The moment we got engaged, however, she began pushing for a quick wedding. I wanted to wait a while, until I'd informed my parents and had them come to Italy for the ceremony, but she wouldn't slow down. I thought it was her eagerness to marry me that caused such insistence and to my everlasting shame I was flattered instead of suspicious…which, as it turned out, would have been the wiser response.'

A heaviness had settled over him. He was coming to the part he had tried in vain to forget, and recalling what came next made his chest feel tight, the memories flooding back to nip at him with sharp teeth. It had been the worst experience of his life—until the day Julia had left Larch House, of course, and it was only for her sake that he allowed the ghost of those miserable days to rise from its grave.

He cleared his throat, wishing it didn't feel so full of powdered glass. 'A couple of days after our engagement I encountered an acquaintance, Dr De Luca, in the street. He gave me his best wishes and then made a discreet mention of having another reason to congratulate me. I didn't understand what he meant and when I asked he replied that as the Bianchi family's physician it was Lucrezia's pregnancy he was referring to, something I had no knowledge of, and as a gentleman had done nothing to cause.'

Julia's gasp was especially loud in the quiet of the night. She started, accidentally brushing against him in her shock, and the brief friction of her arm against his sent a chain reaction right through to his leaping heart.

'She was—and she hadn't told—?'

Samuel only just managed to keep a grim smile from contorting his mouth. 'Yes. And no. I'll spare you the unsavoury details. Suffice to say the child was not mine but Lucrezia had planned to claim me as the father, making a speedy wedding essential. When I confronted her she wouldn't name the other man but confessed all else, leaving me in no doubt that she had never loved me at all. There was nothing for me to do but return to England and so I did, hoping to leave the whole sorry mess behind.'

He finished simply, somehow encompassing his pain with a few scant words. There was no need to elaborate how he had felt during the long journey back, and Julia was sharp enough to know what had gone unsaid, already sifting through to put her finger on the most salient point.

'But the portrait I found? The writing on the back of it? Surely if she had no feelings for you…'

'She didn't mean it. The miniature and the letter were meant to draw me back to her but of course by then it was too late. I was married to you—and my heart, which I'd never meant to give away again, was already in your keeping.'

He sensed her grow very still as his final words hit their target, and at last he looked up from his hands.

Once he might have regretted speaking so plainly but now he had no time for such misgivings. What he had said was the truth and Julia deserved to hear it, his attempts at secrecy already having caused enough damage. If she wanted to know how he felt then he'd tell her, never again trying to keep anything hidden, and there was a strange kind of relief in abandoning himself to his fate—whatever his wife might decide it would be.

Julia's lips parted slightly as though trying to form a reply, although they moved without anything coming out. The blush that always made her look so in-

nocent was clear even in the moonlight but her eyes
held a new question that sent a fresh wave of unease
coursing through him.

'Is that why you called me dangerous, all those
weeks ago in my father's library? Because I reminded
you of her, and you feared I might do the same thing
she had done once before?'

'Yes. I confess I feared the worst. You were even
more lovely than Lucrezia and I saw how half of Guildbury's men wanted you, for your face and the way you
could light up a room just by walking into it. I never
intended to court such a threat ever again after what
had happened in Italy, and I worried that if I let myself care for you, you might be able to inflict the same
pain. Now, of course, I know any likeness is solely on
the surface, but in the beginning I wasn't so certain.'

He saw her mouth tighten and he grimaced inwardly
when she didn't speak, only the rustle of the leaves and
faint music in the distance breaking the loaded pause.

When Julia finally put him out of his misery her
voice was no more than a murmur.

'I'm glad you told me the truth. Thank you for that.'

She gave him one of the sideways glances that always managed to stir the hairs at the nape of his neck,
direct but swift enough he could never be entirely sure
what it meant.

'I'm not sure how I feel about you imagining I'd behave the same way she did. It calls my character into
question when I've never given you any cause to doubt
it. Did you really think I'd dishonour my marriage vows
so easily...or that I cared so little for you?'

Inside the hollow of his chest Samuel felt his heart
lurch forward. Had she just admitted she cared for

him, even at the same time as reproaching him for his insulting lack of faith? He wasn't sure what she was trying to tell him, and the desire to know was so intense it took his breath away, her good opinion now the thing he valued above all else. If by some miracle she had decided to overlook his stupidity there might be a chance they could regain what had been lost—but it seemed now wasn't the moment to find out.

'Julia? Are you out here?'

A hushed call from farther down the terrace made Julia jerk to her feet, and Samuel rose to join her, privately cursing his brother-in-law's timing. It was the worst possible moment for an interruption and he tried to temper his frustration as Harry's shadow fell over them, aware how tense Julia was as she stood at his side.

'Good. There you are.'

Harry nodded at Samuel and then turned to his sister. 'Mother is looking for you. I've stalled her for as long as I can but I thought you might want to see her before she stumbles into something you'd rather she didn't.'

It was a display of tact on Harry's part and Samuel was grateful for it when he saw a flash of relief cross Julia's face. Mrs Livingston was *not* someone he wanted to have poking about in his business and it seemed his wife felt the same, their desire for privacy one thing they had in common at least.

'Thank you. I'll go to her now.'

Julia moved to step past him and he stood aside to let her go. In truth, he wanted to take hold of her hand and pull her closer instead, but with great difficulty he kept himself under control, even succeeding in finding a civil bow for Harry when he turned to walk away.

Just before she followed her brother towards the ballroom doors, Julia looked back.

'It's freezing. You shouldn't sit outside for much longer.'

She smiled, the tiniest movement that still drew Samuel's eye. It was hard to tell whether it was genuine, the moon suddenly dipping behind a cloud to dim even that feeble light, but nonetheless, the beauty of her lips made him want to groan out loud.

'I'll be in momentarily.'

Julia gave a single nod. A chilly breeze made the loose curls at either side of her head sway slightly and she wrapped her arms around herself, rubbing away gooseflesh that had risen on her skin. She seemed to have only just realised quite how cold it was, and Samuel was on the brink of offering her his jacket when she turned away, her white skirts swirling around her like an angel's wings as she went, and this time she didn't look back.

Chapter Fourteen

Samuel didn't bother going to bed when he returned home from the ball. By the time he left it was already the early hours of a new day and sleep would have been out of the question regardless, his conversation with Julia circling too incessantly to allow any rest. Instead, he sat in his darkened bedroom, gazing unseeingly out the window until dawn began to creep slowly over the horizon, and as the birds ventured their first sleepy calls, he got to his feet.

He couldn't sit still any longer. The image of Julia's face as she'd listened to him bare his soul was imprinted on the insides of his eyelids, flashing every time he blinked, and he still couldn't be sure what she had meant by those final words before Harry had come onto the terrace and snatched her away. She'd seemed to admit she cared for him in spite of his mistakes and belated revelations but he had to be *sure*—and the only way to do that was to speak with her again.

A glance in the barely visible mirror didn't show him at his best, his chin roughened by stubble and the circles under his eyes more pronounced than ever.

He looked exactly how he felt, tired and troubled and wondering if he'd made one mistake too many, and he shook his head at the reflection staring back at him in the glass.

'You'd scare her to death if you appeared like this. At the very least you should wait until the sun is fully up before you go banging on Highbank's front door.'

Slightly stiffly, he turned to his armoire, the coldness of the room and sitting unmoving for hours making his muscles ache. The fire had long since died and he hadn't wanted to rouse a servant to come to tend to it, shivering as he finally swapped the previous night's clothes for a clean shirt. The azure silk of the waistcoat Julia had made for him gleamed softly and he studied the way the dim dawn light played over the silver embroidery, each stitch she'd worked so hard on proof that at least once she had liked him enough to think it worthwhile.

But does she still? And was she pleased to see me wear it last night?

They were questions he was powerless to answer, and Samuel gritted his teeth on his uncertainty as he thrust his arms into the sleeves of his old walking coat. The four walls of the bedroom were closing in on him and he felt trapped by his doubts, hesitation and the unknown harrying him like hounds after a fox. If he didn't escape he thought he might run mad, and he tried not to make any noise as he pulled on his boots and eased open the door, glancing swiftly up and down before slipping out onto the landing.

With quiet steps he made his way through the house, down one corridor and another until he reached the stairs. While his mind whirled so unhappily he didn't want to wake the servants. The last thing he wanted was to be surrounded by people, no matter how well meaning, and it seemed obvious where he could go to flee the encroaching walls and be alone with the chaos of his thoughts.

The freezing air hit him like a slap to the face when he stepped out the kitchen door, and he pulled his coat closer around him, watching his breath rise in a cloud of mist. It would be another bitterly cold day and he blew on his bare hands as he looked around the deserted grounds, for this moment at least feeling as though he might be the last person left in the world. He had wanted to be alone—and yet a sudden surge of loneliness swept up from nowhere to realise he'd gotten his wish. Julia should have been there with him, the warmth of her palm pressing against his, and he felt his shoulders tense as he turned up the collar of his coat and paced onto the grass.

He walked blindly, taking scant notice of which direction he'd turned, his head both bowed and filled to the brim with too many thoughts to unpick. A rapid succession of pictures ticked past, all of them featuring dark eyes and shiny black curls, and he was just abandoning any hope of outrunning them when a scent in the air brought him to an abrupt halt.

Is that smoke?

He inhaled deeply. Yes—it was definitely smoke he could smell, drifting towards him in the chilly breeze that was trying to invade the neck of his shirt. He could see it now he was paying attention: a grey plume rising from behind the walled herb garden, close to where the groundsman had a small hut for keeping tools, and straining his eyes he thought he could barely make out a tinge of orange light on the underside of the cloud. There was no doubt that a fire was blazing and he began to walk towards it, a slight edge of concern lending extra length to his stride until he reached the wall.

'Oh. Good morning.'

Hewitt looked up at Samuel's voice, pausing in the act of throwing another armful of ivy into the flames of a cheerfully crackling bonfire. He seemed mildly surprised to see his employer appear out of the dawn gloom but recovered quickly enough, nodding with the same gruff courtesy as always. 'Morning, sir. Were you needing me?'

'No, no. I just saw the smoke and thought I'd come to investigate.'

The groundsman nodded again and without another word tossed his bundle of greenery into the heart of the fire. It roared higher and Samuel watched ash and sparks whirl up into the sky, his eye settling on a heap of boughs piled a short distance away.

'These are the Yuletide decorations?'

'Aye, sir. Taken down last night. I'll be burning them all today to keep bad luck away from the house.'

Something in that lush green sparked a memory, the jewel-toned gleam bringing to mind the colour of Julia's gown the first time he'd seen her dancing at Lady Fitzwilliam's St Nicholas's Day ball. It had been the first time he'd seen her smile, too. That dazzling flash of pink and white that had made him think his heart had ceased to beat before flinging it hard against his ribs, and from that moment on his life hadn't been the same. She'd broken down the barriers between them, first unwillingly and then by showing him forgiveness and patience he hadn't deserved, and as he gazed into the fire, *at last* Samuel knew what he had to do.

'Do you think they'll be doing this at Highbank? Burning things, I mean?'

At the unexpected question Hewitt glanced round, his weathered brow gathering in a faint frown.

'I know they will. The gardener there is my wife's cousin and he told me as much himself.'

Samuel nodded, suddenly unable to speak, but that didn't matter. The idea that had burst forth with such violent brilliance didn't require him to put it into words, and he merely raised a hand to the groundsman before turning away, striding back towards the house as quickly as he could—and wondering which path would take him most swiftly to his study.

Fenshaw had to repeat her question twice before Julia realised she was being spoken to.

'Sorry. I was miles away. The pale yellow, please.'

She watched the lady's maid return the blue gown to the wardrobe and fetch out another in primrose muslin, hoping the colour would help bring some life back to her pallid face. It was expected to feel tired the morning after a ball but she flattered herself that she didn't usually look quite so drawn, the things Samuel had told her out on Lady Donaghue's terrace keeping her awake until she'd heard a distant cock begin to crow.

Now, as Pirate played around her feet and she waited for Fenshaw to fasten her into her gown, she allowed herself a moment to consider—yet again—what she made of his confession. That every word was true she had no doubt, and she wanted to pace the room while she relived them, only her maid's firm hands on the back of her dress stopping her from lurching away. Finally, she'd uncovered the secret she knew he'd been hiding and now all she had to do was decide what would happen next, both of their futures depending on how she chose to respond.

He loved this Lucrezia and she betrayed him, almost tricking him into taking on a child that wasn't his own. Under the circumstances...can I blame him for fearing the worst of me?

It seemed to be taking an age for Fenshaw to finish tying laces and straightening bows, and Julia became aware she was twisting her fingers together with impatient unease, chafing to be set free to walk off the nervous energy that made it difficult to keep still.

She'd be lying if she pretended it hadn't hurt when Samuel called her a threat. For weeks she had thought they were growing closer and to learn he had watched her with such uncertainty left a bitter taste that her early-morning cup of tea hadn't quite managed to wash away. He hadn't trusted her even when she'd given him no cause for doubt, and to think he could imagine her so lacking in moral standards stung, part of her unhappy he'd thought her capable of deceit...although another part understood.

Julia took a deep breath, pulling her shoulders back as she conjured a glimpse of Samuel's moonlit face. He'd looked almost broken as he told her what had happened in Italy, naked emotion playing over his countenance too real for him to hide. There had been pain and raw regret in his voice, and she had longed to take his face in her hands and kiss his poor, sad mouth, only the need to hear the whole truth holding her back. It was clear how much of a grip Signora Bianchi had once had on him, and a spark of anger leapt in Julia's chest, a flicker of some protective instinct flaring to make her fingers lace together harder still.

'There, ma'am. Finished.'

At last, Fenshaw released her. With a word of thanks Julia dismissed the maid from the room and then she stood, the desire to pace melting away as she thought again of Samuel's handsome, granite face. He looked so much softer when he smiled, his laugh always sending a delightful prickle beneath her skin...but he wouldn't have been laughing on his way back to England. His heart must have ached with every rise and fall of whatever creaking boat he'd boarded to bring him home, perhaps even shedding a tear he was far too proud to admit, and suddenly she couldn't bear to imagine his grief.

He would have been devastated. Left all alone with his sorrows and missing the woman he loved...but is it in my power to prevent him from feeling like that again now...?

He had concealed things from her. He had kept secrets and believed her capable of the most insulting things, casting aspersions on her honour he had no right to. But somehow none of that seemed to matter when she thought of his pain. Everything he had done stemmed from the instinct not to be hurt again, and she recognised it as the same aim she'd once held, when she had thought keeping Samuel at a distance was the best way to safeguard herself. In time, of course, she'd realised the opposite was true—that it was only by allowing her husband to pierce her defences that she could find happiness, and it was a lesson it was high time Samuel learned for himself.

Her heart beginning to skip a little quicker, she glanced at the clock on her dressing table. It was still early—too early for him to be awake. The ball had gone on until the small hours and he had still been in the ballroom when she left with Harry, her legs tired but mind whirring like a clockwork toy. She wanted to speak to him at once, feeling there was now no time to lose, but if she startled him awake he might not fully grasp what she was there to say…

That's a chance I'll have to take.

With determination even Mama would admire she crossed the room, Pirate scurrying behind her, flung open her bedroom door—and crashed headlong into her brother's broad chest.

'Watch out!'

Julia reeled back, almost falling over the puppy before Harry seized hold of her arm and jerked her back onto her feet. She leaned against the door frame to catch her breath, too startled to immediately notice the decidedly odd way he was smiling.

'What are you doing, loitering about outside my room? I nearly ran you over!'

'Nearly *fell* over, you mean. As usual.'

Harry grinned down at her and she felt a belated stir of suspicion.

'Why are you looking at me like that? What's wrong with your face?'

'Nothing's wrong with it.'

For half a second he was almost affronted, his countenance never normally described in anything but the most glowing terms, although the next instant the strange smile widened. 'I came up to ask you to go outside. There's something I think you should see.'

He really was behaving peculiarly and Julia hesitated, pulling her skirts straight with an impatient hand as Pirate tugged at the hem.

'I haven't the time at present. Can't it wait until later?'

'No. I don't believe it can.'

Harry shifted restlessly, now all but barring her way, and she studied him more carefully. Like a child with a secret he fidgeted, twisting a button on his sleeve, and for the first time she felt her interest pique.

'What is it? What am I supposed to see?'

'I can't tell you. You'll have to find out for yourself.' Harry shrugged, his determination to avoid answering the question helping her make up her mind. 'In the gardens. You'll know it at once.'

Julia's eyes narrowed but her brother merely continued to stare at her with that same slightly unnerving smile. There was obviously something amiss and it seemed she wouldn't be free to find Samuel until she satisfied Harry's request, her impatience taking on a hint of involuntary curiosity as she suppressed a sigh.

'Very well. If it'll make you happy.'

She moved towards the stairs, pausing to look over her shoulder when he didn't follow.

'Aren't you coming?'

'No. It's meant for your eyes, not mine.'

He shook his head, now holding a squirming Pirate and the grin still in place, and Julia didn't bother to argue as he waved her away.

Probably he's arranged something to try to cheer me up, she thought, descending the staircase into the hall.

He knew she'd been unhappy and in his misguided

way was attempting to help, not realising he was, in fact, detaining her from what she now knew she had to do. Harry had been so kind and it would be ungrateful for her to dismiss whatever he'd done on her behalf, even if the desire to bypass the gardens and seek out Samuel instead chased her all the way to the side door that led out onto the grounds.

She hadn't stopped to fetch a cloak and she wrapped her arms around herself as she stood on the step, the cold air attacking her bare skin. Highbank's lawns stretched out before her in a carpet of frost, every leaf silver and the stone-slabbed patio glistening in the weak sunlight, and taking a rapid scan around her, Julia frowned.

'Well, Harry? What am I meant to be looking at?'

Each murmured word floated in front of her in a little white cloud. As far as she could tell there was nothing out of the ordinary, only the usual sweep of grass and hedges twinkling with ice, and she was about to retreat inside when a flicker of movement caught her eye.

Harry's groundsman had built up a bonfire to one side of the lawn and she watched him walk towards it, a flaming torch guttering in his hand. Carefully, he touched it to the pile of greenery, first in one place and then another and another, the fire taking hold with eager speed—and when he walked away again she saw another man come forward to take his place, the newcomer so familiar she knew at once there was only one person it could be.

For one terrifying, *wonderful* moment, her heart squeezed to a halt.

Samuel?

He was still, only the wind stirring his chestnut hair

as he watched her stumble across the grass towards him, for once not bothering to attempt any graceful-ness in her haste to reach him. It seemed he couldn't have moved even if he'd wanted to. His face was set and his broad shoulders like marble, looking more like a Grecian statue than ever as he stood motionless be-side the fire, every feature chiselled from the line of his nose to the sharp edge of his jaw.

'What are you doing out here? Why didn't you come inside?'

She hadn't meant to speak so quietly but she found her voice was hoarse. All the things she'd planned to say to him fled now he was before her, every nerve and sinew straining forward in an effort to touch, and yet from somewhere she summoned one last thread of self-control. He had to be there for a reason and she wanted to know what it was, the tense seriousness of his face something she longed to chase away with kisses even as she made herself stay composed.

Samuel gazed down at her, the vivid blue of his eyes a fathomless ocean in the morning sunlight. He didn't try to touch her, either, although the slight clenching and unclenching of one hand now showed how hard he was fighting the urge, his battle with himself so in-tense it was almost tangible in the chilly air.

'I needed to see you. There's something I have to show you, and Harry was good enough to say I could do it here.'

His voice was hardly louder than hers, almost lost amid the crackle of the bonfire. The flames were be-ginning to build and orange tongues reached up to-wards the sky, fierce enough to have caught Julia's attention if every last bit of it hadn't already been fixed on her husband as slowly, with a suddenly unsteady-looking hand, he reached inside the pocket of his worn old coat.

He didn't take his eyes from hers as he pulled out a piece of paper. Even without looking she knew it was Lucrezia's letter, and she barely had time to wonder why he was showing it to her before he took a breath, inhaling deeply as if trying to force air into his lungs.

'You wanted to know why I'm here. It's because of this.'

He shook the letter slightly, or perhaps it was a tremor in his fingers that made it move. Either way, Julia managed to spare a glance towards it, the elegant handwriting sending a shard of dislike beneath her bodice.

'I've seen that before. What—?'

At the crease of his brow she fell quiet. That particular relic from his time in Italy wasn't one she was in a rush to see ever again, and she folded her lips into a tight line, suddenly unsure but unable to look away when Samuel dropped it into his other palm.

In silence he weighed it, testing the feel of the paper in his hand. For a moment it lay there, black ink seeming blacker still against white, and Julia had no idea what he was thinking...until at last he spoke.

'This letter, a single piece of paper that I kept for far longer than I should have...it belongs in the past. I have no use for anything that would stand in the way of my future, a future that holds only you.'

With one harsh movement he balled his hand into a fist, crushing the letter into a crumpled mess. The other hand went back to his pocket, once again reaching inside to draw something out, and Julia didn't think her chest could tighten any harder when she saw the little oval frame's glass front gleam in the fire's reflected light.

'This is the same.' Samuel held it up higher, Lucrezia's illustrated eyes finding Julia's and attempting to stare her down. 'Another thing I have no use for. There's but one woman I wish to look at for the rest of my life and it isn't the one in this painting.'

He turned it over, for the briefest of seconds looking down into the seductively smiling face—and then with a single flick of his wrist he cast it into the fire, the screwed-up letter immediately following to be greedily swallowed by the flames.

Julia started, the suddenness of it making her gasp. Both the letter and the portrait popped and blackened, the paper curling at the corners and the oval glass shattering with an audible crack, but Samuel's face didn't change. Between one heartbeat and the next all evidence of Lucrezia Bianchi's presence in his life was destroyed for ever, and Julia felt her mouth fall open with wordless surprise, unable to close it even when he came closer and took hold of her nerveless hand.

'I'm sorry for everything I did to drive you away. I hope that proves, in some small way, that I want nothing and no one but you.'

Julia watched his lips move, the words seeming to come from far away. She could hear them but their meaning was shrouded in a haze, and she blinked when he dropped his head to look directly into her face, blue unwaveringly meeting dark brown in an effort to make her understand.

'What I feel for you is a hundred times more powerful than anything I experienced before. If you'll let me, I'd like to try to help you feel something similar for me in turn.'

Samuel smiled, the upward curve so sweetly uncertain that Julia had no choice but to copy it. Stark wonder gripped her but realisation was beginning to trickle in, finding the tiniest gaps in her amazement to pour forth, and like the bursting of a dam she felt herself give way to a tidal wave of happiness that drenched her from head to toe.

'But... I was coming to tell *you* that before Harry sent me here. Surely you know that I already feel the same...and indeed, that I know I always will?'

She saw his shoulders slump and for one hideous beat she thought it was with something close to dismay; but then she was off her feet, cradled against him and his mouth coming down on hers in a blaze of heat the bonfire had no hope of matching, and she knew she'd been wrong. It was relief that coursed through him, not anything else, and her own joy soared up to the sky where the wintry sun cleaved through the clouds to bathe them in its light.

They clung together, the power of one long-awaited kiss almost bringing both to their knees. Julia pushed her fingers into Samuel's hair and revelled in the scratch of his stubbled chin against hers, knowing it would sting later but too bound up in bliss to care. He held her to him as if he never intended to let go, his hands on her and their breathing falling into perfect synchronicity that matched the twin pounding of their hearts, and although their marriage hadn't been forged willingly both knew the connection between them now was as strong as any love match on earth.

Only when the strength of Samuel's grasp made it

difficult to breathe did Julia break away, swaying when he set her back on her feet. He didn't surrender her completely, however, still unwilling to take his hand from her waist, and she felt her cheeks begin to burn when he brought the other up to trail unsteady fingers down the back of her neck.

'You're cold.'

'Am I? I can hardly feel it.'

She shivered, not sure whether it was a delayed reaction to the temperature or the delight of Samuel's fingertips tracing her nape. Either way, she wanted nothing more than to draw closer to him again, and she didn't hesitate when he opened the front of his coat, nestling against his chest so he could wrap her in his warmth. His unique scent of cedar and smoke was all around her, his presence enveloping every sense as though he was a part of her and not a separate person at all, and neither needed to speak to make themselves understood as they stood together and watched the last traces of his life before love burn down to ash.

How long they lingered there Julia wasn't sure. With her arms around him beneath the cover of his coat she leaned into him, feeling his chest move as he breathed, and the sense of peace that encircled them stretched out in silent beauty until at last Samuel bent his head to drop two words into her pink-tinged ear.

'*Ti amo.*'

She smiled against the smooth linen of his shirt, listening to the steady beat of his heart against her cheek.

'*Ti amo.* For ever, this time.'

* * * * *

If you enjoyed this story, why not check out one of Joanna Johnson's other great reads?

Her Grace's Daring Proposal
The Officer's Convenient Proposal
The Return of Her Long-Lost Husband
A Mistletoe Vow to Lord Lovell
His Runaway Lady